"Ellie, please d⋯ ⋯⋯ make-believe."

"You're assuming I *want* a husband," she retorted. "And that I'm somehow lacking the ability to discern what's real and what's not."

Alexander could never know how wonderful his attentiveness made her feel. Ellie liked being his fiancée. She liked being one half of a couple and the sense of belonging that imparted. And if she'd occasionally imagined what it would be like to be his wife, she'd quickly dismissed the notion. He was too afraid to risk his heart again, and she was too afraid to risk disappointing someone again. Failing at marriage had eaten away at her self-esteem. She wasn't eager to repeat the experience.

"I wanted to remind you. Just in case…"

"Don't worry, I'm not going to tumble into love with you and hang on your heels like an affection-starved puppy dog." Spinning on her heel, she stalked toward the door.

Karen Kirst was born and raised in East Tennessee near the Great Smoky Mountains. She's a lifelong lover of books, but it wasn't until after college that she had the grand idea to write one herself. Now she divides her time between being a wife, homeschooling mom and romance writer. Her favorite pastimes are reading, visiting tearooms and watching romantic comedies.

Books by Karen Kirst

Love Inspired Historical

Smoky Mountain Matches

The Reluctant Outlaw
The Bridal Swap
The Gift of Family
"Smoky Mountain Christmas"
His Mountain Miss
The Husband Hunt
Married by Christmas
From Boss to Bridegroom
The Bachelor's Homecoming
Reclaiming His Past
The Sheriff's Christmas Twins
Wed by Neccessity
The Engagement Charade

Cowboy Creek

Bride by Arrangement

Visit the Author Profile page
at Harlequin.com for additional titles.

KAREN KIRST

The Engagement Charade

HARLEQUIN® LOVE INSPIRED® HISTORICAL

Recycling programs
for this product may
not exist in your area.

 LOVE INSPIRED BOOKS

ISBN-13: 978-0-373-42531-0

The Engagement Charade

Copyright © 2017 by Karen Vyskocil

www.Harlequin.com

Printed in U.S.A.

For You created my inmost being; You knit me together in my mother's womb. Your eyes saw my unformed body; all the days ordained for me were written in Your book before one of them came to be.
—*Psalms* 139:13, 16

To my friend and lunch buddy Christy Barton,
whose love of tea sparked a friendship.

Chapter One

Gatlinburg, Tennessee
September 1887

Alexander Copeland's one goal in life was to be left alone. Not an easy task for a café owner, but he'd managed just fine until Ellie Jameson entered his life uninvited. He hadn't hired the new cook. She had been hired *for* him without his permission. And because of her skills in the kitchen, he wasn't prepared to fire her. Yet.

If only the woman would accept that he didn't wish to be involved in the daily operations. He didn't care whether she was serving roast duck or chicken livers, boiled potatoes or sautéed squash, apple pie or pumpkin fritters. Nor did it matter if she embellished the menu board with dainty little chalk flower drawings and arranged late-summer bouquets in Mason jars to use as centerpieces. Nothing mattered save passing the hours until he could retire upstairs and shut out the world.

At 10:15 a.m., her succinct rap sounded on his office door. He could say this about her—she was punctual and persistent. Snapping the ledger closed, he sank against the leather chair and considered ignoring her.

"Mr. Copeland?" She knocked again, and the burning in his gut spread to his entire abdomen.

Stalking to the door, Alexander wrenched it open and leveled her with a formidable glare. "*Must* we do this again today, Mrs. Jameson?"

"I'm afraid we must." The young widow—she couldn't be more than twenty—smiled in the face of his annoyance. Not a tremulous, placating smile, but a sunny one that brightened her gamine features and made her coffee-brown eyes shine. "As the proprietor of the Plum Café, you should be informed as to what I'm serving your customers."

"My other cook didn't share your opinion. He did his job and left me out of it."

"Perhaps that's why this place earned the nickname the Rotten Plum," she countered.

"Excuse me?"

Twin brows raised a notch. "You didn't know?"

He winced. How could he? He made a point not to interact with the locals, and his employees were hardly going to tell him that to his face.

"No."

Mrs. Jameson's gaze lowered to where he cradled his midsection. "I'm sorry. I thought you knew." She held a glass of frothy milk out to him. "Here you are."

"I've already had my breakfast, Mrs. Jameson." A bland one of lukewarm oatmeal, toast and weak tea, just as the doctor had prescribed.

"Please, call me Ellie," she said, not for the first time. "Trust me, this will help soothe the fire in your belly."

Pressing the cold glass into his hand, she slipped past him and, after crossing to the windows, proceeded to tie back the thick brocade draperies. Bright light filtered through the windowpane, dispelling the ever-present gloom and revealing multiple layers of dust coating the bookshelves along the right wall and the carved wood furniture crowding the room. The once-vibrant Oriental rug covering the plank floorboards had faded to dull reds and browns, and multiple threads had snapped and frayed.

"Might I remind you this is my office? If I'd wanted the draperies open, I would've opened them myself."

She sneezed. "If you choose to ruin your eyesight, that's your business. But I need light to see my list." Pulling out a slim pad and pencil from her apron pocket, she perched on one of the chairs facing his desk, her posture straight and proper, and began to read through the menu items for today's noon and supper meals.

Alexander remained in the doorway. Instead of attending her words, his mind wrestled with the puzzle before him. Few people in this quaint mountain town dared approach him. Since the day of his arrival, he'd discouraged interaction. He wasn't interested in making friends. Most folks respected his wishes. Why couldn't Ellie Jameson?

He contemplated the glass in his hand. This wasn't the first time she'd tried to soothe his ailing stomach. It was as if she studied him for signs of discomfort. Was it some nurturing instinct that spurred her to ignore his unspoken but very clear desire to be left alone? He thought it very likely considering the circumstances of her employment. Several weeks ago, the same day his former cook quit, Alexander had suffered one of his worst episodes since developing an ulcer and had become an unwilling patient of Dr. Owens. Deputy Ben MacGregor and several others had taken it upon themselves to hold cooking auditions without his knowledge. They'd pinned the blue ribbon on Ellie Jameson.

He didn't recall seeing her before she came to work

here—not that he took the time to acquaint himself with his patrons. He'd overheard her tell his waitress, Sally, that she'd moved to Tennessee in May, only four months ago. Beyond that, he knew she was an excellent cook, a dependable and conscientious employee, and far too cheerful for his tastes.

While she continued her recitation, he took the time to study her.

Her hair, worn in a high, girlish ponytail, spilled over her shoulder in nondescript brown waves. Of medium height, she possessed an average, almost boyish build draped in unbecoming gray. Her dove-colored blouse was ill fitting and nearly worn through at the shoulders and elbows. Her skirt was of a darker, charcoal gray and several inches too long, so that the hem skimmed the toes of her old black boots. Her only piece of jewelry was a slim gold wedding band.

Alexander thought of his own ring, hidden in his dresser drawer upstairs. Wearing it would invite questions he wasn't prepared to answer. He didn't need to see it every day to be reminded of what he'd lost. *Not lost,* he thought bitterly. No, it had been ripped away from him.

She finished speaking, and her expectant gaze met his. "Does that sound agreeable?"

"Uh, sure. Yes, very agreeable." He rubbed the stubble along his jaw. "Now, if that will be all, I've got work to do."

Tilting her head to one side, she arched a single brow in a way that dispelled the illusion of youth. She clearly suspected he hadn't heard one word. "It's been a while since we've offered fish. Would you have time today to catch us some? I could fry it up tomorrow and serve it with corn bread, snap beans and coleslaw."

She'd requested his input before, but nothing that required action. "You want me to go fishing?"

"I think folks will enjoy a fish fry, don't you?"

He shrugged and, leaving the drink on his desk, wandered over to the window. Using his handkerchief, he rubbed clean a saucer-sized circle. The alley between his establishment and the post office didn't see much foot traffic. The other building's exterior log wall dominated much of the view. Above the roofline, a brilliant blue strip of sky was visible.

"It's a gorgeous day," she enthused. "There's a consistent breeze that eases the sun's heat and carries with it the remnants of summer. The humidity is low. Doesn't feel like rain, either. I—"

"Fine. You'll have your fish."

At her silence, Alexander turned in hopes she'd quit the room. Instead, she'd abandoned her chair to take up position in the middle of his office, her person a study in grays and browns broken only by faint strokes of pink on the apple of her cheeks and a rosebud mouth that was, in its delicate perfection, her one intriguing feature.

Startled by the thought, he said in clipped tones, "We're finished here, are we not?"

"Before I start on the noon meal, I'd like to show you something in the dining room."

Emitting a resigned sigh, he gestured with an impatient flick of his fingers for her to lead the way. The sooner he listened to her concerns, the sooner he'd be rid of her.

To most folks, Alexander Copeland was an irascible recluse who couldn't be bothered with his customers' needs or wants. In the brief time Ellie had worked for him, she'd come to the conclusion that he was a hurting soul who desperately needed a friend. Someone to gently nudge him from the nest like a baby bird.

In the spacious dining room, she watched him pace restlessly from one window to the next, his remote blue gaze surveying the various aspects of Main Street. The café was currently closed for the two-hour break between breakfast and the noon meal, an opportune time to broach the subject of sprucing up the place.

He ceased his restless movements and directed his full attention to her. Despite his recent health problems, Alexander Copeland cut a commanding figure. Over six feet tall, he favored austere, formal clothing at odds with his tousled, collar-length raven hair and habit of shaving every third or fourth day. His features were classically handsome. His light blue eyes were ringed with darker blue and fringed with lush black lashes any girl would envy. Noting how his black vest shot through with silver threads over an ice-blue shirt complemented his coloring, she recalled the gauntness of his appearance upon his return from the doctor's not so long ago. Sensitive to others' suffering, she was grateful he was following his prescribed diet. While he could stand to gain a bit more weight, he was well on the way to complete recovery— physically, anyway. Whatever tormented his mind remained—that much was obvious.

"What is it that requires my personal attention?"

Arms stiff at his sides, he looked around the room, his gaze snagging on the back wall and the large blackboard where she'd written the day's menu. Did he disapprove of her drawings? Or perhaps it was the Bible verse she'd included? According to her assistant, Flo Olufsen, Mr. Copeland hadn't darkened the doorstep of the church since his arrival.

"It's the curtains, sir." Ellie indicated the maroon draperies that should've been replaced years ago. "They're in bad shape, as are the tablecloths. Their appearance gives a poor impression of the state of the restaurant."

There were twelve tables in total, all rectangular in shape. Four windows overlooked the street and two windows flanked the fireplace on the alley side. Alexander inspected the cloth on the table closest to him. When his finger pierced the worn material and opened up a hole, his face puckered in bewilderment. Ellie couldn't squelch a giggle.

He straightened immediately, his mouth tightening.

Feeling chastened without him ever speaking a word, Ellie hurried to cover the gaffe. "I was thinking we should choose material of a lighter, neutral hue that would brighten the room," she said. "Nothing too feminine, of course. And it would have to be sturdy. You won't want to be replacing them every year."

"You've given this a great deal of thought."

"I want the Plum to be a place where folks feel comfortable. Somewhere they can be assured of a fresh, hot meal in an inviting environment."

He skimmed his fingers along the mantel and inspected them. "Are you responsible for the cinder-free fireplaces?"

Thrown by the question, she said, "Sally and I did the work while you were indisposed."

"It was your idea, though."

"Yes."

"And the windows? You scrubbed them, as well."

"We did, yes."

Folding his hands behind his back, he rocked on his heels. "For a new employee, you're awfully committed to the success of my café. Neither Sally nor Flo, whom you might say I inherited from the former owner, have shown a thimbleful of the initiative you have. While I appreciate your commitment to excellence, I have to wonder at your motivation."

His gaze probed hers and, for a wild moment, Ellie wondered if he might've guessed her secret. But that was silly. No one else in the entire world knew about the precious baby she carried.

"I need the work," she stated baldly. "I happen to enjoy cooking for people. It's a rare occurrence to find a paid position doing what you love. I'd like to keep it."

"You're a recent widow, I understand. My condolences."

Ellie stammered out something unintelligible, her tongue suddenly tied. It was his first mention of her loss. She'd gotten the impression he expected her to burst into tears if he broached the subject. He'd be wrong.

Her marriage to Nolan Jameson had been fraught with difficulty and failed to be the loving union she'd hoped for. She had mourned his sudden passing but rejoiced at this unforeseen chance to finally be a mother, to have a child of her own to raise. Her last two pregnancies had ended in tragedy. She'd beseeched God morning, noon and night on behalf of this baby, praying this time would be different.

"Tell me, do you have someone in mind for the changes you've mentioned?"

"I'm a decent seamstress. I'd be happy to do it."

His dark brows lifted. "Will you have time?"

Ellie's days were long and arduous. Six days a week, she woke before dawn in order to be at the café by five to start breakfast. The morning serving hours were from seven to ten. After a brief coffee break, she and Flo prepared the noon meal, available between the hours of noon and two. The afternoon break was longer, as supper didn't begin until six o'clock. By closing time at nine, her energy was at its lowest point.

"I'll make time," she told him. "I can utilize my afternoons. Flo may be willing to take over the desserts for a week."

"I'm not sure the customers will thank me for that." He shot her a dry look. "Very well. I'll inform Mr. Darling to expect you at the mercantile. Put the supplies on my account."

"Don't you want to approve the fabric choice?"

"I trust your judgment." He made to walk past her and paused. "I'll pay you extra wages, of course. Expect it with your next earnings."

Overjoyed, for she would need yarn and thread to crochet blankets, and fabric to sew clothes for the baby, Ellie seized his hand and cradled it between hers. "Thank you, sir. You're a godsend. First the cooking position, which I relish, and now this…" Her throat grew thick. "You can't know what a blessing you've been to me."

The roughness of his palm registered, as did the nicks and fine scars across the top expanse. She'd expected the slippery smoothness of a businessman's hands. Without thinking, she traced the faded pink lines intersecting his skin. "You hurt yourself," she murmured.

Alexander's lips parted. Then his jaw hardened to stone. Yanking free, he glowered at her like a bear whose honey supply had been disturbed.

"It's an old wound," he gritted out.

Cheeks stinging, she sucked in air as an alarming bout of nausea assailed her. She knew how standoffish he was. This was one of the longest conversations they'd shared. He barely tolerated her presence, and here she'd been *caressing* his skin. How could she have been so forward?

"I apologize. I—I didn't mean to…" *Act with an ab-*

solute lack of professionalism? Make them both uncomfortable?

"It's already forgotten."

Striding from the room, his steps continued past the office and storage room and into the kitchen. The rear door slammed. Cringing, her stomach revolted and, hurrying to reach an empty pitcher on the hutch, she thanked the Lord no one was around to witness her humiliation— most of all, Alexander Copeland.

Chapter Two

He'd nearly come undone at an innocent display of gratitude. His overreaction had caused the young widow a great deal of embarrassment. Her pained expression had remained with him throughout the day, despite his best efforts to put it from his mind. Hiking through the forest at a brisk pace hadn't done the trick; nor had sitting on the riverbank waiting in vain for the fish to bite. Alexander was convinced his brother and sister wouldn't recognize him either by his appearance or his actions.

A deep sigh escaped his lips as he passed the almost indiscernible outlines of the vegetable garden and modest barn behind the café. He met Flo Olufsen on the kitchen stoop. The jolly sixty-year-old had come with the purchase of the café. A jill-of-all-trades, Flo's tasks varied from day to day depending on what Ellie required of her. While she didn't pester him, she didn't spare him from her dry wit.

A circle of light spilled from her lantern. Frizzed corkscrew curls sprouted in all directions, faded strawberry mixed with gray, and her carpet-like eyebrows rested above twinkling blue eyes.

"Evening, boss." She grinned, revealing a missing

front tooth. "The kitchen's tidied and ready for another day of business tomorrow."

"Thank you. Good night."

His fingers had closed over the knob when her voice stopped him. "Oh, you should know Ellie's asleep at the table. Poor thing's all tuckered out. Said she was going to rest for but a minute before heading home. Next thing I knew she was sound asleep."

Alexander stared. "Why didn't you wake her?"

"I saw you coming along the trail. My Eugene is waiting for me. He gets out of sorts if I'm too late getting home." Waggling her fingers in the air, she bustled around the corner and disappeared into the alleyway.

Wonderful.

His steps measured, he entered the darkened kitchen. Spanning the entire width of the building, the room was divided by a natural walkway to the hallway smack in the middle of the far wall. The cooking was accomplished on a pair of cast-iron stoves to his right. A square table was situated nearby for food preparation. Opposite the stoves, a waist-high counter affixed to the wall held a dry sink, carving and bread knives, spoons and other utensils. An ice cabinet sat beneath the alley window. On the left side, stairs tucked against the wall led to his living quarters. Beyond that, another, larger table was situated before a pie safe and floor-to-ceiling shelving holding cooking and serving dishes. It was at that table where he discovered his cook.

Slumped over the surface, her face was hidden in the crook of her elbow. A single wall lamp flickered beside the hallway entrance. Her dark hair spilled in an unruly waterfall over her shoulder. Her even breathing suggested she was in the throes of sleep.

Alexander propped his fishing pole against the table.

"Mrs. Jameson?"

No response.

Frowning, he propped one hand on the chair and bent closer. "Ellie? It's time to go home."

Making a protesting warble in her throat, she turned her head so that he was afforded a view of her milk-white cheek and pert nose. She looked extremely fragile to him in that moment, nothing like her usual energetic, upbeat self. Annoyance flared. He wasn't supposed to be making personal observations about his hired staff.

Giving her shoulder a firm shake, he repeated her name once more.

"Hmm?" Slowly sitting up, she stretched like a cat after a nap in the sun. Her vision must have cleared, for she appeared startled at the sight of him. "Oh! Alexander... I—I mean, Mr. Copeland." Glancing about her, she passed a hand over her face. "I didn't mean to fall asleep. I was more tired than usual."

Watching her gain her feet, Alexander wondered if he was working her too hard. He experienced a pang of guilt. While he was the proprietor and could do as he saw fit, it went against his upbringing to allow others to shoulder the majority of the hard labor while he sat behind a desk balancing ledgers. The state of affairs hadn't bothered him before she'd come around. But then his previous cook had been a stout, gruff man in his late forties who could shoulder fifty-pound sacks of flour without breaking a sweat.

Ellie pushed her chair in, took one step toward the door and swayed on her feet. Alexander caught her around the waist. Her palms found his chest to balance against. Her mouth slack, her big doe eyes blinked up at him.

"I'm sorry. I got a tad light-headed."

The scent of vanilla surrounded him like a warm hug. "Can you stand on your own?"

She nodded. Her hands fell away, and he released her.

"I'm fine," she said, smoothing her hands along her skirt. Then she gasped. "What time is it?"

"A quarter until ten."

"I have to hurry." Brushing past him, she selected a kerosene lamp from an upper shelf and quickly lit it. "My in-laws aren't thrilled about my working. They'll pitch a fit if I come home late."

Alexander realized he had no idea where she lived. "How far is it?"

"About a twenty-minute walk," she said matter-of-factly.

He hid his consternation. In a bustling city with lots of people around and gas streetlamps, that might not be a problem. In mountainous, sparsely populated terrain, a single woman walking alone at night courted trouble.

"Do you have a horse? Or mule?"

She opened the door, giving him a glimpse of the star-studded navy sky. "No. I don't mind walking, though. Helps clear my head."

No wonder she was exhausted. Walking that distance after a good night's sleep wouldn't be a burden. However, after a full day of slaving over a hot stove, her feet had to be sore and her body begging for rest.

"I'll take you."

She twirled the reticule dangling from her wrist in endless circles. "I don't want to trouble you. I'm accustomed to walking."

"No trouble." Waving her onto the stoop, he locked the door behind him. The cooler air hinted that autumn was around the corner. "I'll just be a moment."

He had the team hitched and ready in a matter of minutes. Once Ellie was settled on the high seat, he climbed aboard and listened to her instructions. They rode along the back lane past darkened businesses. His passenger fell silent. Considering her typically chatty nature, Alexander attributed it to fatigue.

Glancing at her profile, he noted the weary slump of her shoulders and the tight clasp of her hands in her lap. He'd bent the truth a bit. Giving her a ride home was inconvenient and awkward. Outside of the café, he hadn't been alone with a woman since before leaving Texas. In fact, he'd had limited interaction with anyone. Alexander had always been one to enjoy his own company, but his hermit-like existence would shock his brother and sister.

Grimacing, he absently rubbed his midsection. What had stirred these thoughts of Thomas and Margaret? Nothing good could come of dwelling on everything he was missing.

"Are you in pain?"

"What?"

She pointed to his middle. "You do that a lot."

Resting his forearm on his thigh, he shook his head. "Force of habit."

"How long have you suffered stomach troubles?"

Since my wife and son were murdered.

Curling his fingers into a fist, he said aloud, "A couple of years."

"That must be difficult."

"My flare-ups happen when I'm not careful with my diet. Or when I go long stretches without sleeping." He clamped his lips shut. Why had he told her that?

Thankfully, she didn't pepper him with questions, and his tension ebbed. The clop of the horses' hooves competed with whirring wheels. When the distant yowl of coyotes echoed through the mountains, she didn't react.

"I had a great-aunt who suffered from ulcers. She was adamant that cabbage juice was the only true remedy."

Stifling his curiosity about her background, he kept his focus on the dark lane as they entered a thick-growth cove. The avenue was barely passable. More than once, his black bowler was nearly lost to overhanging branches. She apologized.

"Howard, my father-in-law, has been promising to trim this for weeks. As you've surely heard, the list of farm chores is endless."

Images of his family's vast ranch surged unbidden in his mind. Farm or ranch, living off the land took energy, determination and raw grit. Homesickness rose up so fast he felt robbed of breath. What he wouldn't give to see those rolling green pastures dotted with cattle, the ranch house and stables framed by boundless cerulean skies. And his siblings… His throat became clogged with emotion as he imagined how they'd changed. They exchanged letters every now and then, but it wasn't the same as seeing them in person.

Memories of the fire that had stolen his home and his wife and child threatened, and, in order to stave them off, he sought conversation he normally wouldn't have.

"I heard you arrived in the area in May. Where are you from?"

If she was startled by his interest, she didn't show it. "Originally Lexington, Kentucky. Beautiful country. My parents died when I was ten, so I went to live with my grandparents in a different part of the state. Their farm abutted the Jamesons' property. That's how I met Nolan. My husband."

Like him, she was no stranger to loss. "My mother died giving birth to my youngest sister," he said. "I was eight."

"I'm sorry. Is your father still alive?"

"His heart gave out on him the year I turned twenty."

Lionel Copeland had seemingly enjoyed good health. His death had blindsided everyone. Thomas and Margaret, their cook and mother-figure Rosa and even the ranch hands had turned to Alexander for reassurance that their way of life would continue as it always had. While it had been an immense burden for one so young, he'd embraced his duty without complaint.

"Loss like that stays with you, doesn't it?" she sighed. "The normal days are hard enough, but the momentous occasions are worse. Those are the days you really grieve their absence."

Again his thoughts turned to a painful place. His wedding day had taken place four years after his father's passing, and yet he'd craved his steadfast presence. He would've given anything for his father to have had the opportunity to meet Sarah. Then there was the day Levi was born...

He must've gasped aloud, because Ellie angled toward him. "Is something wrong? Are you hurting?"

Alexander glanced into her liquid brown gaze. The wagon lanterns swinging from their hooks had light patterns playing across her face. He felt suddenly like a man who'd been encased in ice, his mind and body numb, and now the ice was thawing and he was beginning to sense every pinprick of discomfort. He gritted his teeth. *I'm not ready. I can't relive the nightmare. Not yet.*

"I'm perfectly well, thank you," he told her in stilted tones.

With a skill born of practice, he locked away his past and concentrated on his surroundings, soaking in details he could transfer to paper later. He'd taken to sketching in his free time, mostly nature scenes and animals. He didn't possess natural talent, but his work no longer resembled a child's scribbles.

Unfortunately, Ellie did not sense his need for retreat.

"Nolan was excited about this move. Everyone was, including me. I had hoped it would provide us with a fresh start. We couldn't have known what lay ahead." Her voice hitched, and she cleared her throat. "The men started on Howard and Gladys's cabin first. Nadine, Nolan's sister, was insistent that she and her husband, Ralph, would have theirs built next. Within a month, they had both cabins finished. And then they started on ours. They were felling trees one drizzly June day, and Nolan was standing in the wrong spot. I wasn't there… I didn't see what happened. I was dressing a rabbit for stew I'd planned to serve that evening."

Up ahead, lights shone in the windows of two dwellings situated on opposite sides of a stamp-sized yard. Relief coursed through him. He hadn't asked to travel memory lane with her. Getting sucked into other people's problems was a sure way to lose his hard-won control. Living their pain brought his own rushing to the surface.

As he guided the team to a stop, she didn't seem to notice his lack of response. She appeared to brace herself as the door on their left banged open and an older couple already in their nightclothes emerged onto the porch. The gray-headed man with square features sported a rifle.

"Do you have any notion what time it is?"

The woman Alexander assumed was Ellie's mother-in-law studied him with ill-concealed malice. Probably in her early- to midsixties, she was tall for a woman and big boned. Her dark hair hung to her waist and was striped with wide swaths of silver.

Ellie hurried to disembark. "I apologize, Gladys. I accidentally dozed off after my shift."

"You know not to bring strange men here." The man balanced his weapon against his hip.

"This is my boss." Ellie's voice was low and strained. "I've told you about him." Not looking at Alexander, she waved her hand between them. "Alexander Copeland, meet my in-laws, Howard and Gladys Jameson."

He touched his hat brim. "I'm sorry for the disturbance."

Shooting him a baleful look, Gladys gestured behind her. "Get inside, Ellie."

Even in the darkness, Alexander could sense her resistance.

"It's late," Ellie hedged. Motioning to the other cabin, she said, "I'd like to go to bed. How about we talk tomorrow?"

"We'll talk now."

Spinning on her heel, the older woman stalked inside, holding the door ajar. Howard reeked of suspicion.

Something inside Alexander demanded he seize his employee and take her back to town.

"Thank you for the ride, Mr. Copeland." Her reticule balled in her hand, she started to follow her mother-in-law.

"Ellie."

Her eyes widened. "Yes?"

"Do you have need of anything more?" *Will you be all right?*

She hesitated. "No, sir."

She continued inside the cabin. Howard joined them, shutting the door firmly without a word of goodbye. As he set the team in motion, he was startled at the sight of a man on the other cabin's porch. Shrouded in shadows, he didn't nod or wave, and his intent gaze followed Alexander's progress. Must be the brother-in-law she'd mentioned. Apparently, these Kentucky natives weren't keen on visitors.

Beyond the cabins, a crude shelter housed several horses. Ellie had indicated she didn't have a mode of transportation. He realized it was more a case of not being allowed to make use of it.

The situation hauled him back years to another young woman who'd been bullied by her father and his twisted crony, Cyrus Pollard. He'd rescued Sarah from both men by marrying her, but there'd been consequences. If Ellie needed help, she had resources, men like the sheriff or Deputy Ben MacGregor. Alexander wasn't about to get involved.

"Are you lookin' to sink your hooks into that highfalutin businessman?"

Gladys had spun to face her, her hair in disarray and her bloodshot eyes shooting accusations. Harold remained by the door. Ellie felt hemmed in.

Shock ate at the bone-deep weariness weighing her down. She yearned for her bed. "Certainly not. I'm not in the market for a new husband."

"You don't behave like a woman who's in deep mourning," Gladys spit. "If I didn't know any better, I'd say you're relieved my Nolan's dead and gone. You act as if four years of marriage meant nothing to you."

"That's not the case, Gladys. I'm as sorry about what happened to him as you are."

Guilt wormed through her defenses. Of course she hadn't wanted any harm to befall Nolan. Whatever his faults, he'd been a faithful husband, a hard worker who provided for her needs. Her physical ones, anyway. She'd never had to worry about a roof over her head or enough food and clothing.

But part of what she's saying lines up with the sense of freedom you feel, doesn't it?

Not long after the wedding, Nolan began displaying a troubling side to his personality. He'd become suspicious and controlling and had doubted her commitment to him and their marriage. He'd forbidden her to socialize with her friends and had limited her outings to church services and the occasional trip to the mercantile—always in the company of him or one of his family members. The isolation had chafed. She'd battled loneliness and had turned to God for comfort and strength.

If only Nolan had kept his misgivings to himself, she might've received support from her in-laws. But he'd complained to them to the point they'd become hostile. The youngest child, Nolan had almost died at the age of three. Because of this brush with tragedy, his parents and older sister had cossetted him. They thought he hung the moon and stars and refused to attempt to see Ellie's side of things. Their treatment of her had grown more antagonistic since Nolan's passing, and she worried for her child's quality of life in such an environment.

"If you loved my son, if you respect us at all, you'll give up your position." Grief made the lines in Gladys's visage more pronounced.

"I did love Nolan." Maybe not in the way God intended for a wife to love her husband, but she'd loved him as a fellow human being. She'd wanted good for him. Had tried to please and honor him. "And I can't express how grateful I am to you for providing me with a home. However, I can't do what you're suggesting. I enjoy cooking. I haven't done much of that since we got here. More than that, I need the income."

"For what? We feed you. Clothe you. We need you

doing chores around here. Poor Nadine is working her fingers to the bone."

The stench of Howard's cigars permeating the room made Ellie's stomach churn. "She wasn't complaining when I paid her my portion for room and board. She's bought enough fabric for three Sunday dresses since I started work."

Gladys shot forward and gripped Ellie's forearm so hard she yelped. "Don't you sass me, girl. My Nolan may be gone, but that doesn't give you the right to disrespect us. This is *our* home you're standing in, don't forget."

How could she? The Jamesons hadn't welcomed her into their fold. They'd treated her like an outsider from the start. "You're hurting me."

Howard finally spoke. "It's late."

He moved to stand beside his wife. Tall and muscled from years of physical labor, his craggy features were so like Nolan's it made her chest twinge with sorrow. She wished she'd been better at making her husband happy. She wished they'd had a stronger marriage.

"We can discuss this tomorrow morning."

Uttering a huff of disgust, Gladys released her and trudged off to bed. Ellie didn't waste time making her escape. "Good night, Howard."

Outside in the inky-black night, she breathed in fresh air tinged with scents of earth and pine and lightly rubbed the sore spot on her arm. She gazed at the star-studded heavens. *You hung those stars, God. You placed the planets in the sky. My problems seem mighty to me, but to You they're easily managed. Lead me, Father. Give me wisdom.*

She put a protective hand over her stomach and felt a rush of joy tempered with uncertainty. *Please God, I beg You, let me keep this one. My husband is lost to me.*

The other babies are in the arms of Jesus. I want this child with every fiber of my being. I promise to love him or her and teach them to love You.

"Ellie."

She jumped. "Ralph! I didn't know you were out here."

"I didn't mean to frighten you."

"Is there something you needed?"

Quiet, gentle-giant Ralph Michaels had been a surprising ally. While he didn't possess the backbone to go against his wife and mother-in-law, he'd provided subtle support, especially since Nolan's passing.

The lack of a lantern made it difficult to make out his expression. "I know your secret."

Her heart slammed against her ribs. Was he referring to her desire to find a place of her own? Couldn't be. She hadn't voiced that to anyone, which meant...

"You know about the baby?"

"I saw you being sick the other morning out behind the barn, and again the other night."

Pressing her hands to her throat, she pleaded, "I beg you to keep this between us. I'm not ready to tell Nadine or Gladys."

"I haven't said anything."

"Then why..."

"You should leave this cove." His eyes gleamed with purpose. "I love my wife. I'm aware of her faults, however. Never could figure why she and Gladys treated you the way they did."

"I wasn't good enough for Nolan. I failed to make him happy."

"They worshipped him," he agreed. "I'm afraid of what they'll do once they learn you're carrying his child."

Apprehension coiled tight. What if they tried to turn her own child against her? If she hadn't been good enough for Nolan, she certainly wouldn't be a satisfactory mother for his child. The fact that Nadine had never been able to conceive added an extra layer of worry.

His fingers brushed her upper arm. "Do you have enough money saved for a place of your own?"

"I'm not sure. I haven't spent any besides the portion I've been giving Nadine."

"You should make inquiries in town," Ralph said softly.

Her mind spinning, she agreed. "I think you're right."

She'd been toying with the idea for months—now it seemed she had to put thoughts into action. Ellie would go to any lengths to protect her child.

Chapter Three

Ellie was patting out the biscuit dough the next morning when Alexander descended the stairs earlier than usual. Her pressing problem was momentarily forgotten as embarrassment stung her cheeks. She could only imagine what he thought about her tactless in-laws.

"Good mornin', boss." Flo cracked another egg into the bowl of flapjack batter. "Would you like breakfast?"

He stopped on the bottom tread, his inscrutable blue gaze locked onto Ellie. "I already ate."

Shrugging, Flo went back to cracking eggs.

Alexander was in the habit of fixing his own breakfast in his apartment. No doubt he stuck to bland foods like oatmeal or scrambled eggs with toast. She wasn't sure what he'd done for lunch and supper before she came, but since the day he'd returned from the doctor, she'd prepared special dishes that wouldn't aggravate his stomach. He ate them alone in his office, a sad state of affairs in her opinion. Not that what she thought would make a difference to him.

As usual, his formal attire accentuated his natural reserve. Clad almost completely in mourning colors—midnight-black vest, pressed black trousers and polished, round-tipped shoes—a bottle-green dress shirt provided welcome color. His clothing fit his whipcord-lean frame to perfection. His glossy raven locks were combed off his forehead, the ends curling around his collar. He'd shaved today. Ellie admired the clean planes of his handsome face before jerking her gaze back to the biscuits.

I'm happy his health seems much improved, that's all, she assured herself.

His footsteps didn't carry him to the hallway, as expected. Instead, he approached the table near the stoves where she worked.

"Mrs. Jameson."

She frowned, wondering exactly when she'd come to dislike being called that. "It's Ellie," she countered. "You call Flo and Sally by their first names. Why do you refuse to use mine? Did you have a schoolmate named Ellie when you were young? A girl who teased you unmercifully? Or an old, crotchety aunt named Ellie who pinched your cheek too hard and made you eat beets?"

Flo's chuckling filled the sudden silence. Alexander looked taken aback. "You're the first Ellie I've encountered."

"Then may we cease with the formality?"

"Ellie, I'm going into my office now."

"Can I get you a glass of milk? Or chamomile tea?"

"No milk. No tea. No weak coffee. Under no circumstance do I wish to be disturbed today. I do not want to hear the day's menu or be consulted about decorations. Is that clear, Ellie?"

Irritated, she slapped the dough with more force than necessary. Flour puffed about her fingers. Why must he be so determined to resist her attempts at friendship? "Perfectly clear, sir."

"Good." Turning on his heel, he stalked toward the hallway.

"Oh, Mr. Copeland?"

Shoulders tensing, he twisted around, one haughty brow lifted in impatience. "Yes?"

"Does fire warrant your attention?"

"Excuse me?"

"Fire. Do you wish to be told if there's a fire?"

Flo ceased stirring the batter, humor touching her fleshy features.

Alexander opened his mouth to speak.

Ellie cut him off. "What about a robbery? Would you like to be informed of such an event? Or an altercation between customers?"

He tilted his head to one side, an errant lock of hair sliding into his eyes. "Did you skip breakfast?"

Her fist slipped from her hip. "Sir?"

"I've noticed you have a tendency to lose your equanimity when you skip a meal." He made a circling motion to indicate their workspaces. "Perhaps you should eat something."

He quit the room, his office door closing with a decided click.

Flo's chuckles brought Ellie out of her stupor.

"What just happened?" Ellie spread her hands wide.

"Our boss revealed he's not as oblivious to goings-on as we thought." She winked. "He's right, you know. You do get tetchy when you're hungry."

"Humph."

Ellie tried not to take her frustration out on the dough. Her customers wouldn't be satisfied with biscuits as hard as river boulders. She contemplated the puzzling exchange all while bustling about the kitchen. Part of her was inexplicably pleased that he'd paid enough attention to notice something as personal as her moods. The other part quailed at the prospect. What else had he concluded but hadn't voiced? Could he have added her extreme fatigue and frayed emotions together to equal her current condition?

She wasn't sure why the thought of his knowing unsettled her. Pregnancy was a sensitive time for a woman, especially one without a husband. Alexander was her boss. Not only that—he'd created an emotional barrier between himself and his employees. He was neither amiable nor approachable. Alexander Copeland was not a man to invite confidences. Hard and aloof, he didn't possess finer feelings. Why, he probably had never even courted a lady!

By the time ten o'clock rolled around, Ellie was eager to embark on her mission to find lodgings. Ralph's warnings resurfaced, dislodging her consternation over Alexander. She had more important matters to attend to, like securing a future for herself and her baby.

After explaining her intentions to Flo, who readily agreed to start on the potato gratin that would accompany the roast at the noon meal, Ellie went to inspect the room for rent at the post office. The owner of the building, Lyle Matthews, was a pleasant man who'd likely be a good landlord. However, the room was narrow and musty and the weekly fee far beyond her means. She thanked him for his time and, disappointed but trusting God would provide for her needs, hurried across the street to the mercantile to pick out material for the café.

The proprietor and his wife, Quinn and Nicole Darling, were exceptionally helpful. No matter how busy, the couple remained patient and kind and treated each of their customers with respect. Today, Nicole laid out bolts of fabric for Ellie to peruse. She came close to choosing a ridiculous lime-green cotton printed with pink birds simply to irk Alexander. She reined in the impulse and, for the curtains, chose a sensible, soft yellow that would lend cheer to the space. The tablecloths would be white with matching yellow overlay. With her purchases recorded in Quinn's ledger, she was on her way out the main entrance when a board of announcements caught her eye.

The papers consisted mostly of ads for prized bulls and assorted livestock, farm equipment and workers. Her hope had fizzled by the time she read the last one.

"Excuse me, miss."

Ellie scooted out of the way as a heavyset farmer removed an ad for a rabbit hutch and, with a nod, ambled down the aisle. She looked at the board again and realized a second paper had been hidden by the one he'd taken. As she peered closer at the wrinkled note, her heart leaped with excitement. She ripped it from the nail and hurried onto the boardwalk.

After leaving her purchases at the café, Ellie walked to Mrs. Calvin Trentham's house. Located near the church, the white clapboard house boasted a shingled roof and black shutters. Late-summer flowers provided bursts of violet, orange and green along the foundation. Thick groves of deciduous trees dominated the landscape and gave way to the steep, forested mountainside a couple of acres behind the house.

Ellie's chest grew tight. The farmhouse was very similar to her grandparents', the last place she'd felt completely safe and free to be herself. She squared her shoulders and knocked lightly on the door. Her summons was answered by a diminutive woman with gray coronet braids and periwinkle-blue eyes set in a thin face.

"May I help you?"

"Good morning, I'm looking for Mrs. Trentham?"

"That's me."

"My name is Ellie Jameson. I saw your note at the mercantile. Do you still have a room to let?"

Blinking in surprise, the woman chuckled. "I posted that months ago. When I didn't get any takers, I figured Mr. Darling had tossed it in the waste bin." Waving Ellie inside, she closed the door and gestured toward a room to their left. "Would you care for coffee?"

Clutching her reticule in her hands, she shook her head, her ponytail tickling her neck. The scents of cinnamon, nutmeg and yeasty bread clung to the air, putting her in mind of cinnamon rolls. Her stomach rumbled. If she wasn't queasy, she was starving. There was no in between.

"No, thank you. I can't linger. I work at the Plum, and I'm needed back to help with the noon meal."

"I patronized the place years ago. Hated to see Mrs. Greene leave." She nodded in understanding, her gaze keen. "Are you from here originally? I don't recognize the surname."

"I arrived in Gatlinburg in May. My husband passed in June, and now I find myself in need of alternate lodgings."

Mrs. Trentham made a commiserating noise and patted Ellie's hand. "You poor dear. I lost my Calvin a decade ago. We were together for forty-five years." Glancing about the neat room made cozy with quilts and colorful knitted throws, she said, "Our children have all moved away. The quiet gets to me sometimes. That's why I decided to rent a room. I've been praying for just the right person." She smiled, little wrinkles fanning out from her eyes. "You're the only one to answer my ad. How about I show you around and then you can decide if it suits you?"

"I'd like that."

While not large, the house boasted a separate kitchen and pantry, main living room and two bedrooms. The room Ellie would reside in had two windows, both with views of the rear property, pretty rural scenes. Blue-and-white-checked curtains echoed a blue, white and rose quilt covering the bed. An oversize wardrobe dominated one corner. A slim table carved from pine held a kerosene lamp and pitcher and bowl for morning ablutions.

Mrs. Trentham tapped the cedar chest at the foot of the bed. "I store extra mattress covers and blankets in here, but I could clear it out for your things. What do you think? Will it suit you?"

Ellie turned from the window. "I like it very much. But there's something you should know." She sucked in a breath and took the plunge. "I'm expecting a baby. Come March, you'd have not one but two boarders."

Her face lit up. Clapping her hands together, she enthused, "How wonderful for you! A child to remember your husband by. I wouldn't have placed that ad if I hadn't craved company. A baby in this house would bring it back to life."

"A baby fussing in the middle of the night won't bother you, Mrs. Trentham?"

"Please, call me June." Her expression became reminiscent of bygone times. "My husband used to say I slept like the dead. My sleep is rarely disturbed."

Ellie pushed aside her lingering concern. They'd adjust once the time came. She couldn't let this opportunity pass her by.

"Then it's settled. I'll take it."

Alexander was perfectly aware he was behaving like an adolescent. His younger brother would tease him unmercifully for hiding out in his office and waiting for

Ellie to leave before making his escape. Shifting on the fallen tree that served as his seat, he watched as one by one the stars popped out in the post-sunset sky. His fishing string bobbed in the water. His lamp cast golden light on the bank but did little to disperse the shadows. Night blanketed the countryside in complete darkness.

He smothered a yawn and considered going home. Ellie had asked for fish, however, and it felt wrong leaving empty-handed again.

In his peripheral vision, a second man-made light registered. Balancing his pole against the log, he stood to his feet and studied the figure traversing the field. He was about to have company.

"Hello there," he called.

The light stilled. He could make out the figure of a woman. "Mr. Copeland?"

Shock washed over him. "Ellie? What are you doing out here on your own? I thought you'd gone home."

Her steps were slow. "I did."

The brush of tall grass against her boots joined the frogs' chirruping and occasional hoot owl. When she reached him, the evidence of tears made his mouth go dry. Curious emotion locked his chest in a vise. Aside from her periodic bouts of testiness related to hunger, the young widow was consistent in her sugarcoated optimism. Ellie Jameson looked at life through rose-colored glasses. Seeing her in such a despairing state was so unusual he wondered briefly if he'd nodded off and was engaged in a rare dream.

Circumventing him, she set her lamp down, spread a quilt on the bank and lowered herself to the ground, using the tree trunk as a support for her back. Her head fell against the trunk, and a deep, shuddering sigh escaped her. Alexander returned to his spot and resumed his seat.

"Did something happen?" Bewilderment tightened his voice.

"I informed my in-laws of my decision to move." Staring straight ahead, she spoke in a monotone. "They didn't take it well."

Dismay flooded him. "You're leaving Gatlinburg?"

She turned her head, her brown eyes appearing coal black. Her ponytail had long since lost its starch. The ribbon was close to coming undone and tendrils of hair had escaped to tease her ears and cheeks. She looked young and vulnerable...and alone, like him.

"No. I don't have the resources to return to Kentucky. Even if I did, there's no one left there to return to."

Her words eased the tension in his body. "That's a relief." When she regarded him quizzically, he rushed to add, "I won't have the tedious task of searching for someone to replace you."

"I wouldn't want to inconvenience you," she muttered.

He winced. "Where are your new accommodations?"

"I'll be staying with a widow named June Trentham. She lives near the church."

"That will save you some time."

"Yes."

Her gaze dropping to the quilt beneath her, she traced patterns with her fingertips. She seemed troubled.

Since leaving Texas, Alexander had determined not to get involved with anyone's problems. He'd learned in the worst possible way that doing so led to disaster. Up to this point, he'd stuck to that decision. The wisest course of action would be to gather his things and bid her goodnight. Ellie Jameson was a grown woman capable of seeing to her own affairs.

But what true gentleman would leave her in this isolated spot?

"Why are you here, Ellie?" he said at last.

"The river is peaceful, don't you agree? It's a good place to come when you have troubles weighing on your mind."

"It's not safe for you to be wandering these mountains alone."

She paused in her efforts to tighten her hair ribbon. "What do you think I've been doing every night?"

"Until yesterday, I had no idea where you lived. Which begs the question—why don't you make use of one of those horses I saw on your property?"

"The Jamesons don't approve of my working. I suppose denying me a horse was their way of trying to dissuade me."

Alexander shot to his feet and began to pace along the water's edge. He couldn't recall the last time he'd been angry on someone else's behalf. Granted, the situation smacked of bullying, something he hadn't ever been able to abide.

"You aren't leaving that cove simply to save yourself travel time, are you?"

"No." She lowered her hands wearily to her lap. "My relationship with my husband's family has never been easy. Things got worse after his death. Gladys and Nadine blame me for Nolan's accident."

"I thought you said you weren't there."

"I wasn't. They accused me of rushing him to complete our cabin. They think he was in too much of a hurry to take proper precautions."

He admitted that he'd judged Ellie for her lack of obvious grief. She hadn't fit his idea of a grieving widow. Truth was, he didn't know much of anything about her or her circumstances.

"Your husband's death was a tragedy. Blaming you for what happened is ridiculous and small-minded."

"They made up their minds about me a long time ago, I'm afraid."

Knowing Ellie's personality, things must've gotten untenable for her to decide to leave.

"I'm assuming you had an argument tonight. Are you comfortable that things have calmed down enough to return?"

"They kicked me out." She lifted a shoulder. "I can't go back."

The familiar burning sensation spread through his midsection. "What were you planning to do? Pass the night on the riverbank?" His outrage at her in-laws sharpened his tone.

She jutted her chin. "It's still technically summer. The temperatures are pleasant. I have my grandmother's quilt to protect my clothes from grass stains. And it's quiet. Why shouldn't I stay here?"

He narrowed his eyes. "I thought you were a reasonable person."

"I don't have another choice, all right?"

At the telltale wobble in her voice, concern leaped to life. "Let's go. I'm taking you to Mrs. Trentham's."

"She's not expecting me until tomorrow."

"Does she strike you as an unsympathetic person?"

"No, she seems all that is kind."

He grabbed his pail and rod—yet another failed fishing attempt—and held out his free hand to her. "Then she'll understand, as I do, that you cannot possibly sleep in the elements exposed to any manner of danger."

Ellie's uplifted gaze, stamped with uncertainty, switched from his outstretched hand to his face .

He wiggled his fingers. "Come. We'll stop by the café and saddle a horse for you."

"Why are you involving yourself in my troubles? You've gone out of your way to distance yourself from everyone."

Her fatigue must be why she was speaking plainly. Unhappy with the development, he adopted a stern stare and his haughty employer voice. "As my employee and the reason the Plum is once again packed with customers, you are my responsibility. I can't have you in the kitchen if you're overtired. You'd be a danger to yourself and others."

Her mouth pursed. Reluctantly, she clasped his hand and allowed him to assist her to her feet. As they walked through the silent countryside, Alexander took comfort in the fact this was a singular event, a onetime kindness. He would settle the widow in her new home and tomorrow everything would return to the way it was before.

Chapter Four

Ellie could tell by the sun's slant that she'd overslept. Although reluctant to leave the soft bed, the prospect of Alexander's ire prodded her out of it. He'd gone out of his way to be a gentleman last evening, and this is how she repaid him? She rushed through her morning routine, only to discover the one outfit she'd left the cove with was missing.

She padded through the quiet house and found her hostess seated at the kitchen table with a cup of coffee and her Bible open before her. Her coronet braids neat as a pin and not a single wrinkle in her sprigged cotton dress, June radiated cheerfulness that Ellie found refreshing.

Her smile was bright as she marked her place with a handmade bookmark. "Good morning, dear. How did you sleep?"

"A little too well, I'm afraid." The mantel clock had confirmed her fears. It was past nine o'clock. "I haven't slept this late since I was a child."

"You needed rest."

Fiddling with her housecoat belt, Ellie shook her head. "Not at the expense of my job. Mr. Copeland will not be pleased. And poor Flo's had to prepare everything on her own. I'll have to make it up to her somehow, but first I need to find my clothes. Have you seen them? The wardrobe was empty. I looked under the bed to see if they'd fallen—"

June went to the stove and uncovered a plate crowded with biscuits, sausage and eggs. "I spot-cleaned them for you. They're hanging in the pantry." She indicated the empty seat across from her own. "As for Mr. Copeland, it was his idea to let you sleep for as long as you wanted."

Ellie's jaw went slack. Such thoughtfulness coming from a man who made it his mission to remain indifferent to everyone and everything around him?

"That doesn't sound like him."

"Heard it with my own ears." She winked. "He was very concerned about you. Does he know about the baby?"

"No." At least, she hoped he didn't. Sinking into the chair, she picked up a fork. "I'm not ready to tell him."

Shooting a significant look to Ellie's midsection, she quipped, "Before long you won't have a choice."

Absently rubbing the slight thickness in her middle, she tried to imagine how such a conversation would go. She tried to picture Alexander's lean, handsome features wreathed in happiness, his mouth curved in genuine delight. Unable to manage it, she tucked into her breakfast, more ravenous than she'd realized.

June refused to let her clean the dishes. After expressing her thanks, she quickly dressed and left for the café. The September morning was pleasantly warm. About half of the trees sprinkled throughout the fields and mountainsides were displaying their fiery autumn colors. The rest remained stubbornly green. Robins chirped and squirrels sprang from branch to branch as she passed by. Near the church, a group of white-tailed deer emerged from the forest, graceful creatures that delighted Ellie no matter how many times she encountered them.

Her steps were light the remainder of the way. For the first time in a very long while, she felt refreshed, as if a heavy burden had been lifted from her shoulders. Fragile hope trickled through her. Sure, she was apprehensive about the birth, as well as the prospect of being solely responsible for her child's well-being, but she trusted God to provide. He'd sustained her through a troubled marriage and blessed her with employment and now a nice, comfortable place to live. He'd give her the strength to deal with the future.

Unsurprisingly, Alexander was closeted in his office when she arrived. Ellie watched his door like a hawk waiting to pounce. By two o'clock, her patience had evaporated. A plate of food in one hand, she read the paper he'd attached to the smooth wood surface.

"Do not disturb."

She scowled. He was wrong if he thought a flimsy piece of paper would prevent her from her goal.

He took his time answering the door. When his towering form filled the doorway, his closed-off features inches from hers, a quiver of awareness vibrated in her middle. His eyes were so very blue, the inner ring made more vivid by the darker, outer one. When they were locked onto her like this, she felt slightly dazed by their beauty. His black locks were like rich silk against his pale skin. His mouth fit his carved features, but it was also full and soft-looking, too.

The faint scent of soap that clung to his clothes wafted to her, mingling with that of the sliced beef and cabbage on his plate. She switched to breathing through her mouth. Being sick all over her boss's polished shoes was a humiliation she couldn't afford.

"Ellie." His expression was one of long suffering. "Did you not see my sign?"

"I saw it. You have excellent handwriting." Lifting the plate, she said, "It's long past noon. You missed your lunch."

His lips compressed. "This may come as a surprise to you, but I am able to see to my own needs."

"And I'm not?" she quipped.

"I'm not sure to what you're referring."

"You informed my hostess not to disturb me this morning, did you not? Without consulting me."

His gaze searched her features with disconcerting intensity. Then he stationed himself behind his desk. Ellie took that as an invitation and, stepping inside, closed the door. When she'd placed his meal between a thick sheaf of papers and his pen holder, he said, "You didn't enjoy the extra sleep?"

"I didn't say that." A rueful laugh escaped. Without waiting for his permission, she sat in one of the chairs, tugging her apron down to cover a stain on her gray skirt. "I feel more refreshed today than I have since arriving in Tennessee. For that, I thank you."

He hesitated, staring at her and then the food. Apparently accepting she wasn't going anywhere, he sank into the leather chair and started eating without saying grace. She didn't recall seeing him at church. Was he not a believer? Or had his walk with Christ suffered due to whatever trouble had befallen him?

Since she likely wouldn't get an answer to those questions, she didn't bother posing them.

"Flo said the crowd was sparse this morning."

The café did the most business during the dinner hour.

Lunch was brisk, as well, with bachelors making up the majority.

"I'll have to take your word for it."

His ongoing disinterest in his own business flummoxed Ellie. He must have wealth independent of this venture, which meant the Plum's success or failure wouldn't impact his livelihood. The same couldn't be said for his employees.

"Have you owned other restaurants?"

"No."

Perhaps it was his inexperience guiding his inattentiveness? But that didn't make sense. Alexander struck her as a shrewd man.

"What did you do before this then?"

He was silent for several long beats. A muscle ticked in his square jaw. His focus on his plate, he said quietly, "I owned a ranch in Texas."

"*Texas*? You don't fit the image I have of a rancher."

Alexander's gaze collided with hers. "I left that life behind a long time ago."

The pain he couldn't quite hide—emotional this time, not physical—underscored her conviction that he needed a friend.

"Do you have family there? Friends?"

His throat working, he laid his fork down. "I appreciate what you're trying to do, but I'd rather not discuss my past."

She noticed he'd only eaten half the food. Standing, she said, "I didn't mean to disrupt your meal. It's just that…"

He arched a brow. "Just what?"

"Well, I—"

His full attention made her self-conscious of her shabby clothing and her unsophisticated hairstyle. She suddenly yearned to be admired by this man, which was wholly impossible and not thoughts an expectant widow should be thinking!

Balancing his elbows on the surface, he steepled his hands. "You may as well speak your mind," he drawled. "You usually do, eventually."

"Pardon my bluntness, but you seem very alone. I think you could use a friend. Yet you do nothing to encourage friendships."

His gaze promptly lowered, thick lashes resting against the hollows beneath his eyes. "It's the way I prefer to live my life. Less chance of complications."

"The loneliness doesn't bother you?"

"A small price to pay for peace."

His expression didn't share the conviction of his words. He didn't seem peaceful in the slightest.

"I know what it is to be lonely," she admitted. "It wasn't by choice. Living with my grandparents, I led a full life. We were involved in our church and were friends with most of the neighbors. I didn't stop to wonder why the Jamesons weren't part of our circle." She brushed her fingers over the faded lace edging on the apron that had once belonged to her grandmother. "I was young and naïve. After my grandmother's passing, I was overwhelmed by everything that needed to be done. The funeral service. The sale of the farm—I wanted to stay but I couldn't work it by myself. Howard's offer to buy it seemed like an answer to prayer. His property abutted ours. I'd still be close, you know? And then Nolan proposed…my future went from being scary and uncertain to being assured."

Lost in memories that stirred sadness and regret, she belatedly registered Alexander's piercing regard. His thoughts were impossible to decipher.

"The Jamesons restricted your social interactions?"

The inquiry surprised her. It wasn't his habit to pry. "They did. I resisted at first, but it only angered Nolan and made life uncomfortable. So I adjusted."

"You shouldn't have had to." He pushed the food around on his plate.

"I was compelled to cut off my friendships. No one is requiring you to." She made an encompassing gesture. "I'm discovering that Gatlinburg is home to plenty of caring folks, but they won't force themselves on you. You have to invite their company."

His fork clinked against the plate, and he gave up the pretense of eating. "I'm not sure what gave you the impression that I'm discontent with my current lifestyle. I don't need anyone, Ellie."

The resignation with which he spoke, combined with the hint of sadness in his eyes, prompted her response. Why wouldn't he admit the truth? "You need Flo and Sally. You need me. You need customers."

His gaze became hooded. "You mistake my meaning."

"But—"

He stood to his feet like a king expecting immediate obedience. "I believe we're done here."

Ellie smoothed her apron. "You've been more than kind to me. I simply wanted to offer you…" She swept her hair behind her shoulder and made a dismissive gesture. Why would a man like him value *her* friendship? "I wanted to express my gratitude for everything you've done."

His chest rose and fell in an exaggerated breath. "I didn't do anything out of the ordinary."

"Still, your thoughtfulness means a lot, especially after the past four years." She clamped her lips shut. He didn't wish to hear any more about her disappointments. "I'll, ah, go get started on that rhubarb pie for tonight."

Alexander didn't attempt to stop her. Her mood dampened, she left him to his solitude.

Raised voices coming from the dining room startled Alexander, and his pencil skidded across the page, marring the sketch of a black bear and her cubs. Irritated, he left his office and walked through the short hallway, pausing on the threshold. The tables were full of customers enjoying their evening meal, an unheard-of phenomenon before Ellie. At the moment, they were focused on three people in the corner near the fireplace.

His waitress, Sally Hatcher, wore a cowed expression as a patron, a man taller than Alexander and who likely outweighed him by a hundred pounds, shook his finger in her face. Gauging from the wet stain on his shirtfront and bits of coleslaw scattered on his person, Sally had had a bout of clumsiness. The man's face was mottled.

How anyone could be angry with the earnest, softhearted eighteen-year-old was beyond him. At only an inch or two above five feet and thin as a fence post, Sally was the type of girl who provoked protective feelings in most men.

The man let loose another verbal lash. Sally's big brown eyes filled with tears. Her head lowering, her wispy, corn-colored hair slid forward to hide her flaming cheeks. With a disgusted sound, Ellie inserted herself between waitress and customer as a living barrier. The sight made Alexander's throat close up. He felt the crowd's attention switch to him as he wove through the tables to reach them.

"It was an unfortunate accident, sir." Ellie projected a calm front, but Alexander detected her underlying distress. The irate man was at least a foot taller than her. "Sally didn't mean any harm. I'm sure you've had mishaps before. None of us are immune, unfortunately."

"How am I supposed to finish my dinner with my shirt wet through and smellin' of vinegar?" he growled.

Ellie's forehead wrinkled. "I understand that would be uncomfortable. If we had a shirt to give you, we would."

"My meal is ruined, and I want to know what you're gonna do about it."

"Leave her alone, McCauley," someone from another table muttered.

Alexander pulled Sally aside. "Go fetch something to clean the food off the floor," he murmured.

"Yes, sir. Right away." She fled the room.

As she at last registered his presence, the color in Ellie's cheeks surged and waned. He couldn't resist the silent appeal for help in her coffee-brown gaze.

Moving close beside her, he stuck out his hand. "Good evening, sir. I'm Alexander Copeland, the proprietor of the Plum. I see you've met with a mishap."

"Any fool can see that," he snapped, indicating his chest.

"I apologize for the inconvenience. If you'd like to accompany me to the kitchen, we can get you cleaned up. And of course, your meal will be on the house."

His unkempt brows formed a deep V.

"You're welcome to your choice of dessert, as well." Ellie piped up. "We have rhubarb pie and fried apple pies."

"Go with the rhubarb," another patron called out. "Finest pie I've put in my mouth."

"Harry!" the lady beside him complained.

"Oh, not as fine as yours, my dear."

A few chuckles filtered through the room.

"I'll take you up on your offer," Mr. McCauley consented. "Rhubarb it is."

Alexander had managed to calm a customer. Glancing at Ellie, he acknowledged she was the reason he'd gotten involved. Once he had the mess sorted out, he joined her at the stove where she was sprinkling salt and chopped herbs into a fragrant potato soup.

"In the future, I want you to alert me immediately if another scene like that one arises."

Dusting her fingers on her no longer pristine apron, she tilted her head to one side, causing her ponytail to swing wide. "Sally and I are accustomed to dealing with unruly customers."

He grimaced as once again he pictured her squaring off against the giant of a man. "It's my responsibility."

Clearly mystified, she nodded. "All right. I'll let Sally know."

"Thank you."

He was about to turn away when he noticed she was wearing the unflattering gray blouse and skirt beneath her frilly apron, the same clothes she'd worn several days in a row. Suspicion wound through him.

He made sure Flo was properly occupied on the other side of the room before voicing his thoughts.

"I don't mean to be insensitive, but is that your only outfit?"

Her eyes rounded before she became inordinately interested in the simmering soup. "At the moment it is."

While he knew he'd embarrassed her, he couldn't let the matter drop. "Did your in-laws prevent you from taking your belongings?"

The spoon's stirring slowed. "H-how did you guess?"

The soft pink hue tingeing her cheeks mirrored her rosebud mouth and lent a feminine delicacy to her features. She wasn't beautiful, exactly, but definitely intriguing.

Shaking off the thoughts, he answered her. "They're spiteful enough to forbid you to utilize one of their horses for transportation. Based on your comments of how they took the news, not to mention the fact you had only a quilt with you the other night, it was a logical conclusion."

"Ralph snuck the quilt out to me. He wasn't able to get anything else," she said. "I don't wish to be an embarrassment to the café. Once I save up enough money, I'll buy fabric to make new clothes."

Without thinking what he was doing, he grasped her chin and gently tipped up her face. "You're not an embarrassment, Ellie. That's not why I asked. As I said before, I've had brushes with bullies and I detest such behavior. I won't allow an employee of mine to be treated that way."

Moisture gathered in her molten eyes. "Oh."

Her warm breath fanned over his fingers. He had but to move his thumb an inch to test the texture of her bee-stung lips. Lowering his hand and shoving it in his pocket, he edged back a step.

"Immediately following breakfast tomorrow, I will accompany you to collect your things."

Blinking fast, she laid the soup spoon on the table behind her. "That's not necessary—"

"Oh, but it is." His tone brooked no argument. "I'll let you get back to work."

Slipping outside into the tranquil evening, he gazed up at the stars, the same stars that overlooked his Texas ranch and the graves of Sarah and Levi. The familiar weight of grief and anger squeezed his heart.

"I don't know what Your purpose is in bringing her here, God, but I won't be part of it. I'll do this thing for her, and that's it. No more."

Chapter Five

She was going to be sick. "Please pull over."

Alexander shot her a dubious look. "The turnoff isn't far ahead."

"Please, hurry!"

He must've recognized the panicked note in her voice, because he hauled back on the reins and directed the team to the lane's edge.

"Let me assist you."

Ignoring him, Ellie scrambled down from the buggy and dashed into the woods. The trees and profuse underbrush hid her wretched state. Many minutes later, when she was somewhat reassured her stomach had settled, she trudged over ferns and fallen leaves, mortification seizing her. Alexander would have questions.

She'd awoken that morning with a vague sense of dread. There was no way of knowing how this confrontation would pan out, but having her boss there as a witness added a layer of anxiety to an already problematic situation.

He was waiting for her when she emerged into the lane. Standing on her side of the buggy, he swept her with his gaze, uncertainty an ill-fitting mantle on the usually unruffled gentleman.

He took a single step forward. "What's the matter? Are you ill?"

"I'm afraid my nerves got the better of me. It's quite embarrassing, losing my breakfast within my boss's hearing. Let's agree to forget about it, shall we?"

His frown deepened. Turning away, he removed a canteen from beneath the seat and held it out to her. "You looked peaked. Perhaps a couple of sips of water would help."

After she'd finished, he withdrew a handkerchief from his vest pocket and dampened it. "Here."

Touched by his patient manner, Ellie wiped her face. The damp cloth felt wonderful. Although mid-September, the days weren't much cooler than those they'd experienced in the height of summer.

When she made to return it, he said, "Use it for as long as you need. Are you ready to resume our journey or do you require more time?"

She forced a smile. "I'm ready."

Alexander didn't immediately move aside. Beneath his bowler hat, his expression was difficult to read. "I could go without you. Spare you the trouble."

Stunned, she worked to form a reply. "That's kind of you to offer," she said at last. "However, this is my battle to fight. While I don't relish the thought of you having to witness this ugliness, I'm grateful for your presence."

A peculiar emotion passed over his face. With a dip of his head, he lightly gripped her arm and assisted her into the buggy. The conveyance jerked into motion, and Ellie pressed her hand against her tummy, praying it would quieten. Her body tensed as the twin cabins came into view. Nadine was on her porch churning butter. Spying them, she moved to stand on the steps, arms crossed over her chest and her eyes flashing.

She waited until they'd disembarked to demand, "What do you want, Ellie?"

Tall like her mother, Nadine had flyaway blond hair offset by sunbaked skin stretched over harsh cheekbones. She wore plain, everyday work clothes that accentuated her slenderness. When Ellie had accepted Nolan's proposal, she'd been thrilled by the prospect of gaining a sister. Unfortunately, Nadine hadn't returned the sentiment. It was almost as if she'd been jealous of Ellie's intrusion into their family unit. Prone to grumbling about everything under the sun, she'd found plenty to complain about concerning Ellie.

Drawing strength from Alexander's watchful presence beside her, she said, "I've come to collect my things."

"My folks aren't here, but I'll tell you what they'd say. Get off our property and don't come back."

Ellie felt Alexander stiffen beside her. "You know it isn't fair to prevent me from having them."

"Consider it payment for room and board."

"I did pay you, Nadine."

Ralph walked around the cabin, a box of tools in his hand, the sun shining on his balding head. His initial surprise turned to wariness.

"Ellie." His gaze slid to Alexander. "Who did you bring with you?"

She made the introductions. Neither man moved to shake hands.

"Ralph, I don't want her here," Nadine implored her husband. "Make them leave."

Alexander stepped forward. "We'll do as you ask as soon as you grant Ellie's request."

"This is none of your business," she snapped.

"She's made it my business." A vein ticked in his temple. He looked even more forbidding than usual. "Now, you can act in a reasonable manner or you can continue this foolishness, in which case I'll be forced to involve the sheriff."

Ralph hastened to his wife's side. "He's right, you know," he ventured in a gentle voice. "It's not right to keep Ellie from taking her belongings. She's family."

Nadine jerked away. "That woman has never been part of this family, and you know it! If not for her, my brother would still be here…" she choked out, tears threatening.

Ralph attempted to console his wife. Alexander angled his body toward Ellie, partially blocking her view of the pair. She hoped her expression didn't tell the story of her deep dismay and the sense of failure that cropped up in her weakest moments. She hadn't been good enough for Nolan or his loved ones.

"Let's go for a walk." Curving an arm about his wife's waist, Ralph directed her toward the forest, surreptitiously signaling for them to hurry about their business.

When they were out of earshot, Alexander touched Ellie's sleeve. "Let's not delay."

Upset by Nadine's outburst, she didn't speak as she climbed the steps and entered the cabin. The smell of Nadine and Ralph's breakfast lingered in the close air, bacon and eggs cooked in animal fat, mixed with the strong hint of disintegrating firewood. Breathing through her mouth, Ellie walked to the far corner where her bed and dresser were situated. Alexander remained in the doorway, a silent guardian. She placed her clothes and a handful of books inside a small crate she'd stored beneath the bed. A framed photograph of herself and Nolan was wedged between her keepsake box and a mirror and brush set.

Picking it up, she experienced a rush of sorrow at the reminder of the naïve girl she'd once been.

"You should take that." Alexander's rumbling voice behind her made her jump. "If you want to."

She traced her image. "I'm glad that girl didn't know what lay ahead."

"Were they always this hostile?"

"Not in the beginning." She placed the frame with her other things—her baby would wish to see what her father looked like. "Nolan developed a marked mistrust of my loyalty. His doubts spread to the others. While not ideal, life was tolerable in Kentucky. The cross-state move put tremendous pressure on us all. The trip was arduous and the living conditions once we arrived were strained." Living in canvas tents in the height of spring had been fraught with multiple challenges. "After his death, I believe their grief exacerbated their already poor opinion of me."

He studied the ring on her finger. "How long were you married?"

"Four years."

"I'm not sure how you endured it."

"I wasn't in any physical danger. They weren't nice to me, it's true, but God saw to my needs. I had a roof over my head and clothes to wear. Food to eat. In my lowest points, I reread the account of Job. He lost everything, and still God sustained him."

His blue eyes went flat. "I commend your fortitude and generosity of spirit."

His demeanor hinted at his own troublesome trials. His past was a complete mystery, and he preferred to keep it that way. Why? What terrible wrong had he committed or had committed against him?

"Mr. Copeland—"

"I believe we've passed the formality stage, don't you? Call me Alexander." His gaze quelling any questions she might pose, he inventoried the room's contents. "Do you have everything?"

"The furniture Nolan and I shared is being stored in the barn, but I don't have need of it."

Replacing his bowler hat on his head, he lifted the crate. "Then let us not tarry."

Outside in the yard, Ellie scanned and rescanned the woods. When he'd secured her things behind the seat, he turned to assist her. She placed her hand in his strong one. To take her mind off his heated skin and the tingle of pleasure the contact wrought, she said, "I'm glad Howard and Gladys aren't here. The scene would've been much uglier."

He lifted the right panel of his suit jacket. "I came prepared."

Ellie plopped onto the seat. "I've seen you with your hunting rifle, of course, but I had no idea you owned a six-shooter. That's a nice model. My grandfather owned one, only his had a pearl handle."

Alexander circumvented the horse and, once in the buggy, took hold of the reins. "I had quite the collection back home. You never know what or who you'll encounter on the vast range." He uttered a low command, and they were on their way.

Ellie tried to imagine him in cowboy gear. It was a stretch. His austere business attire fit his personality and role as café proprietor. "Tell me about Texas."

His features shuttered. "I don't like to discuss my—"

"Past. I know. I'm not asking you to divulge your secrets, Alexander." It felt good to voice what she'd been calling him in her head. "I'd simply enjoy hearing about a place I've only read about in books and newspapers."

He sent her a brief, considering glance.

"It's only fair," she tacked on. "You've had a front-row seat to my sideshow."

A sigh gusted out of him. Once they were on the lane leading to town, he obliged her. "I grew up on a cattle ranch smack in the north central frontier of Texas. My father bought the land several years before he met my mother. He built the barns and workers' quarters first. He didn't bother with a proper house until later, when he found his bride and realized he'd need a place to raise a family. I was the first to come along. Next was Thomas, then Margaret." He fell silent, his brow knitted in deep thought.

"How wonderful to have siblings. I always lamented my lack."

Remembering her childhood longings, she wondered if her own child would ever have a brother or sister. For that to happen, she'd have to meet a man worth taking a chance on. Her marriage to Nolan had been such a disappointment. A trial, even. Ellie wasn't sure she could take the risk.

"Yes." He roused himself from his musings. "It has its advantages."

"How long has it been since you've seen them?"

"Several years."

"Any plans to make a trip home?"

He cast her a sharp look. "Texas is no longer my home. I will not be returning."

"I see."

Only, she didn't. Whatever trouble he'd endured was linked to his home state. Ellie doubted he'd ever open up to her, but that didn't stop her from wishing he would.

Sundays were Alexander's only days of true solitude. The café was closed for business. Most of Gatlinburg's residents attended church services in the morning and spent time with family and friends in the afternoon. He relished the quiet and the fact he had the building all to himself. No whining customers. No intrusions upon his time. No doe-eyed waif of a cook who poked and prodded his armor with disturbing regularity.

On his knees in the vegetable garden, pulling weeds and plucking beetles from his cabbage plants, he scolded himself for getting involved in Ellie's troubles. He couldn't seem to help himself, however…old habits reasserting themselves. Well, he was done. She had her belongings. She had a place to stay. She didn't need a reluctant protector.

The knowledge didn't keep him from getting angry every time he recalled her emerging from the woods after being sick. That awful gray outfit had washed out her complexion. Even her delicately-shaped lips had lost their color. She'd looked miserable. And he'd felt the insane urge to shelter her in his arms until she'd recovered.

And then there were her troublesome in-laws. He'd been tempted to deliver a scathing set-down to that woman, Nadine. Ellie's goodness, her lack of bitterness, astounded him. Her bravery, too. Sarah would've jumped at the chance to let him take control of the situation. Not Ellie. Although anxious, she'd tackled her dilemma with reason and self-control.

"Good afternoon."

Surprised to see the object of his thoughts at the edge of his garden, Alexander thumbed his old Stetson farther up his forehead and squinted into the late afternoon rays slanting over the mountains. His mouth dried up like the ranch's creeks after a drought. Ellie looked different today. Gone was the nondescript outfit and perky ponytail. She'd paired a crimson, high-necked blouse with a sturdy navy skirt whose only nod to femininity was a wide ruffle along the hem. Dangly silver and amber earrings adorned her dainty ears. Her brown hair rippled about her shoulders, the top section pulled back and tied with a crimson-and-navy polka-dot ribbon. The hairstyle softened her gamine features, and the rich hue of her blouse made her coffee eyes shine. Bathed in the tawny light of approaching autumn, she was as pretty as a picture.

"How old are you?" he blurted.

Her brows lifted a notch. "Twenty-two. Why?"

"I assumed you were much younger."

She adjusted the bundle in her arms. "How old are *you*?"

"How old do you think I am?"

She inspected him openly until he felt his ears burn. Did she realize how expressive her eyes could be? Admiration shone in the sparkling depths. No one had regarded him like that for a long time.

"Thirty."

"Close." Dusting his gloves on his pants, he stood and gathered the piles of weeds. "I'm twenty-eight."

Ellie watched as he dumped the weeds in an old seed bag to be discarded later. As he walked to her side, a gentle breeze teased her loose strands, forcing her to shift her burden in order to dislodge them from where they'd snagged on her mouth.

"What's this?" he said, indicating the mound of fabric.

"The new cloths and curtains. I thought I'd switch them out if you don't mind."

Alexander wasn't as perturbed by her unannounced visit as he should've been. He stuffed his gloves in his back pocket and held out his hands. "Let me carry that inside."

She released them into his hold, and he caught a whiff of her light verbena perfume.

"You finished these in record time."

She fell into step beside him, her rosebud mouth curving in a bright smile. "June insisted on helping me. I tried to share my earnings with her, but she refused. Said I had to save up money for the—"

He shot her a side glance. "For the what?"

Moistening her lips, she said, "For the future."

"You're a widow like her. Makes sense she'd be sensitive to your position."

"Yes," she softly agreed.

They entered the unusually quiet café. Passing through the kitchen and hallway and into the dining area, he was very aware of her proximity, the differences in their heights, the way she walked and gestured and carried herself. Being alone with Ellie was becoming a habit, one he was growing too comfortable with and must take efforts to curtail.

When she started to drag a chair over to the first window, he intercepted her.

"You take care of the tables. I'll see to the curtains."

Finger to her chin, she studied the room. "How about we work together? You remove the old curtains, and I'll hand you the replacements."

"All right."

While they worked, she gave him a commentary on that morning's services. Apparently a bird had gotten inside and had interrupted the sermon, swooping toward women's hats and causing mayhem as a few of the men attempted to capture it. She described the scene in such detail, Alexander couldn't help smiling.

"I've never seen you there," she mused. "Why don't you attend?"

His smile faded. Rolling the ratty curtains into a bundle, he twisted to hand it to her. Why must she persist in stirring up painful issues? First she'd questioned him about Texas. Now this.

He stepped down from the chair, bringing him close enough to notice her thick, curling eyelashes and a tiny scar edging her lower lip. Once again, he became distracted by her loveliness.

The change in her wasn't *that* dramatic, he reprimanded himself. Ellie was simply the first woman he'd spent any significant amount of time with since arriving in Tennessee several years ago.

"I haven't gone to church in ages," he said. "I have no desire to sit and listen about God's goodness and love."

Compassion softened her eyes. "I've suspected for some time that you suffered a horrible hurt, something you haven't shared with anyone. But God sees your private struggle. He'll give you the grace to work through it, if you let Him."

Alexander couldn't deny he craved freedom from the burdens coiled around him like heavy chains. Her gentle understanding and the conviction of her words tempted him to let go of the hatred he carried for his enemy, the disillusion directed toward his Creator, the guilt and anger he felt over his own actions.

Her small, soft hand curved around his forearm. "You don't have to shoulder your burdens alone, you know. You could talk to me. Or Duncan. Reverend Munroe. No one will judge you."

"Please, Ellie, don't press me on this."

Her countenance pensive, she gave a reluctant nod. "I can still pray for you, can't I?"

Startled, he was trying to form a response when there came a rap on the door. Moving blindly to release the latch, he stared at the couple on the boardwalk wearing matching grins.

"Alexander." Duncan McKenna clapped him on the shoulder. "We were passing by and saw you through the window. Mind if we come in for a minute?"

He absently moved aside as the auburn-haired Scotsman escorted his wife, Caroline, into the midst of their redecoration project. The pair was partly responsible for hiring Ellie. While he hadn't been happy about their meddling, and he'd been pulled into his new cook's affairs, he no longer resented their actions. The Plum was better because of it.

"How are you getting along, Ellie?" Caroline inquired, her blue eyes softening with fondness. "We've come in to eat several times, and we've yet to be disappointed."

A blush tinted her cheeks. "Satisfying customers is my top priority. It's nice to hear I'm succeeding."

"I'm still learning my way around the kitchen. Eating here is a treat for both of us, trust me."

Laughter rumbled deep in Duncan's chest. Taking hold of his wife's hand, he placed a gallant kiss on her knuckles. "You're improving every day, my love."

The affection passing between them made Alexander uncomfortable. He glanced at Ellie but was unable to gauge her reaction. She'd only recently lost her husband. Did it pain her to see a couple so deeply in love with each other?

He ran his finger along the empty spot where his wedding band once rested. The hole Sarah's death had created was complete. He made it a point not to dwell on how much he missed having a connection to another person.

The blonde's next words brought him out of his ruminations.

"Ellie, have you considered offering classes? I'm certain young women on the verge of marriage would pay for your instruction."

"Don't most girls learn to cook from their mothers? Or grandmothers, as I did?"

"There are some whose mothers aren't around or aren't able to impart their knowledge. Others might wish to further what skills they possess. I'd be your first student."

Ellie's hand drifted to her midsection in a protective gesture, something she did often, he realized. The move struck him as familiar, somehow.

"I'm not sure. I'd have to give it some thought."

Alexander spoke up. "I have serious reservations about such a plan. While a valid one, Ellie is stretched thin as it is. Most of her time is spent planning and preparing meals."

Caroline's gaze reflected concern. "I didn't think about that."

Ellie simply looked surprised he'd voice an opinion.

Duncan's grin had a sly slant. "We share your concern for Ellie's well-being. She's been an asset to this community." Rubbing his hand along his jaw, he scrutinized Alexander. "For you, in particular. You're looking much improved."

When he'd been confined to the sickbed over at Doc Owens's, the Scotsman had been his only visitor.

"I have benefited from Ellie's nurturing nature," he conceded. "She's made it her mission to nurse me back to health and is always on hand with a glass of cold milk to soothe my upset stomach."

A spark of mischief entered her dark eyes. "Don't let him fool you. Alexander isn't the least pleased with my interference."

Duncan laughed outright. "Oh, I've had a taste of his displeasure. You've a thick skin, ma'am."

"Most of the time," she agreed, her gaze skittering away.

Alexander studied her. For so long, he'd been mired in his grief to the point of being oblivious to others' feelings. Although he hadn't been outright cruel, he hadn't exactly been kind. Shame shafted through him.

"We'll let you get back to work," Duncan said. "Caroline and I are taking a ride into the mountains this afternoon."

When Alexander remained silent, Ellie followed them to the door. "That sounds fun." A gust of wind pushed through the opening, tugging at her ribbons. "Have a wonderful time."

Caroline's smile encompassed them both. "Thank you. We'll see you around."

"Thanks for stopping by."

They left hand in hand, heads together as they engaged in conversation. This time, Ellie couldn't hide a wistful expression. She leaned against the closed door and sighed.

Alexander resumed his spot on the chair. "Let's get this over with so you can enjoy what's left of your day off."

She complied without a word of objection. They worked in disconcerting silence until every last cloth and curtain had been replaced. What was she thinking about? he wondered. The McKennas and their happy life? Was she considering finding a replacement husband? Alexander hadn't spoken to anyone of his adjustment from husband to widower. He'd walked the lonely road of grief alone.

"You did a good job, Ellie." He felt the need to express his gratitude. "The soft yellow color makes a big difference."

He hadn't realized how dreary and depressing the

heavy maroon fabric had made the room seem. Sunlight passed easily through the swaths of cotton she'd chosen. If he'd been invested in his own business, he would've made the necessary changes himself.

"Thank you." She smiled. "I had hoped you'd be pleased."

"I am." He gestured toward the hallway. "Let me walk you out."

"What about the discards?"

"I'll take care of them."

Outside at the garden, she paused near his cabbage plants. "I can help you finish the weeding, if you like. I interrupted your chore."

The breeze ruffled his hair. He impatiently brushed it out of his eyes and studied the sky. The towering white clouds didn't appear to hold rain.

"I appreciate the offer, but I can do it on my own."

Her smile had a sad quality. "Then I bid you good day, Alexander."

She was about to turn away when another strong gust whipped her hair and flattened her skirt, molding the material to her slender body. Almost immediately, she moved to cover her midsection, but not before he saw the distinct bulge that couldn't be explained by anything other than a developing pregnancy.

Cold shock shivered through him.

Her eyes grew round, her lips working in distress. "Alexander…"

The heat of denial raced through his veins. He felt disoriented. Sarah's laughing face exploded in his mind's eye. Memories rushed at him. The day she'd informed him he was going to be a father and the indescribable joy he'd felt. Her frequent sickness and complaints about her growing girth. Then, after months of anticipation, the day came that his beautiful baby boy had entered the world. He'd been giddy with pride.

Alexander's muscles locked up. He had no idea what his expression revealed, but he could plainly see Ellie's trepidation.

"Why, Ellie?" he scraped out. "Why didn't you tell me you were expecting a baby?"

Chapter Six

Ellie had expected mild surprise, not outright dismay. "I was going to tell you. Eventually. You have to understand it's not an easy conversation to strike up."

His beautiful blue gaze was locked on her middle as a riot of emotions herded across his face. She folded her hands at her waist to impede his view.

"What would you have had me say, Alexander? We're serving chicken and dumplings for supper and, oh, by the way, I'm expecting my late husband's child in the spring."

"That's why you were sick the other day," he murmured. "Why you've been exhausted."

"You don't have to worry about the café. I can work right up until time—around mid-March. I'll require a couple of weeks off, of course, but when I'm able to return to work, I can feed the baby during the breaks. I assume she'll sleep a lot in the beginning. I haven't yet figured out what I'll do once she's older and toddling around."

His gaze bored into her. Ellie fought the impulse to avert her face. She'd dreaded this moment, and now that he knew, it was somewhat of a relief.

Shoving his hand through his dark locks, he clamped

his lips together and shook his head. "I'm sorry, I can't have you here. You'll have to find alternative employment."

Ellie's jaw sagged as Alexander pivoted and strode toward the stoop.

"What?" He was firing her?

Rushing through the grass, she seized his hand and refused to let go.

"I deserve an explanation."

He stiffened.

"I don't understand your reaction at all," she charged. "This baby isn't going to affect your life that much. You're hardly ever around, and when you are, you're holed up in your office." She increased the pressure on his fingers. "Please. I need this job."

"You can let go of my hand now," he pushed through wooden lips.

She slowly released him.

He twisted to face her, remorse etched in his features. "My wife and one-year-old son perished in a fire three years ago. It takes everything I have not to relive that nightmare day in and day out. I can't live with the reminder of what I've lost. *I can't*."

Alexander's stoic mask slipped, and Ellie glimpsed the depth of his brokenness. The word *fire* penetrated her mind, and she connected it with the scars on his hands. Alexander must've been at the scene. He would've done everything in his power to save them.

"I had no idea you'd even been married," she murmured, her heart aching. "Or had a child."

She knew what it meant to lose a precious little one. She hadn't gotten a chance to hold her babies in her arms, but that didn't make her mourning any less powerful. Her heart broke for Alexander. This was the answer to her long-held question—he eschewed the world in order to avoid further pain. While she didn't agree with his method of coping, she understood what drove him.

"Now you do." He heaved a sigh. "I truly am sorry, Ellie. You've been an asset to the Plum." The finality in his voice troubled her. He started to turn away.

"Please listen!" She wasn't too proud to beg. "I can't go back to that cove. Ralph figured out my secret and advised me to leave. He's right. Gladys and Nadine will see this baby as their last link to Nolan. You've witnessed their dislike. I fear they'll try to turn my own child against me."

"Surely there are other jobs you could do. Perhaps at the mercantile."

"I didn't see any advertisements when I was there searching for lodging. Not anything suitable, anyway. Besides, who's going to cook for you? Do you really want to host another town-wide cooking contest? Start fresh with someone new?" She leaned in. "I've mostly left you alone."

He arched a brow in challenge.

"I said mostly," she defended. "What if the next person you hire is more interfering than me?"

His troubled gaze shifted to the forested mountain peaks and a pair of vultures riding the air current in a circular pattern over unseen remains.

"I promise I'll stay out of your way," she pressed. "No more daily intrusions."

"I don't know, Ellie…"

"At least let me work until the baby's born." By that time, he'd see that having her around wasn't as difficult as he imagined. They'd be under the same roof, but they'd rarely see each other.

His gaze skewered her. "No more requests, right? No more visits to my office?"

"None. Unless I have a pressing problem, and then I could merely slip a paper beneath your door. We could converse through written messages."

The corners of his mouth turned down. "Don't be absurd."

"What? It could work. You wouldn't have to see my face or…" She squirmed at the thought of what she might look like in the ending stages of her pregnancy. "Or any other part of me. Just my handwriting."

"I know my issues are putting you in a difficult position." He scrubbed his hand down his face. "I know it, and yet I can't help how I feel. I'm sorry."

"You're willing to try, though."

"I'm willing to try. For you." He once again considered her midsection. "And for your baby."

Ellie couldn't help herself. She rose up on tiptoe and hugged him.

And for the briefest of moments, he hugged her back.

His arms were strong, his broad chest a steady support. Her head fit perfectly in the curve beneath his chin. His sudsy-clean scent flooded her system with pleasant sensation. Alexander felt like home, a wonderful, warm place of acceptance.

Too soon, he gently peeled her arms away.

Bewildered by the depth of her longing to remain in his embrace, she quipped, "I suppose hugging my boss breaks the rules."

Clasping his hands behind his back, he regarded her as one would a troublesome child.

"You will be taking the morning shift off from now until March."

"I can't afford to have my pay cut!"

"You won't."

"I don't understand."

"Expectant women need more rest than usual, especially in the later months."

Ellie dearly wanted to pry. She had so many questions about his past. What had his wife been like? And here she'd assumed he hadn't ever courted a lady. He'd been a husband and, for a brief time, a father.

"I appreciate your concern, but I can't abandon Flo. She can't handle the breakfast rush alone."

"She won't be alone. I'll help her."

"You?"

"I can do the secondary preparation and the dish washing while Flo does the actual cooking." At her continued skepticism, he said, "That's the deal, Ellie. Take it or leave it."

Seemed she didn't have a choice.

Alexander's steps were measured as he approached the McKennas' place. The reason for his visit was a valid one, but he wasn't accustomed to seeking out others' help, not in his former life or this semblance of one he'd crafted.

The stately green Victorian home was situated amid old-growth trees. Meticulous flower beds hugged the foundation. It used to belong to Caroline's parents, the Turners. They'd given it to the newlyweds before relocating to Virginia. This was a house built for large families…he had no doubt the blissful couple planned to fill the rooms with their offspring.

Ellie's impending motherhood had knocked the wind from his sails. He'd reacted poorly. It wasn't until after she'd gone that he'd considered the impact this would have on her life. He'd thought only of his own discomfort. Instead of congratulating her, he'd promptly fired her.

His selfish behavior shamed him. This wasn't the man he'd been raised to be. For the first time since the fire that claimed his wife and son, he wondered what Sarah would think about the decisions he'd made.

"Good afternoon." An elderly man of Native American heritage rounded the corner of the house with bunches of yellow and orange mums in his arms. His wispy black hair bounced with each step. "I'm Wendell. May I help you?"

Alexander lifted a hand in greeting. "Afternoon. The name's Alexander Copeland. I'm looking for Duncan. Is he around?"

"He's in the stables. I'll take you to him."

The man led him past the house to the long rectangular building in the back. Duncan was leading a dappled gray horse out of the nearest entrance.

"Alexander." He stopped short. "Is everything all right at the Plum?"

"There's no emergency. I, ah, have a matter I'd like to discuss with you."

"Certainly." He thanked Wendell, dismissing him, and motioned for Alexander to walk with him toward the paddocks. "What's troubling you?"

"It's that obvious?"

"You wouldn't have paid me a visit otherwise."

His attention on the distant orchard, he pushed out the words. "Ellie's going to have a baby."

Saying it out loud cinched the knot in the middle of his chest even tighter. He should've pieced the puzzle together sooner. The idea of her experiencing the highs and lows of pregnancy, of actually bringing a child into the world all on her own did strange things to his head.

Duncan let loose a low whistle. "Is she now?"

"Yes."

"And that prompted you to come here because…"

"She doesn't have the best relationship with her in-laws. In fact, it's best if she stays away from them, which means she lacks a means of support. A young woman like her…a recent widow, alone and expecting her first child, she'll need friends."

They reached the paddock gate, and Duncan led the horse inside. Alexander waited for him to rejoin him. The Scotsman's blue gaze assessed him from beneath his Stetson.

"Why has this rattled you?"

"There are things you don't know about me."

He barked out a laugh. "No one knows much more than your name. That's the way you've wanted it."

"It's what I prefer," he responded stiffly. "No reason in airing my mistakes before a town full of busybodies."

"'Tis true that some folks would jump at a bit of juicy gossip like wolves on a carcass. No' all, though. There are good people here, Alexander. People who'd offer you true friendship."

"This isn't about me. I came to ask a favor for Ellie."

He cocked his head. "Does she ken you're here?"

"No."

He considered that. "What would you like us to do?"

"I was wondering if Caroline could befriend her. Maybe introduce her to other young ladies her age."

"As the head of the Benevolence Society, most of her time is devoted to charitable endeavors." Leaning against the fence, he folded his arms and lodged one boot on a lower rung. "However, she's on a first-name basis with most of the women in Gatlinburg. I'll talk to her. She likes Ellie. I'm certain she'll be happy to help."

The tension in Alexander's gut eased. Ellie was a likable person. She wouldn't have trouble forming lasting bonds.

He tried to imagine how Sarah would've coped with raising a child alone. He couldn't fathom it. She'd been a dependent sort. He hadn't minded being her strength and support in the beginning—it had fed into his ego. But no one man could be *everything* to his wife, and he'd wound up feeling discouraged and even resentful.

He couldn't help admiring Ellie's courage.

"Do you ken if Ellie's got marriage on her mind?"

"Her husband's only been gone a few months."

"She may view it as a matter of necessity. Ellie's far from home. She has no family, at least none she can count on. I *widnae* be surprised if she's considered the notion."

Alexander refused to examine why the notion unsettled him. "I have no idea. She hasn't mentioned it."

Not that she was prone to sharing her private thoughts with him. He wondered exactly when she'd been planning on telling him about the baby. Until she'd grown too big to hide it any longer?

Shaking off the ridiculous twinge of hurt—because really, he hadn't fostered an open, trusting relationship with her—he removed his hat and fanned his heated face.

"Ellie is a fine woman," he admitted. "Any of the local bachelors would be blessed to have her as a wife."

"Including you?" Duncan prompted.

"I'm not getting married again." Ever.

"Again?"

Alexander closed his eyes. "I was married once. She died."

He felt a heavy hand on his shoulder. "You have my condolences."

Opening his eyes, he encountered compassion in the other man's gaze. Putting his hat back on, he nodded, grateful when the Scotsman didn't press for details.

"Caroline's out at the pond resting from our afternoon ride. Care to join us?"

"No, thank you." He hadn't forgotten what it was like to be a newlywed. Privacy with one's spouse was something to be treasured. "I've got to get home."

But to what? No one awaited his return, not even a pet.

That hadn't bothered him until recent days. Until Ellie. With her innocent doe eyes, engaging smile and generous spirit, she had drawn him into her world and made him care…a circumstance he wasn't at all comfortable with or even happy about. As the ice protecting his heart thawed, the numbing effect lost its potency and the grief lying dormant clawed to the surface.

He'd intended to avoid dealing with his tragedy. Had he known the consequences Ellie's appointment as his cook would wreak, Alexander might've hung a For Sale sign in the window and moved to parts unknown.

Chapter Seven

"You feeling okay, boss?" Hugging the egg basket to her chest, Flo looked as if he'd just announced he was running for president.

"Where's Ellie?" Sally twisted her hands together. "She didn't quit, did she?"

Alexander sucked in a bolstering breath and continued rolling up his shirtsleeves. "I'm fine, Flo. And no, Ellie did not quit. As you both are aware, she's been working herself a bit too hard lately. I've given her the mornings off for the foreseeable future."

Flo's knuckles went white on the basket handle.

Sally gasped. "But who's going to cook?"

"Flo, can I count on you to do the majority of the cooking? I'll fill in where I'm needed both in the kitchen and the dining room."

"Yes, sir." She wore a resigned expression. Not a good sign.

"Sally?" he asked.

Still wearing a bemused expression, the eighteen-year-old slowly nodded. "Anything for Ellie."

The innocuous statement was a telling one. His employees were devoted to their fellow worker, not to him.

He'd left the running of his business to others for far too long. If he wanted to earn their respect, he was going to have to change his ways.

"I have utmost confidence that together, we can maintain the Plum's current standards. The customers have come to expect a clean, pleasant environment and tasty food—and that's thanks to Ellie. While we may not be able to match her excellence, I believe we can put out quality fare."

The women exchanged doubtful glances. "Yes, sir."

"I appreciate your willingness to work with me. Flo, feel free to alter the menu as you see fit. If you'll be more at ease limiting the options to two or three items, that's fine. Sally, I'll keep the coffee coming and assist you in busing tables." He rubbed his hands together. "Now, where can I find an apron?"

"Um, we supply our own," Sally hedged, waving her hand to the yellow-and-white-striped one covering her sapphire-blue dress.

"We don't have extras? In the storage room, perhaps?"

Flo's chin jutted, her frizzy curls quivering. "We asked you last year if we could order the professional ones, but you said no."

"I see."

The buxom woman's features took on a sly slant. "You can borrow Ellie's. I'm sure she wouldn't mind."

He followed her pointed finger to the full-body apron hanging from a nail beside the hallway entrance. On a background of pale pink, tiny red roses marched across the fabric. White eyelet ruffles enhanced the feminine garment. He'd seen her wearing it, of course, and had even thought it lent much-needed color to her gray outfit.

"I suppose there's nothing for it."

Looping it over his head and tying the ribbons behind

his waist, he ignored the ladies' reactions and made a mental note to order plain white aprons at his first opportunity. A glance at the clock told him they had no time to waste.

"Flo, what do you need for me to do first?"

Although initially hesitant to order him about, the women soon grew used to it. Alexander found himself participating in a myriad of tasks, everything from cracking eggs into a bowl for scrambled eggs, slicing bread loaves for toast and wiping tables in the dining room. His customers' reactions were pretty much the same across the board—outright shock that quickly turned to amusement.

He told himself it was a small price to pay. Ellie was home getting much-needed rest, which meant he didn't have to see her and be reminded of what he'd lost and would never have again. *Not to mention you won't have to confront those pesky feelings of concern for her. Was she endangering herself and the baby by being on her feet all hours of the day? Was she eating enough? How was she supposed to provide for herself once the baby came?*

Alexander could worry himself into another ulcer flare-up if he wasn't careful.

She's not your responsibility, he reminded himself.

Amid the hushed hum of conversation around him, he heard another customer enter and assumed Sally would greet him or her. The thud of boots approaching pulled his attention from the table he was wiping free of crumbs.

The man sporting an ear-to-ear grin could pass as Duncan McKenna's younger brother. But while Duncan hailed from Scotland, Gatlinburg's deputy was a Georgia native. Ben MacGregor's hair was a dark red and his bright green eyes held a perpetual glint of mischievousness. He'd been part of the four-person team who'd hired Ellie.

He stopped in front of Alexander and propped his hands on his waist, the badge pinned to his tan vest glinting. "I never dreamed of seeing you like this, Copeland. Nice apron."

"Have a seat, Deputy." He finished cleaning the table and pulled out a chair. "The menu's on the board. Can I get you a cup of coffee?"

"Coffee would be great, thanks."

Hooking his Stetson on the chair beside him, he made himself comfortable and waited for Alexander to bring his beverage. The young bachelor didn't have family in the area and either didn't like to cook or didn't know how, so he ate many of his meals at the Plum. Other times he ate with various families in town. Friendly and amenable, Ben MacGregor was a popular choice of dinner guest among those families with marriageable daughters. At least, that's what he'd overheard Sally say. Judging by the pert blonde's blushes and shy smiles whenever the deputy was near, the waitress harbored her own hopes at possible romance.

Alexander set the cup before Ben. "I forgot to ask if you take cream or sugar."

His eyes twinkled over the rim of the cup. "Neither." Uttering a satisfied sigh, he rested his forearm on the table. "Where's Ellie?"

"She's taking the morning off." Before Ben could pepper him with questions, he said, "She'll be here for the noon meal. What can I get you? The biscuits and gravy are popular this morning."

Ben's good humor dimmed. "She's not ill, is she?"

Did being nauseated from pregnancy count? "She's fine."

"I've never known her to take time off." He glanced out the window at the passersby. "Maybe I should pay her a visit."

Jealousy seared him. Caught off guard, he battled to school his features. Alexander refused to give in to the emotion. He had zero designs on Ellie. After his conversation with Duncan the previous evening, he'd stewed until the wee hours over whether or not she was contemplating marriage. He accepted that she shouldn't be alone. Ellie deserved a solid, responsible man who'd take care of her and the baby.

The deputy wasn't that man. Ben MacGregor possessed a reputation as a notorious flirt. He didn't hide the fact that he wasn't interested in commitment. That didn't stop the more determined young ladies from trying to change his mind, however. No, Ellie needed someone who'd cherish her. Someone who'd make up for her poor excuse of a first husband.

"I doubt she'd thank you for interrupting her first morning off." He strove for a nonchalant tone.

Ben's gaze swiveled around to punch Alexander's. He studied him for long moments. Gone was the carefree air that he wore like a second skin. In this moment, Alexander saw a different side to the debonair deputy.

"I suppose you're right," he said at last, lifting his cup to his lips. "You're her boss, after all. You'd know her preferences better than me."

Unsure what conclusions Ben was making, he asked again for his order.

Sally appeared at Alexander's side. Popping a cinnamon drop into her mouth, she tucked an errant blond strand into her single braid and beamed at Ben.

"Mr. Copeland, I'll be happy to take over. The deputy is my most loyal customer."

Ben's seriousness vanished like a puff of smoke. Dimples flashing, he winked at her. "Morning, Sally. Don't you look like a ray of sunshine today."

The eighteen-year-old stood taller and, batting her eyelashes, giggled and brushed aside his compliment. She inquired after someone named Pinto—probably a horse—and they launched into a conversation he had no part of.

Alexander suspected heartbreak lay ahead for his youngest employee. Hadn't anyone warned her not to hang her hopes on a man who wasn't looking for serious romance? Thoughts of his sister Margaret invaded. Was she as susceptible to charm as Sally? Was Thomas supervising her interactions with potential beaus?

Leaving the pair in order to clear another table of dishes, he considered taking Sally aside and offering a word of caution. He wasn't aware of her family situation. Perhaps she didn't have anyone to guide her in such matters. His sister did, however, and it was time to write Thomas and remind him of his responsibilities. Pushing aside a twinge of guilt over his hurried flight from Texas and his sparse correspondence in the intervening years, he entered the kitchen with his arms full of dishes and stopped short.

"What are you doing here?" His gaze shot to the clock. "You're an hour early."

Ellie greeted Flo, who stood over the stove stirring a fresh pan of red-eye gravy, before approaching him. She looked quite fetching this morning. Her shell-pink blouse brought a bloom to her cheeks and sparkle to her eyes.

"I'm accustomed to waking before the rooster's crow. I remained abed for at least half an hour, attempting to reclaim sleep, but it was no use." Her wide, sunny smile made his chest seize with longing. "One can stare at the ceiling rafters for only so long. Besides, my stomach becomes queasy if I wait too long to eat breakfast."

As soon as the words were out, she blushed and shifted her reticule to try to hide her middle.

"You're wearing your hair different," he blurted.

Her lips parted. Lifting a hand to the loose bun at the base of her neck, she said, "June suggested I try something new. Ponytails are for girls, not a widow on the verge of motherhood." She winced and lowered her gaze to his boots. "Listen to me. I'm supposed to be taking your mind off that particular topic, not dwelling on it."

Alexander heartily disliked himself in that moment. He was being selfish and unfair. He deposited the dishes on the table to his right and turned back to her.

His voice pitched low, he said, "I owe you an apology."

She whipped her head up. "I don't know what for. You haven't done anything wrong…except borrow my apron without asking." Humor simmered in her eyes. "Pink is your color."

A reluctant smile spread across his face. "I'm ordering new ones for everyone at my first opportunity. Plain. No ruffles."

She reached out and adjusted one of the straps, her fingers brushing against his bare neck. He felt that innocent touch to the soles of his feet. He wanted to trap her hand there and prolong the fleeting connection.

"That's a shame," she said lightly. "I happen to like ruffles."

Dazed by his response, he somehow found his voice. "I shouldn't have made you feel like you have to hide your condition or pretend you aren't experiencing one of life's most joyous events. I'm sorry."

Her eyes shimmered with telltale moisture. He recalled how prone to tears Sarah had been during her pregnancy. For once, the memory didn't evoke devastating grief. He was too wrapped up in concern for the woman standing before him.

"It's all right, Alexander. I understand."

The rise and fall of conversation and clink of silverware in the dining room filtered through the hallway.

"Hello, Ellie." Sally bounced past them with a distracted wave. "Flo, is that gravy ready yet? I need to get Ben's breakfast out to him before he's called away on lawman business."

The ding of the front doorbell registered. "I have to seat them," he told Ellie, surprised by his desire to continue their conversation. He was supposed to be keeping his distance.

"I'll help."

"No, you are going to plant yourself at that table with a cup of tea, and you aren't going to move until that long hand reaches ten o'clock."

"I'm already here. There's no reason I shouldn't pitch in."

"That wasn't the deal we agreed to."

"But—"

"Ellie." He planted his hands on his hips. "I won't be swayed on this. Either you do as I suggest or you leave the café and don't return until breakfast is over."

"Has anyone told you that you're a stubborn man?"

"More than I can count, but not usually one of my employees."

Rolling her eyes, she shook her head and flounced to the table. While he admired her more refined hairstyle, he found he missed the perky ponytail swinging back and forth. Sinking into a chair positioned where she could survey the entire kitchen, she shot him a long-suffering glance.

"Is this better, boss?"

Chapter Eight

"What did you do to Mr. Copeland?" Beneath the fringe of her bangs, Sally's brown eyes reflected awe. She hooked a chair with her foot and scooted it away from the table.

Flo's expression turned shrewd as she maneuvered her large girth into the seat on Ellie's right. Due to her exertions over the hot stove, her strawberry-and-gray curls were limp and her ruddy complexion shiny with perspiration.

They'd waited until Alexander left the café to confront her.

"Yes, do tell. Before you came along, it would've taken a stick of dynamite to rout him from his office. Now he's busing tables and scrubbing pots. I think he's taken a shine to you."

"Alexander barely tolerates me," she denied.

Flo wagged her finger. "A man who doesn't like a woman doesn't look at her the way the boss looks at you, Ellie."

Bubbly delight cascaded through her before she caught herself. She craved Alexander's friendship, nothing more. She couldn't afford to be vulnerable to any man. Choosing Nolan for a husband had led to heartache and disillusionment. With her baby's well-being at stake, making wise decisions was paramount.

Looking into her fellow employees' curious faces, she realized the time had come to share her news.

"The reason Alexander gave me time off isn't because he fancies me. He did it because he believes I need more rest than I've been getting. As you know, my husband died in June." Memories of his shocking accident and the terrible days and weeks that followed rushed in. She sucked in a fortifying breath. "It wasn't until after he'd gone that I discovered I was pregnant."

Sally gasped. "You're going to have a baby? Alone?"

Flo shot the waitress a reproachful glance. "Ellie's not the first young woman to face motherhood on her own. It's not as if she has a choice." She patted Ellie's arm. "You're a strong person with a good heart. I have faith you'll be a wonderful mother."

Ellie's throat clogged with tears. "Thank you."

Sally's thin arms closed about her. "I'm happy for you, Ellie. I can't wait to meet him or her."

She returned the hug, relieved to share her secret with these two women. This pregnancy was the fulfillment of a long-held dream. Concealing it had been a tremendous strain. June Trentham was the only person she'd been able to speak freely with. Now she had two more. Granted, Sally was naïve and inexperienced in the matters of marriage and children. Flo, on the other hand, had birthed six strapping boys, all grown now with families of their own.

They peppered her with questions, which she was happy to answer, and before long it was time to begin lunch preparations. As they left the table, Sally's eyes assumed a dreamy light and her smile turned wistful, an indication she was thinking about her favorite topic—Deputy Ben MacGregor.

"I've made up my mind to ask Ben to the harvest dance."

Flo retrieved a bag of sweet potatoes from the storage bin. "Not a grand idea, my dear. Let the man do the asking, I always say. My boys relished the pursuit."

"He hasn't picked up on my hints." Her nose scrunched up. "I'm tired of waiting for him to act. I have to let him know in no uncertain terms that I'm interested."

Ellie finished tying on her apron, which now carried Alexander's male scent. She recalled the moment she'd touched him—why she persisted in hovering over him like a mother hen, she had no idea—and the reluctant admiration in his gorgeous eyes as he'd inspected her new hairstyle.

Forcing those thoughts out of her mind, she searched for the right words to say. "Sally, have you noticed how friendly Ben is with everyone? Especially females?"

"He's nice, isn't he?" she gushed, unaware of Ellie's intent. "I've never met anyone with a heart as caring as his."

Flo searched the spice bins and landed on nutmeg and cinnamon. "That red hair combined with those deep green eyes doesn't hurt, either," she said, winking.

Sally blushed. "He is a fine-looking man, that's a fact."

"I don't doubt that ninety percent of the available women in this town share your feelings," Ellie said. "While I agree he's a nice man, he's also uninterested in settling on any one relationship."

When Sally's smile slipped, Ellie added, "I'm not trying to upset you, sweetie. I simply don't want to see you get hurt."

"I'm not ignorant of his behavior. I've seen him wooing other girls. Romantic picnics. Buggy rides. Strolls along the river's edge." Her confidence wavered. "I've seen and wished with all of my heart that it was me by his side." Fisting her hands, she vowed, "I've made up my mind. I'm asking him to the social and maybe, just maybe, he'll decide that I'm the girl for him. For always." Blinking rapidly, she mumbled, "Excuse me."

Before Ellie could call her back, she was rushing out the rear door, nearly bowling over a startled Caroline in the process. The statuesque blonde hovered on the stoop.

"I apologize for interrupting," she said, peering around. "I know you're closed right now, but I wished to extend an invitation."

Ellie bid her enter. "Good morning, Caroline. Can I get you something to drink?"

"No, thank you. I can't linger. Would you like to take part in a quilting bee this Saturday afternoon? I'm hosting. There will be refreshments, of course. Consider it an opportunity to get to know a few of your neighbors." She nodded at Flo. "Flo's been to several, though it's been a while."

"Busy at home and work," Flo said by way of apology. "Maybe I'll try to make the next one."

"I hope you can find the time," she said kindly. "So, Ellie, what do you say?"

Delighted by the invitation, she wished she didn't have to refuse. "I appreciate you including me, but I can't. Saturdays are our busiest days."

Disappointment flashed. "Couldn't you at least ask Alexander? It's only one afternoon."

"I'm afraid not. If it was a weekday, perhaps I could consider it."

That resulted in a brilliant smile. "I will consult my calendar the moment I get home."

When she'd gone, Flo looked up from the mound of

sweet potatoes she was peeling. "Since when did Caroline McKenna become your best friend?"

"I first met her when I applied for the position here. Caroline sensed my anxiety and was very kind and reassuring."

Ellie retrieved two tins of pineapple and joined Flo at the table. The town-wide audition day seemed so long ago. She'd prayed God would grant her the job, and He had. "We speak at church, but we haven't had a chance to socialize outside of that setting. Don't you like her?"

"I like her fine. Just wondering why she suddenly craves your presence."

Ellie fell silent as she gathered bowls and utensils they'd need for the sweet potato dish. Flo's suspicions stirred her own questions. Why, indeed?

Ellie was preparing to change into her nightclothes Friday night when June appeared in the doorway. The day had been satisfying but long and tiring, and she yearned for her bed. Laying her hairbrush on the dresser, she summoned a smile, careful not to let her consternation show. June was quickly becoming a treasured friend. Ellie enjoyed their frequent chats and relished hearing the other lady's accounts of her life.

"You have a visitor." June's eyes danced with merriment.

"At this hour? Who is it?"

"Mr. Copeland. He insisted on waiting on the porch. Should I tell him to leave?"

Alexander was here? To see her?

"No. That's not necessary." Glancing at her reflection, she smoothed her long locks, which were thicker and more lustrous now that she was pregnant. "I'll find out what he wants and send him on his way."

Her lined face stretched into a coy smile. "No need to worry, my dear. I may be decades older than you, but I remember what it was like to have gentlemen callers."

"Oh no, this is a business matter, I'm sure." Following her into the living room, Ellie continued, "I hope nothing serious has happened at the café."

Resuming her spot on the sofa, June pulled her knitting project onto her lap. "Take as long as you need out there. I'm not sleepy. I'll be awake for at least another hour."

Preoccupied, Ellie murmured a response and stepped outside, closing the door behind her. Alexander turned around. A kerosene lamp emitted soft light that allowed her to make out the planes of his face, the sharp cheekbones and strong chin.

"Alexander." She clasped her hands at her waist. "Is something amiss?"

"There's no emergency." He held his black bowler in his hands. "I had hoped to catch you before you left for the night, but I was detained." His gaze lingered on her hair. "Maybe I should've waited until the morning to speak with you. I know you're tired."

When he started to put his hat back on and descend the steps, she gestured to the bench swing. "It's nice out. Why don't we sit for a while?"

After a brief hesitation, he said, "You're sure?"

Ellie got comfortable on one end of the swing and patted the empty space beside her. "I'm sure."

The bench rocked gently as he lowered his tall frame onto it and placed his hat between them. "You're right, it is nice out here," he said, noting the expanse of stars winking down on them. "I'm glad you found Mrs. Trentham's advertisement."

"It's been a blessing straight from heaven."

He looked over at her. "I haven't heard you complain once about your circumstances. I admire your fortitude, Ellie."

His praise evoked dangerous feelings. After years of disappointing her husband and in-laws, any positive comments were soaked up like a sponge. Alexander's compliment didn't carry a deeper meaning, she reassured herself. Flo's musings were far off the mark—he did not carry a torch for her.

"Feeling sorry for myself isn't going to accomplish anything. My grandmother taught me to look for the good in life." A pang of sorrow arrowed through her. "She taught me a lot of things."

"She sounds like a wise woman."

"I count myself blessed to have had her and my grandfather to raise me." Unwilling to dwell on sad thoughts, she focused on the present. "What did you wish to tell me?"

"I heard you aren't going to the quilting bee. I encourage you to reconsider."

Among the various reasons he might've had for the visit, this wasn't it. "Who did you hear that from?"

"I ran into Caroline this evening. She expressed regret that you wouldn't be joining her and her friends."

"While I'd like to go, I can't leave Flo and Sally on the busiest day of the week. Especially considering I've been forbidden to work during the breakfast hours."

"That was my decision. I'm not an unfeeling ogre, Ellie. You're allowed to ask for time off on occasion. In the past, Flo has had to help with a sick grandchild and care for her husband when he suffered a leg injury."

"Why is it important to you that I go?"

He didn't answer immediately. The buzzing of cicadas swelled in the night air.

He used his shoe to set the bench to rocking. "Having a baby is a momentous event," he said gruffly. "You'll need support in the coming months. With all the hours you put in at the café, you don't have a lot of time to form friendships."

She placed her hand atop his, tempted to trace the ridges of his knuckles, the pulsing veins and scattered scars. "You're a thoughtful man, Alexander. I've long suspected that behind that gruff exterior beats a compassionate heart."

He surprised her by laughing. The husky, beautiful sound reverberated through her. "You'd be the only one."

"You don't have to pretend with me," she ventured. "We've both lost precious loved ones. I understand what you're going through."

He grew serious again. "The difference is I loved my wife."

Ellie winced at the underlying accusation and withdrew her hand. He assumed that because she didn't wear black and didn't walk around with a long face that she didn't grieve Nolan's passing. Before she could form a response, he stood and wandered to the railing, staring up at the stars.

"You didn't lose a child." His voice vibrated with sorrow and anger. "You have no idea how a tragedy like that tears you apart."

"Actually, I do."

Ellie joined him at the railing. The lamplight washed over features tight with sorrow. In her doe eyes, he glimpsed deep rivers of anguish.

"What are you talking about?" he blurted, the rawness of his voice sounding alien to his ears.

Ellie presented a brave face to the world. Contentment

radiated from her. To see into her private world of pain rocked him to the core.

A curtain of dark hair slid forward to obscure her face. "This isn't my first pregnancy."

He released a pent-up breath.

"I lost my first child during the first year of our marriage. It happened in the early stages. I hardly had time to process the fact I was to be a mother before the dream was snatched away." She pressed her hand against her stomach as if to cradle her unborn child, the gold of her wedding band gleaming in the faint light. "The second loss was harder to bear. I was in my fifth month. The baby…" She swallowed thickly and shook her head. "I almost died. There were days I wished I had."

Alexander felt the blood drain from his face.

During Sarah's pregnancy, she'd had her own fears about something going wrong, especially in the early days. He couldn't fathom the trauma Ellie had suffered, giving birth to a stillborn and coming close to death herself. He had the terrible suspicion that she'd been left to grieve alone. The Jamesons wouldn't have offered her comfort or support.

He nearly reached out and pulled her into his arms. Instead, he gripped the railing until the wood bit into his palms. "How did you find the strength to carry on?"

"God gave me the strength. He was my refuge during my darkest days." She slid her heavy mane behind her shoulder. "I slowly healed and was able to see the good in life again. I'll never forget the babies I lost. That pain will stay with me until my last breath. But I'm more grateful than words can express for this last chance to be a mother."

The sadness in her eyes was eclipsed by hope. They shared many similarities, he and Ellie. They'd both lost their parents. They'd lost their spouses. They'd lost children. The difference was in how they'd coped with these misfortunes. Ellie had endured with grace—like gold in a refiner's fire—while Alexander had grown bitter. Ellie had flourished. He was dead inside.

When his self-recriminations lengthened the silence between them, she said, "I suppose speaking of such intimate matters isn't quite the thing to do with one's boss."

"Please don't be embarrassed. I'm honored you chose to share your burden with me."

"You're not discomfited by such talk?"

"Perhaps I would be if I was a green bachelor." He rubbed the empty spot on his ring finger and wondered when she planned to cease wearing hers. Nolan Jameson didn't deserve continued loyalty. "But I've experienced the reality of bringing a child into the world."

She touched his hand again. He liked the sensation of her cool, soft-as-kitten-fur skin against his. He would've liked to flip his hand over and capture her fingers, perhaps raise them to his mouth and kiss them one by one. Yearning exploded in his chest. Floored, he was reaching to do just that when her next question chilled him to the bone.

"Will you tell me about your son?"

He froze. The memory of holding Levi in his arms, the powdery scent that clung to his clothes and the slobbery kisses he'd gifted Alexander with chipped away at the already dangerously thin ice layer protecting his heart.

"I'm sorry, Ellie. I can't."

"I understand."

She wasn't affronted that he wouldn't reciprocate. Compassion wreathed her features that no longer struck him as passingly pretty. Ellie Jameson was beautiful. He simply hadn't wanted to acknowledge it before. Or maybe she'd grown more lovely to him the more he'd gotten to know her?

"You're the first person here I've told about my miscarriages. I have to admit it's comforting to know that someone else in the world knows about the children I lost. Thank you for listening, Alexander."

Leaning over, she kissed his cheek, murmured goodnight and slipped inside the house. Alexander pressed his hand to the tingling spot where her lips had grazed. His gaze drifted to the window where faint light seeped around the curtain edges. He could hear feminine voices but couldn't make out the conversation. The prospect of returning to the empty café and his quiet, impersonal quarters above did not appeal. Instead, he wanted to follow Ellie inside and join her and her hostess. He wished to see Ellie in better light, to be bathed in her healing presence, to soak up a portion of her goodness and strength.

But he wouldn't. The strict rule he'd set for himself the day he left Texas—that no matter how tempting, he would not involve himself in other people's lives—had been bent one too many times since her arrival. He had to correct his behavior, because the other way led to destruction.

As he walked into the dark night and left their cozy haven behind, he reminded himself of his ruthless adherence to that rule these past several years. A pregnant widow wasn't going to be his downfall.

Chapter Nine

Just for one day, Ellie wished Alexander would resume his role of grumpy café proprietor. On today of all days, when the secrets she'd spilled under cover of last night's darkness made her cheeks sting and that brazen kiss made her palms sweat, why couldn't he disappear into his office and refuse to be drawn out?

She had assured herself upon waking that morning that she wouldn't have to spend more than five minutes in his presence, if that. She'd go in at ten o'clock to relieve him of his duties and then he'd do his famous disappearing act. But it became obvious the moment she arrived that Alexander was not going to follow the script.

"Before you start on anything, Ellie, I'd like to show you something in the barn."

To her relief, his manner was professional, his blue eyes free of, well, everything. The common observer would never guess they'd shared a private, poignant discussion on a darkened porch like a pair of courting adolescents.

He removed her frilly apron from his person and hung it up, his long, tapered fingers careful with the fabric. She imagined what it would feel like to have his hands in her hair. Or framing her face, caressing her cheek. Had he been an affectionate person before the catastrophe that shattered his life?

Ellie smothered that line of thinking as she would a flash fire in a frying pan. Theirs was strictly a working relationship, she reminded herself sternly, even as she recalled the faint hint of stubble that had tickled her lips with that fleeting kiss.

As he strode toward her, she couldn't help but be affected by his striking good looks. Where Nolan had been the epitome of a rough-around-the-edges outdoorsman, his proud features hewn from a mountain, Alexander was lean strength clothed in sophistication, quietly refined yet one hundred percent male.

He stopped before her. "Is this not a good time?"

Without thinking, Ellie reached out and straightened his silk puff tie. The underside of his chin was smooth. A slightly woodsy scent clung to his clothes. His larger hand closed over hers. Neither one moved. The difference between the inner blue rings in his eyes and outer, darker ones was more pronounced than usual. His Adam's apple bobbed.

"Well, don't the pair of you look domestic." Flo reached into the oven and slapped a pan of rolls on the top. The jarring sound jostled Ellie to her senses.

She snatched her hand away. "I, ah, your tie was crooked."

"I figured." His gaze sliding to Flo, he spoke in quiet tones. "Next time, tell me the problem, and I'll fix it myself."

Ellie blinked and stared past him at the swept floorboards. "Of course."

With a curt nod, he led the way outside into the welcoming sunshine and fresh mountain air. The barn doors stood open. She waited on the threshold in case the odors of animals and stale hay upset her stomach. And in case she had another urge to touch his person.

Her skin heated with embarrassment.

Flicking her a glance over his shoulder, he lifted a bulging sack from the floor and brought it over. "I checked my traps this morning and discovered a pair of rabbits. Would you be able to use them today?"

That's right, Ellie. Think about cooking, not how appealing your boss is.

"I can rearrange the menu. I haven't served rabbit stew in quite a while. I can dredge the meat in flour and brown it before adding parsnips and carrots." When she reached for the sack, Alexander moved it out of reach.

"I'll dress them."

"I'm perfectly capable of doing it myself."

"I'm aware of that. However, it's time I start pitching in more than I have been."

A breeze toyed with his midnight hair. He absently pushed it out of his eyes.

The signs of his illness had all but disappeared. Healthy color had returned to his complexion, and the hollows in his cheeks had filled out. She liked to think her ministrations were partly responsible but really it was his commitment to guarding his diet and sleep habits that were key in his recovery. And for him to do that, he had to care at least a little. The man she'd met weeks ago hadn't cared about much of anything.

"It *is* your café," she said lightly. "There's nothing wrong with pride of ownership. Flo and Sally have had only good things to say about your recent efforts. Apparently even the customers are in awe."

Telltale color crept along his cheekbones. "It must be the sight of me in your pink-and-lace apron."

She laughed, her lingering awkwardness dispelled. "I happen to think it makes you look dashing."

"You're being generous." He kneaded the back of his neck and grimaced. "Now, if I could manage to catch those fish you asked for."

"They aren't accommodating you, are they?"

"Maybe it's the way I hold my line." He shrugged, chuckling softly. "To be honest, I never was much of a fisherman. Too impatient."

"You're a man of action."

He got a faraway look. "I used to be."

Ellie pictured him in cowboy gear astride a horse, rifle across his lap and a blade of hay dangling from his lips. Repressing the questions she'd dearly like to have answered, she gestured to the building behind her.

"I'll leave you to your work."

"Ellie?"

"Yes?"

He shifted the sack to his other shoulder. "After our conversation last night, I got to thinking, and if at any time you feel unwell I want you to go straight to the doctor. Don't worry about any costs you might incur. I'll cover those. The important thing is that you and your baby are safe."

Shocked, she stammered, "Th-that's sweet of you, Alexander. I assure you I'm taking proper care of myself."

"Are you?" he challenged quietly. "Before I made the decision to cut your hours, you were on your feet from dawn to dusk slaving in a hot kitchen. If I'd known about your condition, I would've acted long before I did. Now that I know about your miscarriages, I have serious reservations regarding your employment."

His words made her feel like she wasn't as alone as she'd feared. They also sparked misgivings. "You aren't considering firing me again, are you? I thought we'd reached an agreement."

"No." Worry churned in his eyes. "I won't fire you—*if* you promise not to overdo it. I want you taking regular breaks."

Her heart tripped over itself. He acted as if her well-being and that of her baby was his top priority. *Because you're his cook, Ellie. He depends on you to turn out decent-tasting fare for his customers. Don't make this personal.*

"That goes without saying." She covered the spot where her baby was nestled deep inside. "Trust me, there's nothing more precious to me than this child. I've been to see Doc Owens. He reassured me that everything is progressing as it should. More importantly, I feel differently this time."

His attention settled on her middle then flitted away. "Good. I'm glad to hear it."

Sally's calls startled them both. Frowning, Alexander laid the sack on a hay square and strode past Ellie. She hurried after him.

"What's the matter?" he demanded, his long strides carrying him past the garden.

Sally twisted her hands together. Her eyes were wide and frightened. "Flo cut her hand. It's bad."

Inside the kitchen, Flo hunched over the preparation table. Her round face was whiter than parchment. "I made a clumsy mistake, boss."

Ellie stayed near the door with Sally while Alexander snagged a clean cloth from the shelves and deftly wrapped her injured hand.

"Happens to the best of us," he said, aiming a sympathetic smile at the shaken woman. "I'll accompany you to the doctor."

Flo looked to be in a daze. "I don't need a doctor. I'm sure my husband will bandage it up for me. He's not a bit squeamish."

Taking careful hold of her uninjured arm, he steered her toward the door. "I'd feel better if you saw a professional. He can dispense a salve that will help stave off infection. Sally, will you assist Ellie with lunch preparations until I return?"

"Yes, sir." Her voice wobbled. "You can count on me."

As the slow-moving pair came abreast of them, Alexander's gaze melded with Ellie's.

"Leave the rabbits. I'll dress them later."

She nodded. "We'll serve them for supper."

He cocked his head toward the accident spot where blood had spattered on the surfaces. "Do not go near that table, understand?"

"The sight of blood doesn't bother me," she protested.

His brows descended. "Maybe not under normal circumstances. Do you really wish to test your mettle and risk becoming nauseated?"

"My ma has a cast iron constitution except when she's expecting," Sally interjected. "Then any little thing threatened to send her into a swoon."

"Speakin' of swoonin'," Flo groaned and sagged against Alexander's side. "We best hurry, boss. I don't feel so good."

He curved his arm about her stout shoulders. "The cooler air outside will help." Opening the door, he guided her onto the stoop. "We'll take it slow and easy."

Ellie closed the door behind them and went to fetch her apron. The lunch rush would descend in little more than an hour, and she had to start the meal from scratch. She began to cover the mess with towels.

Sally hadn't moved from her spot. "It happened so

fast. One minute she was chattering about her eldest son's birthday celebration and carving up the ham, the next she was staring at her hand like it didn't belong to her."

"She's going to be fine. You'll see."

"I bet getting it stitched up will hurt something fierce." Her gaze became unfocused. "I've never had to get them, but my younger brother had a mishap with an ax when he was twelve." She shuddered. "You should see the scar. Do you think Flo will have one?"

Ellie walked over and cupped Sally's shoulders. "Let's not dwell on the details, okay? Alexander is counting on us to get our customers fed and time is short."

Her brows tugged together. "You're right. He was very kind to Flo, wasn't he? I thought he'd be furious."

Smiling, Ellie lowered her hands and, searching the cabinets, retrieved a heavy stock pot. "He's changed in recent weeks."

Her opinion of him had undergone a huge shift, so much so that she feared she was developing an infatuation. Most inconvenient. He'd be appalled if he thought she was entertaining romantic thoughts about him.

"It's because of you."

"My presence has nothing to do with the differences in his behavior," Ellie said firmly. "He's taken an interest in his business, that's all."

"If you say so."

"I do." Wiping her damp palms on her apron, she said, "Now, would you mind fetching me a couple of onions while I gather the green beans? I hope folks are in the mood for hearty vegetable soup."

To her relief, there was no more mention of Alexander. They bustled around the kitchen in a rush against the clock. It was ten minutes past noon, and the dining room was already half full of customers when he returned and discovered her serving soup and corn bread from one of the hutches.

His enigmatic gaze took in the soup station and the sight of Sally calmly pouring coffee. The menu board advertised a discounted rate for the day's special.

"I'm sorry I'm late." He divested himself of his suit coat. "Doc had another patient, so we had to wait to be seen. I took her home afterward. She was in need of rest after her ordeal."

"Is she all right?" Ellie measured out broth and vegetables into another bowl, concentrating on her task instead of his handsome profile.

"As long as she keeps the wound clean and dry, she should heal quickly."

"I'm glad you were willing to take control of the situation."

"Instead of hiding in my office, you mean?"

She lifted her gaze to him then, surprised to see faint humor edging his mouth. She couldn't help smiling in return. "Yes, that was a refreshing change of events."

Rolling up his sleeves, he nodded at the heavy pot. "Good idea."

"We thought it would save time for me to serve right here in the dining room. Saves Sally needless running back and forth."

"You're full of good ideas."

Before she could respond, Colleen Hatcher approached, her youthful face wreathed in happiness that should've warned Ellie.

"Good afternoon, Mr. Copeland."

"How are you, Mrs. Hatcher?" he said politely.

"I'm wonderful, especially knowing what I know."

Sally was talking to a young couple with a baby. She glanced their direction, and a panicked expression chased the smile from her face. "Mama," she started over. "Remember what we talked about?"

Ellie experienced a flash of discomfort. Something wasn't right.

Colleen ignored her daughter. "I wanted to be the first to congratulate you on your news, Ellie." Her voice boomed to the rafters. "What a wonderful gift God has bestowed on you, a baby to remember your late husband by."

Beside her, Alexander stiffened. The clinking of dishes faded along with the conversation.

Sally finally reached them, water pitcher in hand. "Mama! That was supposed to be a secret!"

Colleen's tinkling laughter assaulted Ellie's ears. "My dear, one only has to look close enough to see the truth." She addressed Ellie. "How far along are you?"

Alexander shifted closer, and his hand came to rest on the small of her back. She zeroed in on his protective touch and reminded herself that she wouldn't have been able to hide the news indefinitely. Still, it would've been nice to control when and how others found out. Once it spread, and it would spread like wildfire, she dreaded Gladys and Nadine's reactions.

"I'm sorry, Ellie." Sally looked distraught.

"It's all right." Ellie forced the dismay from her face. "I agree, Colleen. God has indeed blessed me. If He allows, I'll be welcoming a child in the spring."

The other woman wore a pleased as punch expression. The customers were whispering and staring. The reverend's wife, Carole Munroe, left her corner table.

"Congratulations, Ellie." She clasped Ellie's hand. "I'm happy for you."

"Thank you."

"The ladies at church will want to know what you need for the baby, so start on a list."

"That's very thoughtful, but—"

"I agree, that's extremely generous." Alexander's hand slid up her spine and came to rest atop her shoulder. "Ellie, you will need a great many items, some things you may not have thought of."

There was that concern again, peeking through his professional demeanor and making her feel like he cared about her. Maybe, at some point during these past weeks, he'd come to see her as a friend. The notion pleased her.

"You're right." Turning back to Carole, she said, "Thank you, again. I'll take you up on that suggestion."

When they were once again alone, she quipped, "My ears will no doubt be burning tonight."

"It was bound to happen eventually."

Her in-laws' relative isolation wouldn't protect her from what was sure to be an ugly confrontation. Sooner or later, they'd learn she was carrying Nolan's child. What happened after that was anyone's guess.

Chapter Ten

"Alexander?" Ellie peered at him with a familiar knit of her brow. "There's no reason for you to accompany me if you have other things to do. Mr. Darling will send everything over later. All I have to do is ask."

He blinked and shook his head. "I'm free at the moment," he said, his throat muddy. "I, ah, was lost in thought, that's all."

Gently linking her arm though his, he checked the street before guiding her across. He wasn't sure exactly what was happening to him. The more time he spent in his cook's presence, the more aware he became of her many sterling character traits. This morning, much to his chagrin, the sight of her had jolted him, the activity around him blurring into slow motion.

That couldn't be good.

Two weeks had passed since the day of Flo's accident and the revelation of Ellie's pregnancy. She was well into her fifth month and visibly showing. Her face had rounded out. Her skin glowed. And her rose-hued lips seemed fuller than ever. The boyish waif with the perky ponytail had disappeared. She'd transformed into a beautiful young woman, and Alexander couldn't stop staring. Nor could he stop the growing need to push past the bounds of employer-employee.

He'd thought he was stronger. He'd thought he'd insulated himself enough.

He'd thought he'd hurt so much that he'd never risk hurting that way again.

Glancing at the bright-eyed beauty beside him, he was startled to realize the torment he'd endured in Texas seemed like a whole other lifetime. Guilt immediately flooded him. How dare he forget, even for a second, the sweet boy he'd held in his arms on the fire-scorched grass, the son he'd rocked in his arms and wept over as he cried out to God for a reprieve? And Sarah, his innocent, fragile wife...

On the boardwalk, Alexander immediately drew away from Ellie and, instead of blocking the memories, he welcomed them. He could never forget what it meant to lose everything he'd ever held dear.

Inside the mercantile, a handful of customers browsed the aisles. He told Ellie he'd wait by the sales counter and peruse items in the glass cases while she shopped. Not allowing his attention to linger on her orchid-colored dress and the way it enhanced her figure, he stared out the plate-glass window with a view of the heart of town.

His thoughts turned to his brother and sister and the latest letter he'd received. Margaret had big news to share—she was hoping to tell him in person. Couldn't he come home at last? Even for a short visit?

He hadn't yet put pen to paper, but there was no question of his returning. That would never happen.

The bell above the entrance signaled newcomers. Alexander casually glanced that direction, only to straighten and search the store for Ellie. He wasn't the only one.

Gladys and Nadine were clearly on a mission, and gauging from their expressions, they knew about the baby.

His protective instincts roared to life. Circumventing shoppers, he took a circuitous route to her side.

"Ellie."

She dragged her attention away from the china display and gifted him with a smile. "Bored already?"

"It's not that—"

"There you are, Ellie Jameson." Gladys's voice snapped like a whip, alerting the store occupants to the brewing storm.

Last time he'd seen her, she'd been preparing to retire for the night. The older woman looked far more menacing with her silver-streaked black hair stretched into a tight bun, exposing her eagle-like bone structure.

Trepidation tightened Ellie's features as she turned to face her in-laws. "Good morning, Gladys. Nadine."

The mother-daughter duo glared at her. The open hatred in their eyes set off warning bells inside Alexander. This wasn't a case of simple dislike or even jealousy. They despised Ellie, a fact he had trouble wrapping his mind around.

"Did you think we'd never learn the truth?" Gladys spat. "Do you take us for fools?"

Positioned beside a display of stacked, tinned fruits, Nadine stared at Ellie's bulging tummy with a strange mixture of horror and longing. "How could you not tell us? That baby is a Jameson. He belongs with his kin."

Ellie held herself with dignity and poise. "This baby is mine and Nolan's. No one else's."

The skin tightened across Gladys's cheekbones. "You're wrong if you think you're capable of raising a baby on your own. Stop this nonsense and come home."

"You'll need help, Ellie," Nadine insisted, a hint of

desperation leaching into her voice. "You know you will.
Ralph and I can fill that need while you recuperate." She
briefly glanced at Alexander. "You wouldn't even have
to give up your job. You could continue working while
I care for the baby."

Ellie sucked in a bracing breath. "I'm happy where
I am."

Taking a menacing step forward, Gladys stretched
out her sun-ravaged, age-spotted hand. "You can't keep
us from the baby!"

Alexander's muscles tightened, ready to spring into
action. Out of the corner of his eye, he noticed the proprietor, Quinn Darling, rounding the sales counter and
heading their way.

Ellie set her chin at a militant angle. "Whether or not
you spend time with my child depends on your behavior.
This ugly display isn't helping your cause."

Uncaring of the gathering onlookers, Gladys spewed
disparaging remarks that drew gasps.

"My son never should've married you," she continued, her face screwed into sour lines. "You weren't good
enough for Nolan. You certainly aren't good enough to
raise my grandchild."

Alexander had had enough. Ellie was visibly shaking.
He positioned himself in front of her, a human barrier. "I won't allow you to further harass Ellie. She's a
kind, decent person and has done nothing to deserve your
spiteful behavior."

Quinn's authoritative voice ordered the gathered patrons to continue about their business. They were slow
to heed his command, of course. Before he could reach
their group, Gladys waved her finger beneath Alexander's nose.

"You've been sniffing around her skirt tails for weeks.

What exactly are your intentions toward my daughter-in-law?"

Alexander felt the weight of every single person's gaze. He looked at Ellie but couldn't decipher any one emotion. She'd handled herself admirably in this confrontation, but what would happen when there weren't witnesses? He couldn't stand by and allow her to be bullied when he was in the position to act.

Threading his fingers through hers, he summoned a smile. "My interest in Ellie is easily explained, Mrs. Jameson. I am her fiancé."

His words had the effect of an approaching brush fire. Chaos erupted. Ellie darted through the aisles, bent on escape. Worried, Alexander bypassed patrons and entered the deserted hallway linking the mercantile to Nicole Darling's seamstress shop in the rear of the building. He heard a door open and bang closed. Lengthening his stride, he exited onto the landing of a steep set of stairs.

"Ellie!"

Paying him no heed, she continued along the alley used mainly for deliveries. Beyond the dirt road, the river gurgled a rocky pattern at the base of a hillside alive with autumn finery. Shades of orange, scarlet and yellow reflected on the water's surface.

Ellie crossed a wide, wooden bridge and entered the shaded lane beyond. She was in the cover of trees when he caught up to her.

"Ellie." He reached out and lightly skimmed her back. "You can't run forever."

She abruptly stopped but didn't turn around. Winded, he moved to stand before her, dismayed by the evidence of tear tracks on her cheeks.

"You're upset."

Not meeting his gaze, she dashed away her tears. "I don't know what I am." Her lips quivered. "I underestimated their reaction. I should've known they wouldn't be reasonable, especially Nadine. She's never been able to conceive." Putting her hands to her forehead, she started pacing. Leaves crunched beneath her boots. "She's desperate for a baby. I'm telling you, Alexander, she's not stable. I should've left Gatlinburg. Should've left the state. They never would've found out…"

Alexander intercepted her, settling his hands on her shoulders. The cotton was smooth beneath his palms. "Ellie, stop. Working yourself into a tizzy isn't good for you or the baby."

Her throat working, she lifted her molten gaze to his. "I'm frightened, Alexander."

Ignoring the warning he was repeating history, he pulled her close. She didn't hesitate. Didn't resist. She leaned into him, accepting his comfort as if in the habit of doing so. She clutched his jacket lapels and pressed her cheek to his chest. A shudder wracked her. He curled one arm about her waist, his right hand tucked against her side, and ran his fingertips in soothing patterns along her upper back.

Alexander closed his eyes and basked in the rare contact. Ellie was warm, soft and sweet-smelling, her swollen tummy a slight barrier between them. Her baby meant the world to her. Because he'd walked through the nightmare of loving and losing a child, he would never allow a woman as purehearted as her to suffer the same fate. Not if he could help it.

The longer they stood there locked in each other's arms, the more frantic the distress signal inside his head became. He'd rescued Sarah by marrying her. Here he was claiming to be Ellie's fiancé in order to shield her from her in-laws. Hadn't he learned his lesson?

This situation isn't the same, he reassured himself. *I feel responsible for Ellie because of our working relationship.* He was her boss. Naturally he wished to protect her, to assist her as he would any one of his employees.

Sniffling, Ellie eased out of his embrace. He masked his disappointment by digging in his suit jacket for a handkerchief.

She accepted it with a wobbly smile. "Thank you for what you did, Alexander. For standing up for me. It's been a long time since I had a champion. I asked God for a friend, and He delivered."

Alexander's heart stuttered. Ellie viewed *him* as an answer to prayer?

"I can't say I'm not surprised," she tacked on. "I never expected you to claim an engagement to me."

He held up his hands. "It wasn't planned, believe me. Are you angry? You saw how everyone reacted, like I blasted a cannonball into the crowd."

"I'm not angry. I understand your reasons for doing it." Gratefulness warmed her eyes. "However, I can't condone a lie."

"It doesn't have to be a lie," he blurted, surprising himself. "I will gladly be your temporary fiancé for as long as you require it."

"Why would you do that? I've known you long enough to know you don't readily insert yourself into other people's problems."

"You're right. I don't. But you single-handedly saved the café. I owe you."

"There's more to it than that."

Alexander searched for the right words. "My wife, Sarah, and I grew up in the same town. We went to school together. Attended the same church." He shrugged. "Her father, Elias, had a reputation as being a hard man. I didn't pay the rumors or Sarah much heed. I was too wrapped up in ranch business for that. After my father passed and I assumed the running of it, I started thinking about settling down. It was around that time that I witnessed Sarah being harassed by a much older man, Cyrus Pollard. He'd cornered her at a church social, out of the view of others, and was clearly frightening her."

"He had a romantic interest in her?"

He nodded, sickened all over again. "I came to her aid, thinking Elias would thank me for protecting his only daughter. He was livid. Turned out he'd promised Sarah to the old codger in exchange for land. Cyrus's ranch ran alongside his own. His greed outweighed Sarah's happiness."

"You married her to protect her from both men."

"I loved my wife." If he'd wondered at times if there was supposed to be more to a husband-wife relationship, he hadn't dwelled on it. "She gave me a son."

There was no condemnation in her eyes. She understood his actions.

A snap echoed above their heads, and a black walnut plummeted to the ground not far from where they stood. Alexander snagged the palm-sized nut and, tilting his head back, examined the branches.

Discarding it, he held his arm out. "Let's not risk a headache."

She placed her hand in the inner curve of his elbow and allowed him to guide her back to the bridge. Using the wooden railing as a support, she observed the river below, murky water trickling over moss-crusted rocks and yellowed leaves floating on the surface. A pair of ducks splashed near the far bank.

"Tell me about Sarah."

Alexander pulled his gaze away from the autumn scene. "Everyone who met her liked her." With shiny blond hair, big blue eyes and a face that could've inspired sonnets, her comportment had been that of a damsel in distress. He'd had the thought once that she liked being a victim and immediately felt ashamed. "As pretty as a picture, she'd been born with a delicate constitution. She was sick a lot."

"That must've made it difficult for her to uphold her role as a rancher's wife."

"Fortunately, we had Rosa. My father hired her not long after my mother's passing. She cleaned and cooked and became like a favorite aunt to us all. She was a great help whenever Sarah became ill."

Ellie's soft smile dispelled the troubling memories. "Sounds like you hold a deep fondness for her."

"I'm not sure what would've happened to me and my siblings if we hadn't had her. She tended our scrapes, tucked us in bed, taught us the Scriptures, comforted us when we missed our mother. I haven't seen her since the funeral…"

Grief tried to claim him, suck him under and snuff out the light. He released the railing and started walking without direction. The sight of those plain wooden caskets had almost felled him, and he'd barely made it through that grueling service. Ellie's whispering touch against the back of his hand drew him once more to the present.

She fell into step beside him. Ahead, the mountains framed the wooden buildings of Main Street and, farther in the distance, the church's steeple. A wagon lumbered farther up the lane, weighted down by recent purchases.

"You've never told me the details of what happened."

"Their deaths haunt me. It's not a burden I like to place on anyone else."

She seized his hand and held on, forcing him to stop. "I'm strong enough to hear it, Alexander. Remember what I told you after I shared my losses?"

He stared woodenly at the barber shop sign. "You said it was a relief not to shoulder the truth alone."

"They died in a fire. Where? On the ranch?"

"Yes, on the ranch," he snapped, tugging free. "In a fire that was meant for me."

"Someone wanted to harm you?" Disbelief threaded her voice. "Cyrus?"

"He was only part of the problem. The instigator was my own father-in-law." Hatred burned in his heart with the same intensity of a flaring ulcer. "Elias couldn't resolve the fact I'd spoiled his plans. He wanted rid of me and concocted a plan to do just that."

Her brown eyes were swimming with sorrow. "But Sarah and your son…"

"Levi," he rasped. "His name was Levi."

"They were in the wrong place at the wrong time."

Pinching the bridge of his nose to ward off an encroaching headache, he nodded. "I tried to save them. I was too late."

"Oh, Alexander."

He covered her hand where she'd placed it on his arm. "I failed them, Ellie, but I won't fail you. Let me help you."

Uncertainty tightened her jaw. "I don't know what to say."

"Say yes."

Chapter Eleven

"Congratulations, Ellie!" Mrs. Carpenter waved her handkerchief in the air in a bid for Ellie's attention. Smothering a sigh, Ellie pasted on a smile and sent a longing glance at the deserted alley between the Plum and the post office. Escape was so close.

"Good morning, Mrs. Carpenter. How are you today?"

"I couldn't believe it when I heard about your engagement. Everyone knows Alexander Copeland prefers his own company. I suppose working in close proximity sparked his interest." Her gray eyes were ripe with suggestion. "I tried to catch up with you after church services yesterday, but was waylaid. Tell me, when's the wedding? Have you set a date?"

"No, not yet."

Ellie brought her hands together and was once again startled at the bare spot on her left ring finger. Removing her wedding band had been necessary for their scheme to work. Why it had proved emotional she couldn't pinpoint…it had felt like a final goodbye to that period in her life. Only, she carried inside her a permanent link to Nolan.

She shook off the sentimental thoughts to refocus on the lady awaiting more information. Ellie had fielded this same question dozens of times in the short time since Alexander had fabricated their engagement. Agreeing to his plan had seemed like a good idea—a temporary solution until the baby was born and she'd regained her emotional and physical footing. He'd insisted that he had no interest in courting anyone, so their fake engagement could continue indefinitely. Unable to resist the lure of his protection, she'd agreed despite her qualms.

She hadn't anticipated their charade would be this complicated.

Mrs. Carpenter glanced deliberately to Ellie's protruding middle. "Better remind him time is short."

Her cheeks tingled. "Yes, I'll do that. If you'll excuse me, I have to go inside. Today's inventory day. Lots to do."

"I saw that the café was closed. Well, enjoy your day away from the stove."

"Good day, Mrs. Carpenter."

Ellie entered the building through the rear entrance. The kitchen was empty, and she could hear Flo and Sally chatting in the dining room. They must've started inventorying the items in the hutches. Not ready to face their inquisition—they'd made eye contact at church the day before but couldn't reach her for the crowd—she entered the hallway intent on speaking with Alexander.

She found him in the storeroom, clipboard in hand and a pencil lodged behind one ear. He'd shed his dark jacket and vest and rolled up the sleeves of his kelly-green shirt. The vibrant color was in stark contrast to his inky black locks. She'd been held by this man, had sought and received comfort in his embrace, which he'd readily offered. Nolan had not been a sympathetic man, and she'd quickly learned not to seek it from him.

When he looked up and smiled, his blue eyes warming at the sight of her, Ellie found herself in deep waters. He grew more handsome with each passing day. She could never tire of soaking in his countenance, especially now that he was regarding her as one would a friend instead of an irritating employee who didn't know her place.

"Ellie. You look refreshed. Did you have a relaxing Sunday?"

Closing the door behind her, she leaned against it. "Not exactly."

"What's the matter?" His smile slipped. "Gladys and Nadine didn't pay you a visit, did they?"

"No." Sliding her reticule ribbon free of her wrist, she laid the pink-and-cream pouch with seashell embroidery—another of her grandmother's possessions—on a shelf. "I haven't seen them since Saturday. The problem lies with the holes in our plan."

"What holes?"

"People are pressing me for a wedding date. Some have been very vocal about it. They are expecting us to wed before the baby comes, and I can't say I blame them. That would be the logical course of action."

He clutched the clipboard to his chest. "I admit the thought didn't cross my mind."

"Mine either." She bit her lip. "There's something else."

"Tell me."

"A number of people have cautioned me against marrying you."

He smirked. "Not surprising considering I've avoided them like the plague. I'm sure there are a number of rumors out there as to the cause of my unsociable behavior."

"It's not that." She shook her head. "There's concern

regarding your spiritual condition. You don't attend services."

"Ah." He didn't get angry, as she'd feared. Nor did he appear offended. She did detect a hint of rebelliousness, however, and so was surprised at his response. "That's easily remedied. I'll go with you."

"You will?"

"This was my idea, Ellie, and I'm prepared to see it through."

"*Every* Sunday?"

"As long as my ulcer is behaving, then yes—every Sunday."

Ellie could hardly believe it. Perhaps this plan would benefit not only her, but Alexander, as well. Long-lasting benefits, she hoped. Reaching around, she absently rubbed her lower back muscles, which were becoming stiff and sore with regularity now that her baby was growing larger. A small price to pay.

Alexander's gaze lowered to her belly, then slowly lifted to her face, snagging on her mouth. Indefinable emotion pulsed in the brilliant blue depths. Ellie stilled. The atmosphere between them became charged. What was happening?

He turned away and dragged a hand over his mouth. "I, ah, should get back to the task at hand."

"Of course." Her heart fluttered in her chest. Convinced she was imagining things, she hovered in the doorway. "We never settled on a solution for the wedding date dilemma."

Not looking at her, he said, "Let them wonder. I'm sure they'll come up with their own conclusions."

"Right. Like fictional family members who want us to wait until they can make it for the wedding?"

He kicked up a shoulder. "Could be. Or perhaps you

want to wait until you can wear your grandmother's wedding dress for the ceremony. Most folks tend to have active imaginations."

He still wasn't looking at her, so Ellie took that as her cue to leave. The instant she stepped into the hallway, she was ambushed by her fellow employees.

"We've been waiting to talk to you!" Sally's hushed voice was rife with excitement.

"That's right, and we're all out of patience." Flo linked her arm through Ellie's and guided her through the kitchen and out into the garden. Releasing her, she folded her arms. "What I'd like to know is how you managed to convince that young man to relinquish his solitude in exchange for marriage and fatherhood."

Sally clasped her hands together and gave an exaggerated sigh. "Isn't it obvious? He's fallen in love with her."

Her heart squeezed with a sudden, hopeless longing. Alexander was no longer the brooding boss who did everything in his power to avoid her. She'd gotten to know him, had glimpsed the caring, thoughtful heart protected by layers of fortified armor. She had no doubt he'd make a fine husband and father.

"Our engagement has nothing to do with love," she insisted. "Alexander is a practical man. He's marrying me to provide my baby with a father."

Sally resisted that answer. "He has feelings for you," she charged, pointing her finger. "I know it."

Older, wiser Flo narrowed her gaze. "You expect us to believe that Mr. Copeland suddenly had the urge to play papa? And that he's willing to sacrifice his bachelorhood to do a good deed for you?"

"We've become friends." She absently fingered a pumpkin plant. "Besides, he's at the point in his life where he's ready for a family of his own, just not in the traditional means."

"Humph."

Ellie resisted the urge to squirm. Was guilt stamped across her features? Was there a telltale wobble in her voice? She'd never been good at keeping secrets. No amount of rationalizing could free her from the knowledge that they were essentially deceiving the entire town. Neither planned to follow through on this sham engagement.

What would you say if he asked for real?

Before she could dwell too long on that notion, Alexander came outside and stood on the stoop. "Taking a break in the vegetable garden, ladies?"

"We were congratulating Ellie on her engagement," Sally piped up.

His gaze locked onto Ellie's. "I'm a fortunate man."

Her tummy tumbled. The dip of his husky voice washed over her in a sweet caress. Her scalp prickled. Her emotions were beyond managing.

This charade of theirs was like a hidden whirlpool in storm-swollen rapids, the dangers not visible until one was already waist-deep in the water. Alexander was the whirlpool, drawing her in with his hero-on-a-white-horse behavior. Before long, she wouldn't be able to touch bottom, too far from shore for rescue.

Why had he agreed to this?

The church doors mocked him. To others, walking through those doors led to an uplifting worship experience. For him, they opened up a storehouse of despair-laced memories and anger at God, who'd allowed evil to triumph.

"Alexander?" Ellie was next to him on the stairs, her face a mask of concern. "You look ill."

"I feel ill," he muttered, tugging at his tie.

"When was the last time you were inside a church?"

"The day I buried my wife and child."

She uttered a quiet gasp. "You don't have to come inside."

"I made you a promise, and I aim to stick to it." Even if it meant another trip to the doctor. So far, his stomach was holding up against the onslaught of churning emotions.

"We've never discussed the subject of faith. Do you have a relationship with God? Have you ever placed your trust in Christ Jesus?"

"You ask hard questions."

Fortunately, the churchyard was inhabited only by shuffling horses hitched to wagons. He'd timed their arrival to when the congregation would already be singing hymns. Less time for folks to pepper him with questions.

Ellie said nothing. She didn't make excuses, didn't spare him. Instead, she waited with her small hands folded atop her swollen abdomen, her big brown eyes shining with compassion and caring. He'd never had a female friend before. It was both comforting and confusing. The confusing part stemmed from the fact her beauty seemed to increase with each passing day. Today she was wearing one of his favorite colors on her, a buttery yellow that lent her flowing brown tresses a rich chestnut shine.

"We're engaged," she said simply. "I should know these things."

"Right. I was taught Scriptures from a young age. One of my most poignant memories of my mother is sitting on her lap each night in front of the fireplace, the big family Bible spread out before us as she read to me."

"That's a nice memory."

"After she passed, Rosa filled that gap. She used to sing hymns in her native Spanish and then translate them for us."

She smiled gently. "I'm glad you had someone like her in your life. While I would've given anything to have my parents, I treasured my childhood with my grandparents. They wrapped me in unconditional love. It sounds like Rosa did the same for you and your siblings. Did she attend church with your family?"

He nodded. "I heard the gospel both at church and at home. It wasn't until I was sixteen that I finally acknowledged my need for forgiveness and a personal relationship with the Savior. How old were you?"

Her smile turned nostalgic. "Thirteen. A decision I've never regretted."

His mood darkened. "I never thought I'd feel betrayed by the One who created and redeemed me. Sarah and Levi's deaths were unnecessary. Wrong." He fisted his hands at his sides. "I tried to save them, you know. I was riding in from the fields when I saw the smoke. I didn't immediately panic because Sarah was supposed to have taken Levi to a neighbor's for an afternoon visit. When I passed the barn, I saw the wagon still inside. That's when I went crazy. The ranch hands tried to prevent me from going in. They said it was too late. Too dangerous. But I had to try."

Ellie's cool hands enveloped his right one. "I can't imagine the pain you've endured."

"You asked about the scars on my hands. I got them that day. The smoke was so thick, I could hardly breathe. But I battled onward." Thrust back in that raging inferno, he struggled to draw breath. "I finally located them in the bedroom beside the window. Sarah must've gotten sick and decided to stay home and nap. I believe she tried to get our son to safety but was too weak."

The singing inside ended. Movement indicated the congregation had taken their seats.

She stroked his scars. "You did everything humanly possible to save them."

"You're right. I'm only human. Which begs the question, why didn't God intervene? He could've spared their lives. I would still be in Texas on my ranch, teaching my son to ride like my father did me."

He didn't attempt to hide the hollowness grief had carved inside. Dismay flashed upon Ellie's features before she smoothed the emotion away.

She squared her shoulders. "I understand how you feel. God could've spared my babies. He could've prevented the accident that called my parents to heaven. But He chose not to. Sometimes trials find us, and we can't see any logical reasons why God allows them. We simply have to trust in His divine plan and lean on Him for strength."

Emotion churning in his gut, Alexander reached up and lightly ran his knuckles along her cheek.

"You're a wise woman, Ellie Jameson. A better person than I'll ever be."

Her eyes widened and lips parted—a response to his words or his touch? Maybe both?

"You've suffered a great tragedy. Everyone deals with things in their own way and their own time." She gestured to the doors. "I don't mind going in alone. Wait another week. See how you feel then."

He couldn't deny he was tempted. "No. It's time I started facing unpleasant things instead of running from them."

"I hope, in time, you don't view a chance to hear God's word preached as unpleasant," she said gently.

In answer, he took her elbow and guided her up the steps and inside a building he'd never planned on entering.

Chapter Twelve

That was the longest service in recent memory. Typically, Ellie relished being among fellow believers, but knowing what a trial it was for Alexander dimmed her pleasure. As the yard emptied of families eager for their noon meal, she studied his hard-as-marble profile. He carried himself with the stiff forbearance of a prisoner facing execution.

Their earlier conversation weighed on her mind. One part in particular troubled her—the part about a different outcome of that terrible fire. If he'd remained in Texas, she never would've met him. She felt ashamed for the instant protest that had risen up inside her. Worried, too, because the thought of not knowing Alexander caused her disconcerting sadness, a sign that her feelings were far from platonic.

They were nearing the cemetery and the path that led to June's farmhouse when Sally intercepted them.

"Ellie! Mr. Copeland!" She rushed up, brimming with excitement. "My folks are going to the river for a picnic lunch, and we'd love for you to join us."

Alexander turned to Ellie. The skin across his cheekbones looked tight. "I was planning on a simple lunch at home, but you should go if you feel up to it."

"I think a picnic sounds lovely." She glanced at the clear blue sky above. The day was warm, resembling summer rather than autumn. "In a few short weeks, we'll be stuck inside. We should take advantage of the nice weather. Why don't you go with me?"

He opened his mouth, denial written on his face.

"Mama and my sisters have prepared a delicious spread. Enough to feed an army regiment." With a furtive glance over her shoulder, she leaned in to confide, "I invited the deputy, and he said yes."

Alexander's brows snapped together. "About Ben, I've been meaning to speak to you—"

"Sally! Let's go!" On the opposite side of the field, her brother beckoned. Ben was standing with him.

She let out a squeal. "This is going to be the best day of my life. I've finally worked up the courage to invite him to the harvest dance."

"Are you certain that's a good idea?" Alexander said quietly, his concern mirroring Ellie's. Apparently she wasn't the only one with reservations.

"He's the best man I've ever met," she gushed. "Why wouldn't it be?" Walking backward, she said, "Will you come? Both of you?"

Alexander reluctantly nodded. "We'll be there."

When she'd crossed the field, he held out his arm for Ellie. "I suppose appearing together in public will aid your cause."

She experienced a twinge of disappointment. It would've been nice if he'd acquiesced because he wanted to spend a relaxing afternoon in her company.

Resting her hand lightly upon his suit sleeve, she strolled with him toward Main Street. "An employee sharing a meal with her boss isn't so out of the ordinary, is it?" she quipped.

He didn't speak for long minutes. As they came alongside the livery, he said carefully, "You've got a point."

"I do?"

"It's not enough to say we're engaged." He cut her a side glance. "In my experience, couples headed to the altar display at least a modicum of affection for one another."

Anticipation warred with common sense. "Alexander, are you suggesting we pretend to be madly in love?"

The café's front facade came into view. The windows with gold lettering sparkled, the yellow draperies visible from the street. Twin pots of orange and purple mums had been placed on either side of the entrance. Several benches lined up on the boardwalk outside, offering rest for passersby. Today they were empty.

He inhaled deeply. "Yes, that's exactly what I'm suggesting." His dark brows formed a V. "Although *madly in love* may be stretching things a bit. I'm certain most people consider our match a practical one. We're merging our personal and professional lives. Still, I believe we should at least enact a fondness for each other."

Passing through the alleyway, they reached the barn's entrance. He angled toward her. "Well?"

Ellie met his gaze squarely. "Alexander, I don't have to pretend. I truly am fond of you."

Color crept up his neck. "I didn't mean to imply the feeling isn't mutual. I just meant…" He gave a self-conscious laugh. "This is an awkward business."

"I know what you meant." She opened the barn door. "When we're in public, we'll gaze into each other's eyes. I'll hang on your every word and find excuses to stroke your cheek and run my fingers through your hair."

"And what will I do?"

She laughed at his slightly dazed look. "Easy. You'll act the solicitous gentleman. You'll fill my plate for me, sit *very* close beside me and shower me with compliments. Oh, and don't forget a lady likes to receive flowers."

"Hmm." He walked past her into the barn and strode for his horse. They would take the buggy out to the picnic spot. "Are those the types of things that impress you?"

She hung back, surprised at the serious turn. "That hardly matters now. The baby is my chief priority."

Working without speaking, he hitched the horse to the buggy and led it out into the sunshine. He assisted Ellie onto the seat, waiting until she was comfortable before going on the other side and climbing aboard. Lost in thought, neither spoke until they reached the popular picnic spot. The forest opened up into a huge clearing. In the distance, mature trees edged the river.

Alexander parked the buggy. While crossing the field toward the Hatcher clan, they spotted Ben lounging on a blanket with Sally. The young girl was chattering and gesturing, and Ben was regarding her with an indulgent smile that was more brotherly than anything.

"Speaking of romance, that isn't going to end well, is it?" Alexander said.

"I'm afraid Sally is going to have her hopes dashed. I've tried to point out the obvious, but she's convinced Ben's resistance to commitment can be overcome."

"She's a sweet kid. He'd better let her down gently."

Her fingers tightened on his sleeve. Despite his intentions to remain uninvolved, he cared about his employees' welfare.

"At least her heart will be bruised, not broken—unrequited infatuation is an all-too-common rite of passage in life."

Ben laughed at something Sally said, his green eyes sparkling with mirth.

"He looks wholly entertained in this moment," Alexander murmured. "No wonder females across this town have fallen prey to futile hopes. Why do you think he resists settling down?"

Ellie shrugged. "I have no idea. Aside from his flirtatious ways, the deputy has a reputation as a fair and honest man. He's committed to keeping our citizens safe. He's a faithful churchgoer. It's my estimation that Sheriff Timmons doesn't suffer fools gladly. He wouldn't keep Ben around if he wasn't a top-notch human being."

Their conversation was cut short when Sally saw them and came over.

"I hope you brought your appetites. We're almost ready to eat."

She gestured to the center quilt laden with heaping platters of meats, vegetables and homemade breads. The aroma of fire-roasted pork filled the air, and Ellie was suddenly ravenous.

"Thank you again for inviting us," she said.

"Of course. You and Mr. Copeland work too hard. You deserve to relax now and then."

Ben joined them and, wearing an ear-to-ear grin, enveloped Ellie in a quick hug and then clapped Alexander on the back.

"I hear congratulations are in order." He winked. "I know you weren't too pleased with our interference in your business, but just think what you'd have missed out on if we hadn't hired Ellie."

Ellie wished she could guess Alexander's true thoughts.

Did he regret ever meeting her? She'd been forced on him, after all.

A small gasp escaped as he slid his arm around her. His hand light on her hip, he nudged her close to his side. Despite her expanding form, she fit perfectly against him. His crisp, clean scent and the lean strength of his body sent heady longing spiraling through her. She adored being close to Alexander. Yearning to truly belong by his side struck her unawares.

"I'm a fortunate man," he said huskily. "Ellie is one of a kind."

Blushing, she recalled her role in this charade. Snuggling even closer, she placed her hand on his chest and gazed up at him with adoration. "Better watch out, Alexander. With talk like that, you're bound to inflate my sense of self-importance."

His gaze growing smoky, he took her chin between his fingers. "Impossible, my dear."

Her heart stilled, then thundered against her ribs. Who would've guessed he was such a skilled actor?

His mouth captured her attention. It looked firm and soft at the same time. What would it be like to be kissed by him? Would he be gentle and thorough, or—

Ben's low chuckle scattered her inappropriate ruminations. Feeling heated, she fanned herself with her hand. Alexander didn't seem to notice.

"Tell me, Deputy, don't you think it's time to tie the knot yourself? The appeal of bachelorhood is short-lived."

Defiance surged in Ben's sparkling eyes. "It hasn't lost its shine for me yet. I've no interest in settling down. Not now, maybe not ever." Oblivious to Sally's flagging spirits, he lifted one shoulder. "That happens when you grow up the only male in a household of simpering sisters."

"Surely you'd like a family of your own someday." Sally's brown eyes reflected hope.

"That life isn't for me."

An awkward silence descended. Mrs. Hatcher's summons saved them. And while Ben's mood was restored by a hearty plate of delectable food, Sally remained subdued. Ellie wanted to wrap her arms around her and console her. She intercepted Alexander's frequent, concern-filled gazes toward the girl.

She reminded herself that underneath his gruff exterior beat a compassionate heart. He cared about his workers. As one herself, he viewed her as a responsibility. She couldn't afford to forget that the playacting wasn't real. This engagement was a farce intended to keep her in-laws at bay, nothing more. Perhaps they'd do well to keep their public appearances to a minimum from here on out.

Pretending to adore Ellie wasn't as difficult as it should've been.

She was witty and insightful, earnest and kind. Any sane man would be proud to have her by his side. Alexander's gaze was drawn to her once again. Seated beside him on the quilt with her legs tucked to one side and one hand resting on her tummy, she listened along with the rest of them as Ben regaled them with humorous tales from his years of law-keeping. Contentment smoothed her features and warmed her dark eyes. A slight smile curved her rosebud lips. With her shining tresses and peach-tinted cheeks, she was lush and inviting and too beautiful for words. The attraction budding inside astonished him. For a moment, he let his imagination forge into forbidden territory. Thoughts of kissing another woman hadn't crossed his mind since the day he left Texas, and now his pregnant, widowed cook was inspiring them?

What was wrong with him? As Ellie's boss, he had a duty to look out for her best interests. Normally, his responsibility would be limited to their work environment. He couldn't allow his feelings to become muddied because their interaction had spilled into personal territory.

Children's laughter erupted nearby, moments before a ball rolled into his lap. He twisted around to return it, his mouth drying at the sight of the two boys standing a few feet away. The older one looked to be about seven or eight. He put a protective hand on the younger boy, who couldn't have been more than three. His honey curls shone in the sunlight, creating a halo effect about his cherubic face.

"Levi," he murmured, grief gripping him.

Thankfully no one heard the slip.

"We're sorry, sir," the older one said. "The ball got away from us."

"Ball!" The younger one held out his chubby hands.

"Here you go."

Alexander held it out to the boy, mesmerized by the sweet face. He missed his son each and every day. He'd grown accustomed to the dull ache. But now, so close to a boy who could've been Levi's twin, the emptiness and loss ballooned to a demanding, physical pain that stole his breath away.

The boys snatched the ball and ran back to their playing spot. Alexander felt Ellie's cool hand close over his. Without him saying a word, she recognized his distress.

"Alexander, would you care to stroll with me?"

He tore his gaze from the boys. Compassion turned her eyes a molten chocolate color. Nodding, he stood and bent to assist her to her feet. She murmured an excuse to the others and, linking their arms, directed them to the river. She didn't chatter about inane subjects or prod him for a confession. Instead, she walked silently beside him, her presence alone soothing his tormented soul.

He acknowledged that Sarah wouldn't have been able to accomplish it. She hadn't possessed Ellie's inner strength. His wife had labeled him her rescuer from the start, a label that hadn't changed over the course of their marriage. Alexander hadn't wanted to admit it then, but looking back, he'd found it exhausting at times. To always be Sarah's source of support. To bolster her mentally and emotionally, day in and day out. Whereas Sarah had shied away from adversity, Ellie faced it head-on. As his pa would've phrased it, the woman had pluck.

At the water's edge, they strolled north along its banks, occasionally encountering fishermen or adolescents splashing each other in the shallow depths. A pair of approaching riders picking their way through the woods caught his attention.

"That looks like Caroline and Duncan." Ellie slipped free of him.

Farther upstream, the newlyweds guided their mounts through the water. Calling greetings, they dismounted. Caroline was effusive in her congratulations. Duncan was much more reserved. When he pulled Alexander aside, he didn't waste time voicing his misgivings.

"What's happened between you two?" he said quietly. "You could've toppled me with a feather when I heard the news. You certainly had no intentions on involving yourself in Ellie's life to this extent, that much I ken."

Alexander opted for the truth. The Scotsman had seen him in his lowest point. He wouldn't be fooled.

"This whole thing is an attempt to protect her from her late husband's family?" Duncan's blue eyes reflected shock. "And 'twas your idea?"

"She doesn't have anyone else to protect her."

"You *dinnae* think she can take care of herself?"

"That's not what I'm saying."

"Listen, I understand why you're doing this, but I have to offer a word of caution. Watch that you *dinnae* hurt her. She's in a vulnerable place right now."

Alexander glanced over his shoulder at her. "I would never hurt Ellie."

"Not intentionally. But a woman in her position— expecting her first bairn with no husband and only you for support? And pretending to be in love, to boot?" He shook his head. "It's got the makings of disaster."

His own reservations rushed to the surface. "Don't worry. I'll proceed with caution."

"See that you do."

Chapter Thirteen

What was he thinking?

Ellie couldn't determine what Alexander's silence meant, whether he'd enjoyed the outing or whether he was contemplating calling off their agreement.

A light in the window of June's house beckoned. Near the azalea bushes hugging the porch, she turned to face him. "Do you regret agreeing to the picnic?"

"Why would you ask that?"

"Oh, I don't know. Maybe because you had to dance attendance upon me? Or maybe because of those young boys and what they reminded you of?"

Alexander paced a few steps away and stared off into the distance. The sun had already dipped behind the mountain ridges. Shadows lengthened.

"For years, I've eschewed society. I thought by doing so I could manage my grief." Running his hands along his vest front, he said, "Thanks to this farce of ours, I'm learning it doesn't matter whether I'm alone or surrounded by people. The pain doesn't go away."

Her heart breaking for him, she sought for the right words to say. "It's been my experience that loss and grief can't be ignored. You have to work through it."

"Maybe I wouldn't struggle so much if their deaths had been the result of an accident. I can't let go of the fact that fire was meant for me." His voice thickened. "Elias and Cyrus plotted to get rid of me. Their evil deeds netted disastrous results. I can't stop hating them for it. To be honest, I don't want to."

"Is that why you haven't been going to church?"

He twisted around. His eyes were stormy. "I can't forgive them. I know I'm supposed to, but how can I when they aren't sorry for what they did?"

"Sarah's own father isn't remorseful?"

His gaze dropped. "I haven't seen him since before the fire," he admitted. "I barred him from the funeral."

"Your siblings haven't mentioned him in their letters?"

"I forbade them. Told them I would cease correspondence if they did."

"I think—"

June emerged from the house then. "I thought I heard voices out here. Supper's ready. Alexander, won't you join us?"

"I appreciate the offer," he said. "I should be getting home. Another time, perhaps."

"Yes, please. I'd like to hear all about your plans for the wedding."

Fresh guilt pierced Ellie. June was such a dear lady. A romantic at heart, she was ecstatic over the news of Ellie and Alexander's betrothal.

When they were once again alone, his somber mood deepened. "Ellie, please don't forget this is make-believe. I'm a broken man. I have nothing to offer you."

"You're assuming I *want* a husband," she retorted. "And that I'm somehow lacking the ability to discern what's real and what's not."

Alexander could never know how wonderful his attentiveness made her feel. Ellie liked being his fiancée. She liked being one half of a couple and the sense of belonging that imparted. And if she'd occasionally imagined what it would be like to be his wife, she'd quickly dismissed the notion. He was too afraid to risk his heart again, and she was too afraid to risk disappointing someone again. Failing at marriage had eaten away at her self-esteem. She wasn't eager to repeat the experience.

"I wanted to remind you. Just in case…"

"Don't worry, I'm not going to tumble into love with you and hang on your heels like an affection-starved puppy dog." Spinning on her heel, she stalked toward the door.

"Ellie, wait—"

"Go home, Alexander. No need for you to prolong your time in my company—there's no one around to witness our performance."

Inside the house, she sagged against the door, exhaustion invading her body. She cradled her middle. "You're all I need, my love," she whispered. "It'll be me and you, and that's enough."

"Have you seen Ellie this morning?"

Alexander checked his pocket watch again. He told himself it was simple concern for her causing his unease and not the lingering tension that marked their conversations. If he didn't know better, he'd think she was avoiding him. Ellie, the woman with the heart of a lion who could conquer any obstacle, didn't want to deal with him. His stomach clenched. He waited for the familiar burn, but it never materialized.

Flo continued chopping heaping mounds of cabbage and carrots. Her hand wasn't completely healed, but she was able to work at a slower pace. "She's out behind the barn."

"Is something wrong? Is she unwell?"

She flashed a coy smile. "Your pretty little fiancée is perfectly fine. She's skinning and gutting fish."

"Fish?"

"Yes, sir. We're going to have a tasty spread of fried potatoes and onions, slaw, fried corn bread, corn on the cob and golden fried fish." She used her knife for punctuation. "And the best part? Lemon meringue pie."

Alexander's mouth watered. Not that long ago, he wouldn't have been able to eat such rich fare. Now that his ulcer had calmed—largely thanks to Ellie's nurturing—he could occasionally indulge. He went in search of Ellie. Laughter, a man and a woman's, drew him to a spot behind the barn where carcasses were cleaned. A large oak tree with wide, interwoven branches provided shade from the autumn sun. His stride faltered at the sight of Ellie with Ben MacGregor, their heads bent close as they rid the fish of bones. Something Ben said made Ellie smile and blush. She hadn't been doing much of that in Alexander's company lately.

Frowning, he advanced, eventually garnering their attention. Ben straightened and smiled. A pleat appeared between Ellie's brows, and she seemed to have trouble holding his gaze. She must still be mad at him for what he'd said more than a week ago. Couldn't she understand he'd simply been trying to protect her?

Maybe that warning hadn't been as much for Ellie's benefit as your own.

"Good morning, my dear," he murmured before brushing a kiss against her cheek.

Ignoring her flashing eyes, he nodded at the deputy.

"Morning, Ben." Gesturing to the large pail spilling over with bounty, he said, "What's all this?"

"I like to fish in the early hours before my shift," Ben said. "Today was unusually successful. And since I couldn't possibly eat all of this myself, I offered to let Ellie have it."

"On the condition he eat lunch for free." She nudged Ben with her elbow.

The easy camaraderie between them stirred feelings of jealousy. *She's not really yours, remember? Besides, she knows Ben isn't interested in a genuine relationship. And neither are you.*

He extended his hand, palm up. "I'm not busy right now. How about I take over for you?"

She lifted her chin. "No, thank you. I'm enjoying the chance to be outside in the fresh air."

Ben looked at her, then Alexander. He seemed to come to a decision. Setting his knife on the makeshift work surface, he said, "I've actually got to get to the jail." He used the water barrel beside the barn wall to rinse his hands. "Sorry to abandon you midtask, but you've got the boss to help out."

Her smile was brittle. "I'll see you at noon?"

"Count on it. That is, unless Shane finds something pressing for me to do, like sweeping out the jail cells."

"I'll be sure to set a plate aside for you."

"Appreciate it, Ellie." Tugging at his Stetson's brim, he nodded and would've sauntered away if Alexander hadn't blocked his path.

"There's something I'd like to say."

His eyes darkened. "Let me guess, you're going to warn me off Ellie. I'm aware of my reputation, but do you honestly think I'd try to move in on an engaged lady?"

"It's not Ellie. It's Sally."

"Ah. I'm not allowed to talk to her, is that it?"

Ellie left the work area. "Do you have serious intentions toward her?"

"Of course not," he snorted. "She's just a kid."

Alexander shook his head. "She's eighteen, plenty old enough to have marriage on her mind. She's infatuated with you."

"What?" His incredulous gaze bounced between them. When Ellie nodded, he threw his hands up. "I was careful not to flirt with her. I treated her as I would a younger sister."

Ellie placed her hand on his arm. "For some girls, merely spending time with you is enough to inspire dreams of happy-ever-after."

"Sally's a loyal employee," Alexander tacked on. "I'd hate to see her get hurt."

His lips twisted. "I've already agreed to accompany her to the harvest dance."

"Then you'd better think of a good reason to bow out," he retorted.

Ellie flashed him an exasperated glance before turning her attention to the deputy. "I think that would be best, don't you?"

Ben lifted his hat and ruffled his hair. "I'll do it the first opportunity I get."

After he'd gone, Ellie jammed her hands on her hips. "Did you have to be so harsh? Couldn't you see he was upset by the situation? The man can't look at a girl without rumors swirling."

"Harsh? I was merely being honest."

"Like you were with me?" she scoffed. "You need to learn some tact, Alexander."

She returned to her task. He followed. "You're angry with me. Why?"

"I'm not angry. I'm offended that you think I'd misconstrue your attentions as real. Was that kiss really necessary, by the way?" She tapped her cheek.

"What I said wasn't only for your benefit." Scraping his hand over his face, he admitted, "I've been on my own for several years. Spending time with you has been…well, wonderful."

Her lips parted in surprise.

"I've come to consider you a good friend," he continued. "I never want to hurt you."

"I feel the same."

His chest expanded with a warm infusion of contentment, but he couldn't deny there was an underlying desire for more than friendship. He couldn't act on it. He had to bury it so deep it withered and died. After her baby was born, he'd go back to being nothing more than her boss. He'd have to learn to be content with that.

Chapter Fourteen

"**B**oss, come quick!"

Alexander pushed out of his desk chair, his heart in his throat as he rushed after Flo. Fear seized him when he spied Ellie hunched over the table by the stoves. He couldn't see her face, just the top of her head and her small hands splayed against the surface propping her up.

Flo hovered beside her. "I don't know what happened. One minute she was checking the pies and the next she almost swooned."

"What's wrong?" he demanded, curving his arm around her shoulders. "Ellie, talk to me."

She angled her head to look at him. Tiny beads of sweat dotted her brow. "I'm just a bit woozy, that's all. I got overheated."

He scooped her up in his arms and strode for the door. Ellie gasped and wriggled in his hold. "Alexander Copeland, put me down!" She clutched the front of his vest.

"In a moment." He bit out a command over his shoulder. "Flo, bring a glass of water."

"Yes, sir."

The cooler air was a soothing balm he hoped would ease her distress. He surprised himself by offering up a silent prayer. If Ellie lost this baby…if anything happened to her…

"Put me down," she urged. "I'm too heavy."

"For me to carry across town, maybe," he quipped, desperate to bury the unnerving thoughts. "I believe I can manage to get you to that tree yonder."

Brow knitted, she fell silent as they traversed the yard. He lowered her gently to the ground at the base of the tree so that she could sit with her back against the wide trunk. Crouching beside her, he searched for signs of pain, his focus eventually settling on her belly. Alexander reached out his hand, only to draw back at the last second.

"Do you hurt anywhere?"

She smoothed her hair behind her ear. "No. I'm the teeniest bit nauseous, but being out of that hot kitchen is helping." Then she clapped her hand over her mouth. "My pies. I have to check on them."

"Whoa." He put a restraining hand on her shoulder. "Absolutely not. You're not moving from this spot until I say so."

"Alexander, the judging event for food entries is today. I have to have those pies there no later than three o'clock."

"I'll deliver them."

"But they're still in the oven. They could be burning as we speak."

Flo trundled up and passed her a glass. "How are you holding up?"

Ellie dutifully sipped the water. "I'm feeling much improved. The heat got to me. I won't make the mistake again now that I recognize the warning signs."

"Ellie isn't ready to come inside yet, and she's worried about her pumpkin pies. Would you mind checking them?"

"Will do, boss."

When she'd gone, he once again raked his gaze over Ellie. "Do you need to visit Doc?"

"That's not necessary."

"You're sure?"

"Trust me. If I felt like there was something seriously wrong, I'd already be there."

His worry lingering, he took in the impressive scenery. Vivid blue skies framed the barn and shed. The orange pumpkins and variety of squash in the garden mimicked the colors climbing up the mountainside. Soon autumn would give way to winter and winter to spring. Ellie's baby was due in March. It seemed both an eternity and a blur.

Ellie cupped his jaw, drawing his attention to her. "I'm fine, Alex. I promise."

A smile formed. "No one besides my sister, Margaret, has ever called me that."

The corner of her mouth quirked. "It was a slip."

His leg cramped, so he rested one knee in the grass. "I don't mind."

"How old is your sister? Is she married?"

"Twenty. Last I heard, she had her sights on a certain young shopkeeper in town. Hard to believe she's of the age to marry and set up her own household."

"What about your brother?"

"He's been engaged for over a year, but he's dragging his feet on setting a date. I'm not sure why."

Remorse pounded him. His siblings had paid the price for his decision to abandon his home. They'd depended on him, as the eldest, to run the ranch and provide guidance as they navigated life's major crossroads.

"Have you invited them to visit you here?"

He shot her a dry look. "Until you came along, I wasn't

in the condition for company, especially that of my siblings."

Her smile broadened. "I'm not going to apologize."

He noticed there was color back in her cheeks. "You're looking more like yourself. Still queasy?"

She shook her head. "I feel normal."

"Good."

"That means I can check on my pies?"

"Not so fast." He stood to his feet. "I want you to rest for a while longer."

Due to the harvest festivities, he'd made the decision to close the Plum for the rest of the day. Tomorrow they'd only be open for breakfast. Ellie had entered the pie contest, and Flo had entered jams and hand-knitted shawls. Sally's mother wanted her there to help with the younger siblings.

Half an hour later, Ellie had convinced him she was fine and to escort her and what were sure to be her award-winning pies to the open fields located beyond the church where the harvest fair was held each year. Booths were set up in even rows, leaving ample space for attendees to mingle. Scents of venison and pork roasting above open fire pits mingled with that emitted from fat barrels of tart apple cider. School had been let out early, so kids of all ages prowled the area in search of games and snacks to spend their pennies on.

As he and Ellie made their way to the far end of the fields, folks who'd previously given him a wide berth now smiled in approval. He wasn't sure what carried more weight—his church attendance or his choice of a bride. Knowing how likable Ellie was, he was inclined toward the latter.

They'd delivered the pies when Ellie nudged him and nodded toward a couple who appeared to be arguing beneath a huge maple tree. The petite blonde girl was gesturing wildly while the young man listened, hands up in defeat.

"Sally." He exchanged a concerned look with Ellie. "I wonder what's going on? Ben reneged on the dance days ago."

"She looks really upset," Ellie said. "Should we go over there?"

"If it were my little sister, she wouldn't be thrilled with my interference."

"Look around, Alex. People are starting to notice."

Indeed, folks were staring and whispering. "Let's go."

With Ellie's arm linked with his, they walked over. Ben's glance in their direction reeked of helplessness.

"Is everything okay over here?" Alexander ventured.

Sally spun around, her cheeks wet and her eyes puffy. "You!" Brown eyes huge with distress, she advanced on him. "How could you do it? Who gave you the right to dictate whom I can and cannot socialize with? I've already got a pa. I don't need you poking your nose where it doesn't belong."

The vehemence with which she spoke put Alexander off-kilter. This behavior wasn't typical for sweet, biddable Sally Hatcher.

"Sally, don't blame Alexander for attempting to look out for your best interests," Ellie implored. "He's your boss."

"Not anymore," she scoffed. "I quit!"

Alexander's jaw sagged. "You can't quit. The café—"

"Is no longer my concern." With that, she stalked off in the opposite direction, almost mowing down a kid balancing a fried pie and three cinnamon rolls.

Ben cleared his throat, drawing both their gazes from her retreating figure. "I apologize. If I'd known this would be the outcome, I would've given her the cold shoulder from the start."

Alexander crossed his arms. "Think back on your acquaintance with her. Did you smile and flirt and pay her compliments?"

He stroked his chin and winced. "It's possible."

"You singled her out at the café," he accused.

Ellie sighed. "What reason did you give for changing your mind about the dance?"

"I told her I decided not to go, plain and simple. She kept pestering me until I couldn't take it anymore. I let it slip just now that you didn't think it was a good idea."

Alexander scuffed the ground with his shoe, frustration riding him. He searched the fields for a sign of her. Sally quitting was a disaster for his business and for her financial state. He knew from Flo that the Hatchers had more mouths to feed than they could manage and that her income helped keep food on the table.

It had been ages since someone had been that angry with him. He wanted to fix things but didn't know how.

Ellie couldn't handle seeing Alexander's stricken expression. It reminded her of the early days when he'd shunned everyone in order to live out his private nightmare. While he wasn't completely rid of his past's influence, he was halfway to freedom. He was taking an interest in his café. He involved himself in his employees' lives. He was allowing himself to care. She couldn't bear it if one day he decided to withdraw again.

"How about we go explore the booths?" she suggested. "This is my first official harvest fair in Gatlinburg, and I'm curious what all they have to offer."

His mouth set in a frown, he stared in the direction

Sally had disappeared. "I can't believe she quit. What are we going to do? How will we serve everyone?"

She curled her fingers around his biceps and lightly squeezed. "She's upset. Trying to talk to her now would be futile. Let's give her some time to collect her thoughts, and then we can pay her a visit."

He turned his head, his troubled gaze finding hers. "You're right. Margaret used to have similar episodes. My first instinct was to charge after her and settle our dispute, but Rosa advised me against it."

"So? Shall we browse?"

He inclined his head. "All right. I do believe I'm in the mood for something sweet."

"I smell spiced apples."

They walked toward the closest tables where multiple crafts were on display. "Don't eat anything too rich. You don't want to risk a stomach upset."

"Yes, Nurse Jameson."

He gifted her with a lopsided smile that turned her insides to mush. What would she do if he smiled in just that way more often? How would she resist longing for this relationship to be authentic?

"I know what you're thinking—you're a grown man perfectly capable of taking care of yourself."

He chuckled. "I may have grumbled in the past, but in truth, who could complain about having a woman as beautiful and wonderful as you watching out for them?"

Ellie's entire body tingled at the compliment. She'd never tire of Alexander's praise. Unsure how to respond, she led him to the nearest collection of hand-pieced quilts and crocheted blankets. One in particular caught her eye. Done in pastel green, yellow and pink, the blanket would be perfect for a baby.

Alexander tested the soft yarn. "You like this one?"

The elderly woman seated behind the table looked up from her current project and smiled benevolently. "When is your baby due?"

"March."

"Still cold enough to get some use out of it before spring's heat sets in," she responded.

Alexander leaned close, his shoulder brushing hers. "I'm sure you could use that for several years to come."

The lady overheard and wiggled her eyebrows. "By the time that one's outgrown it, he or she will have younger siblings to pass it along to."

Ellie lifted her hand from the blanket and took a step back. The assumption that she and Alexander would have children together put a pang in the vicinity of her heart. She hadn't known how appealing such a notion was—or how unhappy she'd be at the impossibility of it.

You're being ridiculous, she scolded. *He may never recover from losing his first son. No way would he wish to be a father again.* Rubbing her tummy, she silently wished things were different. Her unborn child would benefit greatly from having Alexander in his or her life. He was thoughtful and practical, caring and loyal.

"Maybe another time," she demurred, steering him toward the next booth.

A few paces away, out of the crafter's hearing, he said, "Let me purchase it for you. I have yet to choose a baby gift."

Ellie was tempted. With one last glance at the beautiful blanket, she resolutely shook her head. "Thank you, Alexander, but I couldn't possibly accept such generosity."

His blue eyes were insistent. "We may not be engaged, but I am your boss. There wouldn't be anything out of the ordinary about me bestowing your child with a gift."

"I can't." She scanned the row of tables and pointed. "Forget about browsing. I'm ready for dessert."

He allowed her to lead him away. He did insist on paying for their treats. They devoured mouthwatering fried dough dusted with sugar and cinnamon while standing in the middle of the aisle, uncaring they were disrupting the flow of foot traffic. Ellie couldn't resist licking the sugar from her fingers. Catching her, Alexander grinned and mimicked her actions. As a matronly figure passed them and assumed a disdainful expression, they burst into laughter.

Their sweet tooth satisfied, they resumed their explorations. Alexander admired hand-carved knives and walking sticks. Ellie browsed household goods but didn't purchase anything. When she spotted an area where folks—mostly of the ten-and-under variety—were painting faces on gourds and carving pumpkins, she persuaded her handsome escort into taking part.

He took a seat in the middle of a makeshift table and smiled at kids on either side of him. Ellie watched as he painted a silly face on the gourd. When the little girl across from him asked what he was going to name it, he tapped his chin as if in serious thought and said "Gordy." She giggled.

Ellie's heart melted. Her imagination threatened to take her to the future, to when her son or daughter was that age. How easy it was to picture Alexander teaching a little boy to fish or reading a book to a little girl. She put a stop to it, but it commanded all her willpower.

"Are you going to join us?" he asked, dark brows lifted.

"Not this time."

He caught her kneading her lower back and immediately replaced his paintbrush in the jar. Tucking his gourd against his side, painted face directed outward to avoid staining his suit vest, he extended his arm to her.

"Let's go find some shade, shall we?"

"Good idea."

"Are you feeling well? You're not too hot?"

She smiled over at him. "I'm fine. My feet are a bit tired, however. I'd enjoy a rest."

"Once I get you settled, I'll fetch you some lemonade."

"You don't have to dance attendance on me, Alexander. I am and always will be *just* your cook." The truth was a painful but necessary reminder. "One you didn't even hire yourself."

He was contemplative as they passed other festival-goers. Entering a sparse smattering of trees on the edge of the full-fledged forest where cut logs had been situated in a circular pattern, he led her to the nearest one. The area was empty, so she had her pick. He rested Gordy the gourd on the ground near her feet, propped by the log.

The air was cooler here in the shade and rich with the scents of moss and decomposing leaves. The kaleidoscope of vibrant green, orange, yellow and crimson was as lovely as a painting. She could remain here indefinitely in Alexander's company.

"Will you watch over Gordy until I return?"

"I won't let him out of my sight," she said.

Her soft chuckle was cut off when she felt a swift, hard kick on her left side. At her soft inhale, Alexander sank onto the log beside her, lines bracketing his mouth.

"What's the matter?"

She shook her head in wonder, pressing gently against the spot in hopes of a repeat. "The baby's kicking." Without thinking, she snatched his hand and guided it beneath her own.

His face hovered near hers, wonder brightening his

eyes. They remained very still, the intimacy of the moment wrapping them in a cocoon of unreality. The booths and distant crowds faded from consciousness. Then, just when Ellie thought the chance was lost, there came another firm kick.

Alexander's growing smile was like the sun emerging from behind a cloud, bathing her in radiant light that warmed her skin and lifted her spirits.

"You're going to make a wonderful mother, Ellie."

Her eyes grew moist. The deep-seated yearning to meet her child was tempered by uncertainty. Would she be able to provide for her? Would she be successful in copying the model of love and nurturing her own mother and grandmother had patterned for her? And then there was the gnawing truth that, once the baby arrived, Alexander would likely retreat. He'd be there for her if the Jamesons caused trouble, but she sensed he wouldn't be as eager to spend time with her and the baby, a reminder of his tremendous loss.

"I pray you're right," she breathed, caught in the approval shining upon her.

He was so close. He smelled divine. And his large hand was still pressed against her belly.

With his other hand, he slowly smoothed her hair off her forehead, sweeping it to the side and out of her eyes. Sparks of electricity raced along her scalp and behind her ears.

"You're beautiful, you know that?" His voice was low and smooth like honey, a timbre she hadn't heard before.

"I don't feel beautiful. I feel ungainly."

"Pregnancy suits you, Ellie."

She gave in to the need to touch him. She caressed his face, starting at his temple and over his cheekbone and down along the hard line of his jaw, clean-shaven today. His eyelids slid closed on a sigh.

Ellie's fingertips played over his chin and, in a surge of boldness, drifted over his sculpted mouth.

His eyes popped open.

"I overstepped the bounds," she started.

He closed the distance between them, bringing his lips to hers and kissing her with an exquisite tenderness she'd never before experienced. A feeling of rightness flooded her. He was a man she admired. A man she felt utterly safe with.

When he lifted his head, his gaze soaked her in, longing fighting with regret. "Now it is I who's overstepped the bounds."

Withdrawing, he stood to his feet and looked down at her with hooded eyes.

She lifted her chin. "I'm not sorry you did. I enjoy being close to you."

His head reared back. "Ellie—"

"I'm being honest. I trust you, Alexander. I feel comfortable with you, like I can do anything and you won't judge me. But I know we can't let that happen again. It's unfortunate, since we're engaged." She somehow managed a lighthearted tone. "But it's the way it has to be."

He looked at once relieved and distressed. She stuck out her hand.

"Help me up?"

His strong grip closed over hers, and he assisted her to her feet, instantly releasing her and locking his hands behind his back.

"I'm suddenly ravenous," she announced, forcing her gaze to connect with his. "Let's find another unhealthy snack before I call it a day."

He hesitated, seeming torn. "All right."

For the remaining hour she was in his company, Ellie played her part of happy fiancée to the hilt. Not for the people of Gatlinburg, but for Alexander. She'd proven she had the grit to withstand tough situations. She could wait until she reached the privacy of her room to let the weight of her disappointment crash over her.

Chapter Fifteen

"Ellie! What a nice surprise." Mrs. Hatcher opened the door wider. "We've just finished supper, but we've plenty of leftovers if you're hungry."

Remaining on the porch, she said, "Thank you, but I couldn't manage another bite. I overindulged at the fair today."

The other woman assumed a knowing look. "Mr. Copeland seems to enjoy doting on you. I had my concerns about my Sally working for him in the beginning, but he turned out to be a fair-minded employer, if you ignored his reclusive nature."

Apparently Sally hadn't shared what had happened earlier in the day. "I actually came to see her. Is she available?"

Leaning out the door, she pointed to the barn. "She's milking, but she won't mind the company."

"Thank you, Mrs. Hatcher."

One of the younger children hollered from somewhere in the house. With an apologetic smile, she waved and closed the door. Ellie went in search of her young friend. Alexander had escorted her home two hours ago. After a much-needed rest on the couch with a borrowed book, she'd told June she had an unavoidable errand to complete. Entering the large structure, she prayed for wisdom. Pushing Sally further away wasn't the outcome she hoped for.

"Hello? Sally?"

A rustling sound came from a stall on the far right end. "Down here," she called.

Ellie found the right one and rested her hands on the top ledge. When Sally didn't look up from her milking, she said, "Your mother said I could find you here."

"I'm busy."

"I won't stay long. I came to see how you were feeling. You were distraught earlier."

The rhythmic splash of milk hitting the insides of the pail mingled with the clucking of the free-roaming chickens.

"I'm still distraught." Lifting her head from the cow's side, she paused in the milking to finally meet Ellie's gaze. She looked more angry than anything. "If not for Mr. Copeland, I'd be going to the dance tomorrow night with Ben. I'm in love with him, you know."

"Is he in love with you?"

Her eyes flared. "H-he hasn't said as much. Some men aren't comfortable sharing what's in their heart. A tough lawman like Ben is bound to have trouble expressing the finer sentiments."

"Sally, when a man is interested in courting you, he won't leave you in doubt. Ben has been vocal about his decision to remain a bachelor. He doesn't want the commitment or responsibility of a long-term relationship."

Lips quivering, Sally averted her face, chin dipping toward her chest. "We'll never know if he might've felt differently about me, will we?"

Hurting for the girl, Ellie went into the stall and

touched her thin shoulder. "Sweetie, Alexander was try-ing to help. He doesn't want you to get hurt."

She sniffled. "He doesn't care about me. All he cares about is his business and who's going to serve his pre-cious customers."

"You wouldn't say that if you'd seen his face after you left. He feels horrible, Sally. He wanted to come after you, but I advised him to wait."

Sally dashed wetness from her cheeks. "Do you think maybe he'll speak to Ben? Take back whatever it was he said?"

Sighing, Ellie lowered her hand to her side. "I'm afraid that's not going to happen."

"I see."

"Alexander's got a good heart. Deep down, I think you know that." When she remained stubbornly silent, Ellie added, "I'd like you to do something for me."

Dejection switched to denial. "I'm not coming back."

"Not that." Ellie held up her hands. "I'd like for you to ponder your interactions with the deputy. Examine his behavior. Ask yourself if perhaps your own hopes colored your perceptions. One last thing—men don't typically like to be told what to do. If Ben has serious intentions to-ward you, he doesn't strike me as the type who'd meekly back away if someone raised objections."

Exiting the stall, she sent her a final glance. "Good evening, Sally."

For Alexander's sake, she hoped her visit wasn't for naught.

Alexander held the plain gold band in the palm of his hand. Alone in his living quarters—when was he not alone up here?—he waited for guilt to rush in. He de-served to wallow in it. He'd kissed a woman other than his wife. The role he'd played in Sarah's ultimate demise, his arrogance in thinking he'd bested their enemies, dictated he remain alone and unhappy for the rest of his days. He didn't feel either when he was with Ellie. Holding her beneath the comforting autumn sun in the shade of a dozen trees, he'd felt more in tune with another person than at any other time in his life. To his shame, he'd do it again in a heartbeat.

The gold band mocked him. *You think you can protect Ellie?*

Closing his fingers around it until the metal bit into his flesh, he shut his eyes and immediately saw the lifeless forms of his wife and child. Just like with Sarah, he'd promised Ellie he'd keep her safe. Was he deceiving them both?

The thought ignited fear deep inside. He couldn't fail another mother and child.

Replacing the ring inside the drawer, he shut it with a snap and went to fix himself a solitary cup of tea, the battle between what he *should* do and what he *wanted* to do raging inside. Call off the engagement and let Sheriff Timmons and Ben guard Ellie? Or continue as they had been, spending an increasing amount of time together that somehow skewed their thinking and muddied their true mission?

Gulping down the steaming hot liquid, he went to bed, expecting to spend hours staring at the rafters overhead. Next thing he knew, the bedside alarm was jangling, jolting him awake. He washed and dressed, no clear answers to his dilemma, before descending the stairs to start on breakfast.

He froze on the bottom step.

"What are you doing here?"

Ellie calmly hung her dove-gray knitted shawl on the

hook and slipped her apron over her head. "Good morning, Alex. How did you sleep?"

He liked when she called him that. Gripping the banister, he was transported to the first time he'd clapped eyes on her. They'd stood in the exact same spots. His ulcer and his lack of the proper precautions had landed him in a poor state of health. Annoyed with himself and dealing with a substantial amount of physical pain, he hadn't welcomed his new cook with open arms. Back then she'd been reed thin and wan, grappling with the unexpected loss of her husband and stuck in a troublesome environment with hostile in-laws.

To him, she'd been nothing more than an irritant, an obstacle to his goal of shutting out the world. Alexander couldn't have guessed she'd shift his very existence and resurrect the hope he'd thought had been destroyed in the fire.

Now, he soaked in her lush beauty. This morning she'd pulled her rich brown hair into a loose twist that framed her face, stray strands teasing the line of her jaw. The deep purple blouse she'd paired with a serviceable black skirt complemented her fair complexion. How fortunate he'd be if she was indeed destined to be his!

"I slept well, thank you," he belatedly answered. "You should still be in your bed. Resting."

Having tied off her apron, she turned toward him, her smile serene. "I am rested. And you can't seat customers, fetch their drinks and food, and cook at the same time."

"Flo and I would've managed somehow."

"You would've had unsatisfied customers on your hands."

He adopted a stern expression. "Have you forgotten what happened yesterday?"

Unfazed, she glanced over at the stoves and shrugged.

"I'll be on alert for the signs of overheating. I'll step outside for fresh air if I need to."

He furrowed his brow.

She laughed. "You worry too much, you know that?"

Flo arrived then, and Alexander explained what had happened with Sally. After expressing her considerable surprise, she got straight to work on the biscuits. He fetched a slab of bacon to slice, and Ellie chose to soft boil the eggs instead of scrambling. She also started on a big batch of oatmeal.

At five minutes until seven, he entered the dining room. Already a handful of men were waiting on the boardwalk, no doubt eager for hot coffee and tasty food to fill their bellies. He unlocked the door and bid them enter. The next three hours were a blur. Again and again, he answered the same question—where was Sally?—his own disappointment deepening as the morning wore on. Sally and Flo were fixtures here. It didn't feel right when one of them was absent.

At one point, he was in the kitchen to brew more coffee when he approached Ellie. "How are you holding up?"

She flashed him a long-suffering look. "I'm fine. How are you?"

"Fine." He watched her pull out another tray of biscuits. "No, I'm not. I'm not suited to waitressing. I thought Sally might show up today."

Laying aside the leather cooking gloves, she reached out and gave his arm a light squeeze. "She fancies herself in love. To her, you're the obstacle to everlasting happiness."

"You're serious?"

"She's young and impetuous. I believe she'll come around."

"And if she doesn't?"

Her mouth twisted. "Then you'll have to hire a new waitress."

From the other side of the room, Flo snorted. "Once her mamma learns what she's done, she'll have a thing or two to say about the matter. You don't give up a position such as hers without so much as by-your-leave. Young ones got to learn responsibility."

She regaled them with stories of her own sons' antics. Alexander and Ellie exchanged a secret smile. Flo's favorite subjects were her children and grandchildren. As soon as he was able to slip away without being rude, he returned to the dining room to tend the remaining five customers. He happened to gaze out the window. What he saw caused his heart rhythm to slip.

"It can't be," he murmured.

There on the boardwalk stood a young woman in elegant yet wrinkled traveling clothes, her expression unsure as she compared the window lettering to the paper in her hand. Disbelieving, Alexander remained stock-still as she pushed the door open.

The bell's ding barely registered. The footsteps behind him in the hall were muted. Ellie's voice reached him, but he couldn't decipher it for the buzzing in his ears.

The newcomer entered, her bonnet's brim framing her matured features and hiding much of the raven waves she used to wear in pigtails. Her wide blue eyes that surveyed the café interior were still bright with intelligence and curiosity. Seconds passed until that gaze finally came to rest on him. Shock registered first, followed by unfettered joy.

Her squeal echoed through the space, and as she rushed into his arms, Alexander found himself drowning in a sea of emotion.

Chapter Sixteen

Alexander's past had come to town. A tight ball formed in the middle of Ellie's chest as she watched the very public, very enthusiastic reunion between him and the stunning stranger. Although his face registered lingering shock, his eyes told another story…he loved this woman. Affection brightened his eyes to celestial blue as he openly studied her.

For a wild moment, Ellie wondered if this was an old flame, someone who'd loved Alexander from afar and who'd ultimately decided to follow him to Tennessee. Or perhaps she was a beloved friend who hoped to be more.

The commotion brought Flo to the dining room. The customers ceased their conversations in order to listen in.

When the pair finally realized they were at the center of attention, Alexander turned to Ellie and Flo. Looking at them side-by-side, Ellie realized her identity was obvious. They shared the same hair and eye color, and their facial structure bore similarities. Ellie's relief was tempered by the fact that one day in the future, she'd be forced to see Alexander with a woman who was not his sister, one who truly was linked to him in a romantic sense. The knowledge was like a dreadful dream that offered no escape. In that moment, she realized her feelings had progressed far beyond friendship.

She loved him.

She was in love with her boss, a man who would never return her feelings.

There wasn't time to process the revelation because Alexander was introducing his sister to Flo. Ellie was next.

He hesitated. "Margaret, I'd like you to meet Ellie, my...um..."

"I'm Alexander's cook," she said by way of rescue. Was that a hint of desperation in her voice? Were her eyes feverish?

Margaret's smile appeared genuine. "It's a pleasure to meet you, Ellie."

"Cook?" Flo snorted. "She's more than that. She's his fiancée."

Margaret gasped, her gaze falling to Ellie's protruding middle. Alexander grimaced and tugged on his suit sleeve ends. Ellie's cheeks burned thinking what conclusions his younger sister was jumping to.

"This is wonderful news!" she exclaimed. "Welcome to the family!"

Ellie found herself caught up in a tight hug. When Margaret released her, her eyes were suspiciously bright.

"Oh, Alex, I can't express how happy I am for you. I thought I'd find you in a terrible state. You left Texas a ravaged man...and your letters, as infrequent as they were, didn't inspire confidence that you'd moved on."

Tears sprang from her eyes. Alexander looked at once discomfited and horrified.

"Please don't cry—"

Margaret fell into his arms a second time. Ellie and Flo exchanged glances.

"All right, everyone." Flo bustled over to the curious patrons. "It's closing time. You can settle your bill with me."

Following her example, Ellie caught Alexander's attention. "Why don't you two visit in your office? I'll rustle up some tea and a snack."

Gratefulness settled across his pinched features. "Thank you, Ellie." Patting his sobbing sibling on the back, he said, "No doubt you're exhausted, Margaret. There's a couch in my office just a few steps away. You're probably hungry, too." He eased away. "Are you hungry?"

Ellie left them to prepare the drinks and food. While thrilled for Alexander—he'd been apart from his loved ones for far too long—she wondered how this extra wrinkle in their pretend engagement would impact them both.

"It appears I'm not the only one with news to share."

Margaret had made herself comfortable on the couch near the windows. Her bonnet rested on the empty cushion beside her. His handkerchief was balled in her hand, her bout of tears passed and curiosity resurging.

Alexander had taken up a stance in the middle of the office, his hands buried in his pockets. The changes in his sister were marked. She'd blossomed into a becoming young lady with more than a passing resemblance to their late mother.

"About Ellie, I know what you must be thinking..."

"That you're blessed to have a second chance at a family?"

"She's a recent widow," he explained, the tips of his ears burning. "She discovered she was expecting shortly after her husband passed in a tragic accident."

Understanding tugged at her mouth. "You've bonded over your shared loss. That's natural."

Indecision churned his gut. Should he confess the truth? Fooling the locals didn't bother him near as much as fooling his own flesh and blood. Pressing his hand against his middle, he chose to change the subject.

"I can't believe you're here. And that you traveled all this distance alone. What was Thomas thinking to allow it?"

She lifted her chin in silent reproof. "I'm twenty years old, Alex. I don't need anyone's permission to come and see my oldest brother. Nor do I need a caretaker." Tugging off her gloves, she splayed her hand midair. A garnet and gold ring adorned her left hand. "As a matter of fact, I'll soon be a married woman."

"Married? To who?"

"His name is Lowell Draper. He's a blacksmith. He's very skilled at what he does. People drive from miles around to patronize his business."

"Why didn't you tell me?" He began pacing. "Or why didn't Thomas?"

Margaret rose to her feet and blocked his path, her demeanor solemn. Gone was the carefree girl he'd once known. "I shouldn't have to share what is probably the most important news of my life in a letter." She placed her hand on his chest. "I've missed you, Alex. We've all missed you."

"I've missed you, too," he scraped out, too many memories bombarding him at once.

"There's more I have to tell you."

He sensed it wasn't a subject he wanted to visit. "What is it?"

Eyes darkening to navy blue, she hesitated. "It's about the fire. And Cyrus."

Pulling away, he stalked to the window and stared unseeing at the alley.

Margaret didn't follow, but she didn't remain quiet, either. "About six months after you left, one of Cyrus's employees came forward. He admitted to overhearing Cyrus discussing the fire and his intent to kill you."

Alexander balled his fists. The bitterness and hatred he'd managed to bury broke free again, choking him. "Let me guess, the sheriff didn't believe him."

The man hadn't believed Alexander's claims. To his knowledge, he hadn't bothered to investigate the matter.

"On the contrary, Sheriff Andrews took him at his word and managed to find one other man to corroborate his story. Cyrus was arrested."

He twisted around. "Cyrus Pollard. In jail. I never thought…" He passed a shaky hand down his face. "Was there a trial?"

"Yes. It took some time, about a year. The sheriff wanted to summon you to testify, but Thomas and I convinced him not to." Her forehead bunched. "I wasn't sure if that was the right thing. I'm still not. However, neither of us thought you'd come home."

He stewed over the revelations. "I don't blame you, Margaret. I'm not sure what I would've done if you had. To be in the same room as my wife and son's murderer—" He broke off. "What was the outcome? Please don't tell me he walked away a free man."

She swallowed hard. He could tell this was difficult for her. "He was convicted and sentenced to jail for the rest of his life."

"That's not a suitable punishment for what he did. If I'd come back there, Margaret, I would've wound up behind bars myself."

"Alex, Cyrus was killed by another inmate two months ago."

Instead of satisfaction, Alexander just felt numb.

"Elias testified during the trial that he had no prior knowledge of the fire. He insisted he would've put a stop to it." She sucked in a ragged breath. "He's a broken man."

"He's not innocent in this, Margaret," he bit out. "His actions played a part in the deaths of his own daughter and grandson."

Fresh tears filled her eyes. "I grieve for them, too. Sarah was my friend. And darling Levi..."

She buried her face in her hands. Alexander wrapped his arms around her and held her as he should've done three years ago. The magnitude of his cowardice registered. He'd abandoned his own siblings and left them to deal with the aftermath of his personal destruction.

"I'm sorry, sis," he murmured, his voice thick. "I was wrong to put my own needs above yours."

Once she'd composed herself, she cupped his cheek and smiled tremulously. "We understand why you had to leave. I'm so very glad I decided to come. You look well, dear brother. And content. You can't know how it gladdens my heart to know you've found someone special. Ellie must be a gem."

"Margaret, I have a confession," he said. "Ellie and I aren't truly engaged. It's a sham."

Her head reared back. "Why? To what end?"

"It was a spur-of-the-moment decision. I only offered out of a sense of duty. Her in-laws are putting pressure on her, and I thought that by offering her my protection, they'd back off."

"I don't know what to say, other than I'm disappointed it isn't real."

"It's not real. Not even close." He ignored the niggling doubts.

"You loved Sarah. Of course you'd be reluctant to risk

your heart again. I don't like to think of you alone, however, far from family and friends."

"I'm fine on my own. As you probably remember, I'm content with my own company. I don't need a wife or children. I had a family, and I lost them. There's no replacing them."

Ellie wished she could redo the past five minutes. She would've taken longer to prepare the tea. Or lingered in the kitchen with Flo in order to give the siblings extra privacy. But she couldn't undo this moment, couldn't unhear Alexander's declaration, couldn't pretend she hadn't seen the fierceness in his brilliant blue eyes or the obstinate set of his jaw. He'd meant it. Every word.

And Alexander knew she'd heard them. He'd belatedly noticed her in the open doorway. He'd looked startled and had opened his mouth to speak before closing it again and averting his gaze.

How inopportune, she thought inanely as she set the tray on his desk, that mere moments ago she'd acknowledged she loved him. Her heart was still in a tender state. After her tense relationship with Nolan, she hadn't thought herself vulnerable to such things. And before she could come to terms with what it meant, here was irrefutable proof that she was nothing but an obligation.

His embrace hadn't felt like one, though. Ellie could almost feel the warm imprint of his hand on her stomach, the smooth, velvet-like heat of his mouth atop hers and the glorious sensation of his fingers caressing her hair.

Attempting to pour the golden liquid into the teacups without sloshing it over the rims, she wondered why exactly he'd deigned to kiss her. Had it been a whim? Had curiosity spurred him on—what would it be like to kiss the poor, penniless widow? Or perhaps loneliness had gripped him and he'd temporarily forgotten she was his particular burden to bear.

Her stomach roiled, and the back of her neck went hot. *Not now*, she prayed.

"Thank you for the tea." Margaret appeared at her side. "I'm famished. I last ate more than five hours ago on the train. The driver I hired to bring me here was sadly lacking in rations." Bending over the desk, she peered more closely at the snacks Ellie had prepared. "Is that blackberry preserves?" Snagging a biscuit slathered with the fruit concoction, she sank her teeth in and groaned. "Delicious. Alex, have a biscuit."

Alexander meandered closer, going around the desk so that he was facing them both. Ellie couldn't meet his gaze. She stared instead at the wall of books behind him.

"I've had my fair share of Ellie's biscuits. Everything she turns out of that kitchen is worth raving over."

"I'll leave you to your conversation," she said, her voice higher than usual.

Margaret protested. "Please stay. I'd like a chance to get to know you."

"Didn't you hear your brother?" she responded. "I'm not an important part of his life. I'm just another employee."

Alexander's sharp inhale was lost to Ellie. Not giving either a chance to waylay her, she rushed into the hallway and closed the door behind her. In the kitchen, she hurriedly exchanged her apron for her shawl.

Unaware of her upset, Flo smiled as she dried the last pot. "Isn't it wonderful that the boss's sister has come to see him? It's about time. He's been alone too long." She winked at Ellie. "Of course, now he's got you and the young 'un."

"Flo, I'm going to go home if you don't mind."

She lifted a shoulder. "We're done for the day. You know, last year the boss didn't close for the harvest festival. You've wrought a lot of changes around here."

Her heart throbbing like a painful bruise, Ellie schooled her features and headed for the exit. "I'll see you in the morning."

"You haven't forgotten about the harvest dance tonight?"

"I—I'm not sure we'll be going. Alexander will want to spend time with Margaret, and I'm sure she's fatigued from her trip."

Flo bustled over. "But what about the new blouse and matching shawl June gave you especially for the dance?"

Ellie shot her a sideways glance. "It'll keep. There will be other opportunities."

Her squinty eyes narrowed. "You're sort of pale. Are you feeling quite the thing?"

Alarm gripped her. If Alexander suspected she was ill, he'd come to June's to check on her. She couldn't talk to him.

"I'm not about to lose my breakfast, nor am I about to swoon. My back is sore and my ankles are swollen, however, and a nice long nap sounds divine right about now. T-to be honest, a leisurely evening at home sounds perfect." She forced a laugh. "I have to face facts. I'm almost six months pregnant. Me dancing at this stage would only serve to provide comedy for the onlookers."

"That's not true," Flo began to protest.

"Please tell Alexander I've decided not to go. The last thing we want is for him to worry about me when he should be enjoying Margaret's visit."

Flo stewed over this, her fingers plucking at the drying towel she held. "All right."

Ellie patted her shoulder. "Thanks, Flo. I look forward to hearing all about it tomorrow morning."

Leaving the café and Main Street behind, Ellie made it to June's front porch swing before bursting into tears. The charade had seemed like a good solution to her problem. In hindsight, agreeing to Alexander's scheme was the worst decision she could've made.

Chapter Seventeen

"**W**hy, Ellie, whatever is the matter?" June padded over to the swing and sat beside her. The scent of rose water enveloped her, putting her in mind of her grandmother.

"I'm in love with Alexander," she wailed, fresh tears flowing.

"Of course you are, dear." Confusion colored her voice. "You've agreed to become his wife."

"How I wish that were the case." Wiping her tears, she risked a glance at the woman she'd come to admire and trust. Alexander had revealed the truth to Duncan and Margaret. Ellie was about to burst with the need to confide in someone.

"I've sensed you've been troubled about something. Why don't you tell me what's going on?"

The entire story came pouring out. While dismayed about Gladys and Nadine's behavior, June was gravely worried about Ellie's state of mind.

Patting Ellie's hand, she said, "You've suffered a great deal at the hands of your late husband and his folks. I hate to think of you suffering further."

"Alexander couldn't have known I'd fall for him. He was simply trying to help."

"Are you certain he doesn't return your feelings?"

Pushing out of the swing—a feat her growing girth was making more difficult—Ellie crossed to the railing and soaked in the countryside arrayed in the fullness of multicolored glory.

"I'm positive."

"There's no chance—"

"None."

"Have you considered telling him how you feel? Perhaps he'd be interested in a marriage of convenience."

Ellie half turned to gawk at the older lady.

"What? It's a common enough thing. Practical marriages benefit both parties. You need a husband and father for your child."

"The problem is Alexander doesn't need or want me." Sorrow weighed on her soul. "I can't repeat history, June. Being married to Nolan was a miserable experience. Even if Alexander did agree to such a marriage, I couldn't survive living with him day in and day out, knowing I have feelings for him while he considered me nothing more than a responsibility."

June was quiet for long moments. "What about after the baby comes? Are you going to be able to continue working with him?"

The prospect of leaving the Plum, of not seeing Alexander every day, made her heart ache. "I don't think I will," she admitted in a low voice.

June came and wrapped her arm around Ellie's shoulders. "You don't have to make a decision today. Come, let me prepare you some warm milk. You'll feel better after a nap." She let June steer her toward the door. "And once you've rested, I'll do your hair for the dance."

Ellie stopped. "I'm not going."

"You could do with an evening of fun, young lady. You can tag along with me and my friends."

"But—"

"Soon enough you'll be on this little one's schedule." Her periwinkle gaze winked with a teasing light. "Enjoy your free time while you still have it."

He'd done the very thing he'd promised not to.

Alexander watched as couples performed a country reel, his mind replaying his and Margaret's conversation and Ellie's crestfallen expression. He'd been almost relieved that she'd left. He'd meant what he said, but there were doubts. Secret longings he couldn't afford to nurture. It frightened him to think what might happen once he met Ellie's child. Already he could picture himself involved in his or her life…a second chance at fatherhood.

Quelling that thought, he searched the crowd for the sheriff. He'd already hurt Ellie with his comments. Cutting things off now would prevent future hurt. There'd be no more ill-advised embraces. No more confusing emotions. They could revert back to their former ways—he'd steer clear of her and leave her safety to the professionals.

"I'm glad you agreed to come, Alex." Beside him, Margaret swayed to the music, no trace of fatigue on her face. "You were frustratingly stingy with your descriptions of Gatlinburg. The scenery is breathtaking, and the residents I've met so far seem friendly enough."

A fat, orange-tinted moon cast weak light over the high mountain slopes. Torches throughout the field emitted patches of light. Off in the distance, a large bonfire created a gathering spot for those who'd rather socialize than dance. The evening was pleasant and on the nippy side, perfect for celebrating the harvest.

All around him, people were enjoying themselves, as he would be if Ellie were with him.

Margaret nudged him. "Isn't that your cook?"

Alexander shifted to the left. Through the whirling couples, he spotted her. "She must've changed her mind," he murmured.

He tried to make sense of Ellie in the arms of another man, smiling the smile he thought she reserved for him, her brown eyes wide and trusting.

"Who's she dancing with?" Margaret asked.

He strained forward, his neck muscles knotting with tension. The man maneuvered her around, and Alexander relaxed somewhat. Nathan O'Malley was a married man. He brought his wife, Sophie, into the café on occasion.

"One of the locals."

The song ended. Alexander took a step forward, only to halt when Nathan handed Ellie off to Duncan. He sensed Margaret's perusal.

"You care for her."

He reluctantly met her shrewd gaze. This side of his grown-up sister would take some getting used to. "I care for her well-being. She's been an asset to the Plum and is a valued employee."

"A nice speech," she countered. "One that doesn't tell the whole story."

Alexander was spared having to defend himself when a young farmer approached Margaret for a dance.

"Why, I'd love to." Her smile dazzled the man, who led her into the fray like a buck who'd found his mate. He hoped Margaret relayed her engaged status before she blazed a trail of disappointed hopes.

Turning his attention once more to his fake fiancée, he remained where he was as she danced with a succession of gentlemen, some married and some not. Telling himself it was concern spurring him to her side, he fetched a lemonade and waited nearby for the music to fade. Fortunately, her partner led her out of the chaos and into Alexander's path.

"Good evening, Ellie."

She stopped short, her smile fading. "Alexander. I didn't think you'd be here."

Her implication was clear. Grimacing, he handed her the cold drink. "Margaret convinced me. I thought you'd chosen to stay in, as well."

With a murmured thank-you to her partner, Ellie left the press of people, all the while sipping her drink. Alexander followed.

"June talked me into coming," she admitted, a little line between her brows as she studied their surroundings.

Since she didn't seem inclined to look at him, Alexander took advantage of the opportunity to drink in her loveliness. Her dress was new. A becoming peach hue, it flattered her feminine curves. Her dark tresses spilled over her shoulders, the top section secured with a ribbon.

The impulse to smooth her hair over her shoulder, to cup her nape and urge her close was difficult to resist. He yearned to hold her in his arms again and shut out the world. But he couldn't. He closed his eyes and forced himself to think of a way to tell her his decision—the engagement had to end. Together, they could confide in Sheriff Timmons about her in-laws.

Duncan's quiet greeting pulled Alexander from his thoughts.

"Ellie, do you know those two couples over there?"

The concern tightening Duncan's jaw became more pronounced when Ellie located the people in question and put a trembling hand over her mouth.

"That's Howard and Gladys Jameson, my late husband's parents." Her gaze shot to Alexander. "Ralph and Nadine are here, too."

Alarm threading through him, he searched the crowd and saw them near the tables. They weren't taking part in the festivities, they were scrutinizing the dancers. Hunting someone.

"I overheard them talking," Duncan said. "They mentioned your name. Considering what Alexander told me, I figured they were your in-laws."

"Their presence here isn't typical." Ellie had gone pale.

"You think they're here to cause trouble?" Duncan shared a look with Alexander indicating he'd assist in any way necessary.

"They don't like that they've lost control of Ellie," he said. "There's no telling what they'll do to try to get it back."

Alexander regretted his words when Ellie sucked in a sharp breath. He settled his hand low on her back and edged closer. "Try not to worry. I'm not going to leave your side."

She nibbled her lower lip. He hated seeing her distressed. "Do you feel up to another dance?"

"You want to dance with me? Now?"

"They think we're engaged. We should put up a solid front."

Her eyes widened. "We've barely spoken."

"You've danced with several men but not with your fiancé."

She was apparently too distracted to note the hint of jealousy in his tone. Duncan wasn't. He smirked at Alexander.

"We can't let them think we're having problems," she murmured.

"Or that you're uninterested in getting to know your future sister-in-law."

News traveled with lightning speed in this town. Everyone in attendance had likely known Margaret's identity within half an hour of their arrival.

Duncan promised to keep an eye on her in-laws while they danced. Alexander held out his hand and waited. She placed hers in his and allowed him to guide her to where the couples were preparing to dance to a new, slower tune.

"I do want to get to know Margaret," she told him.

Alexander placed his hand on her waist. The last time he'd danced had been in a setting much like this, only the woman in his arms had been his wife. He couldn't think of Sarah now, however, not when Ellie was so close, her light, fruity perfume teasing him and the memory of their kiss in the forefront of his mind.

Enchanted by the molten depths of her eyes and humbled by the absolute trust she placed in him, Alexander didn't have to pretend devotion. Goodness radiated from Ellie Jameson. She was the type of person who people wanted to befriend. He had to be careful not to let his physical attraction—wholly unforeseen and shockingly intense—overcome common sense.

His thumb caressed her side, skimming her ribs. "I'm not sure my idea was the right one."

She stumbled. "You don't wish to dance?"

Steadying her, he guided her along the edge of the dancers, far from her in-laws. "I meant the engagement. I'm wondering if we made a mistake."

It took her full concentration to follow the music's rhythm while keeping her emotions hidden. His doubts compounded the hurt his earlier words had inflicted.

Alexander regretted offering to help her. What a burden she must be…and now his sister had come after years apart, and he had to give awkward explanations for their relationship.

She faked indifference. "Let's call it off. Your sister already knows the truth, as do Duncan and Caroline. June knows now, too. The pretense has become tiresome, don't you agree?"

His eyes darkened. "Ellie, you know the outcome of my last attempt to protect someone." Regret marred his features. "I'm not a lawman. I don't want to give you a false sense of security."

"And I don't want you to feel trapped. The Jamesons are my problem, not yours."

His fingers flexed on her waist. "Trapped is the last thing I feel."

The music faded. Alexander released her, and she instantly missed his comforting nearness.

"There's Shane now," he murmured, his mouth close to her ear. "We should tell him everything."

Involving the sheriff made sense. Releasing Alexander from his duty, no matter how much she'd miss these moments with him, was the right thing to do.

She nodded her assent and they wound their way through the crowd. Alexander clasped her hand in a firm hold and, despite her anxiety revolving around the Jamesons' purpose for being here tonight, she felt safe with him.

The sheriff was closer to the bonfire, standing with his wife and another couple. A pair of adorable twins were sleeping in matching prams. Rubbing his wife's back, Shane stooped to kiss the newborn in her arms. He looked enamored and very, very happy.

Alexander apologized for the interruption and asked

if Shane could spare a moment. Instantly switching to lawman mode, the ruggedly handsome blond man led them several yards away to a secluded spot.

"What's the trouble?" His intent gaze focused first on Alexander, then her.

"Ellie's received threats from her late husband's family."

Without looking their direction, Alexander explained where they were standing. Shane surreptitiously checked them out.

"What kind of threats?"

"They had an abnormal connection with my husband, Nolan." Settling her hand atop her belly, she said, "I'm afraid they will transfer that to my baby."

"They've already tried to pressure her to return to their cove," Alexander inserted.

Shane's brows descended. "And they weren't happy when you declined?"

Ellie shook her head. "Their presence tonight makes me uneasy. They don't want to make friends among the townspeople. In Kentucky, they refused to allow me to see my friends. I was only permitted to venture into town in the company of one of them."

At this, Alexander's grip on her hand tightened and his expression became thunderous. "Sounds like a prison."

Shane looked none too pleased, as well. "It's important you don't find yourself alone with them, Mrs. Jameson."

"There's something else you should know," Alexander said. "Our engagement is a front to keep them at bay. I thought if they knew Ellie wasn't alone, they'd be reluctant to act."

To Ellie's surprise, the sheriff didn't scoff at the revelation. "I agree. A fiancé—whether real or make-believe—is a good deterrent."

"We're considering dropping the act."

"Don't. Not yet, anyway." His gaze narrowed on the couples. "I'll inform Ben of your situation. We'll be on alert to any shenanigans on their part." He looked at Ellie once more. "And if they approach you, I want to know about it. Ben and I will pay them a visit if they do."

Ellie hated to impose on Alexander for any longer. She opened her mouth to speak, but he cut her off.

"I'll do whatever it takes to keep you safe." A half-hearted smile graced his mouth as he gestured behind him. "What do you say, my dear? Shall we go put on a show for our audience?"

Chapter Eighteen

The sheriff's advice didn't evoke the slightest bit of resistance in Alexander. While ending the engagement was wise from an emotional standpoint, he was confident he could proceed with more extreme care than he'd employed up until this point. He must exercise control over his mind and heart, for Ellie's sake. He'd managed to guard his heart for three years. What was another few months?

"Don't be upset," he told her. "I'm not."

They'd left the sheriff and his family behind and were returning to the heart of the festivities. Alexander noticed that Howard and Gladys were in deep conversation. Nadine and Ralph, on the other hand, were observing the goings-on with stony expressions. Were they planning on approaching Ellie with more threats?

"You're essentially trapped by your own conscience," she quipped. "No matter how much you might wish yourself free of this quagmire, you'd never act on it."

His sister's approach prevented him from replying. Margaret looked from him to Ellie and back again, her smile smacking of self-satisfaction.

"Ellie, I'm glad you decided to come." Linking arms

with her as if they were long-lost friends, Margaret said, "I saw the two of you dancing together. You make quite the handsome couple."

Ellie blushed. "Have you been enjoying yourself?"

"Very much. I haven't wanted for a partner all evening. Turns out farmers aren't that different from ranchers. Excellent manners and eager to please." Winking at Alexander, she said in a conspiratorial tone, "I have to say, I'm not accustomed to seeing my brother in the role of café owner. What's he like as a boss?"

"Speaking of manners, it's rude to put her on the spot," he protested.

Ellie smiled, and for the first time since noticing her in-laws' presence, the worry about her eyes dissipated. "Oh, I don't mind answering as long as you reciprocate. I'd like to hear about Alexander's ranching days."

Margaret laughed outright. "It's a deal."

"When I first came to work at the Plum, trying to get your brother out of his office was like pulling teeth. He was most stubborn." Her gaze found his, and he was struck dumb by the fondness he witnessed there.

"Not surprising," Margaret observed. "His stubborn nature must've followed him all the way from Texas. He can be quite dictatorial when he puts his mind to it."

"So I've learned." Ellie's smile widened.

Alexander rolled his eyes, but he couldn't dredge up indignation.

"Anyway, he finally left his haven to join us lowly employees, and he's proven to be a fair-minded, thoughtful boss."

"I'm glad to hear you say so. His ranch hands might argue with the label 'thoughtful,' however."

Thoughts of Billy, Fred, Sonny and Edgar rushed in. Suddenly he wanted to pepper Margaret with questions.

How were his men? The ranch his father and grandfather before him had loved almost as much as their kin? Through her letters, she'd offered snippets of information here and there, but it didn't compare to a face-to-face conversation.

"It's a shame your brother Thomas couldn't come. I would've liked to meet him," Ellie said. "Are he and Alex very much alike?"

"He insisted he couldn't leave the ranch." Her tone indicated she didn't agree with his decision. Did that mean Thomas was nursing resentment toward Alexander? He wouldn't blame him. He'd dumped the ranch in his younger brother's lap without permission. Riddled with grief, he'd fled his hometown and state and hadn't looked back.

Tipping her head to the side and studying Alexander, she said, "Physically, they both resemble our father. Their personalities are quite different. Alex has always tended to be a loner, comfortable with his own company. He knows what he likes and does it. Thomas is more social and can be as temperamental as a steed with a burr under his saddle."

"What Thomas needs is to marry and produce heirs," Alexander supplied.

"He's proposed to a wonderful woman. For whatever reason, he's leery of seeing it through. I'm afraid he's going to lose her if he waits too much longer." Margaret showed Ellie her ring. "I'm getting married in December. That's partly why I chose to visit—I'd hoped to convince Alexander to attend my wedding."

"A Christmas wedding," Ellie breathed, "how romantic."

Suddenly, he had two pairs of expectant gazes directed at him.

"You aren't thinking of missing your only sister's nuptials?" Ellie charged.

He caught the hint of vulnerability on Margaret's face and wished he hadn't. "I'm afraid it's impossible."

Margaret's posture sagged.

"If you're worried about the café," Ellie said, "I'm sure we can find someone to help out in your absence."

"It's *you* I'm worried about." Had she forgotten the sheriff's instructions? The threat to her and the baby?

Her expression softened. "I'm not incapable of seeing after myself."

"Let's discuss this later, shall we?" He'd set his mind against ever returning home. Drawing out the discussion would only hurt Margaret. It was her first day in Gatlinburg. She deserved to enjoy herself. "I find myself in need of food and lots of it."

Ellie glanced at the quiet woman beside her, sympathy marching over her features. "I could eat. How about you, Margaret?"

"Sure."

Alexander searched out their nemeses and saw they were making their way to the church where wagons were parked. Relieved, he set out to cheer his sister. Recalling her love of sweets, he tempted her with assorted pies to follow up their main meal of roasted chicken and potatoes. When they'd found empty seats, he left them to procure drinks.

Four others were in line before him. The girl at the front paid and turned, a mug of hot apple cider in one hand. Her gaze encountered his, and her jaw sagged.

"Mr. Copeland!"

"Good evening, Sally." He offered her a gentle smile. "I'm glad I ran into you."

Her brows hit her hairline. "Y-you are?"

"I brought your final pay with me." Fishing the envelope from his suit jacket, he handed it over.

Head bent, she studied the blank exterior. Finally, she lifted her head. "Thank you, Mr. Copeland." Glancing at the others who were subtly listening in, she said, "Do you have a minute to speak privately?"

"Of course."

They made their way to the end of the refreshment area.

"What's on your mind?"

"I owe you an apology. I treated you with disrespect, and I shouldn't have."

"Apology accepted." He inclined his head. "And I apologize for interfering."

"Ellie was right. You did it to protect me."

"She spoke to you?"

"She came to see me that night." Her expression turning sheepish, she said, "She helped me realize the truth. Ben's not the man for me."

"She didn't tell me."

"Mr. Copeland, do you think…that is, my folks aren't happy that I quit. I understand if you don't want to hire me back—"

"I'd be greatly relieved if you'd agree to come back, Sally. You're efficient and hardworking, but most important, you care about the customers. They miss you, and so do I."

Blinking rapidly, she looked elsewhere. "I'll be there tomorrow morning."

"Good."

A lad about Sally's age rushed up. "Hi, Sally, would you like to dance?"

"Um, sure, William. I'll just drop this cider off with my folks first."

William grinned. "I'll walk with you."

Alexander watched them leave. The lad chattered and gestured, eliciting laughter from his dance partner. Sally's disappointment over Ben would soon fade, he was certain.

His spirits somewhat lighter, he purchased the drinks he'd promised and spent the next half hour listening to Margaret regale Ellie with tales from the past. Afterward, they escorted Ellie home and returned to the café. He bid his sister good-night.

She paused in the entrance to her room. "Alex?"

"Yes?"

"Who were those people you and Ellie were avoiding?"

"You noticed that?"

"Are they the reason you concocted this scheme?"

He sighed, hating to see the worry in her eyes. "Her in-laws' goal is to control her and ultimately steal the affections of their grandchild."

"That's horrible." Her fingers dug into the doorjamb. "I'm glad she has you."

"See to it that you don't concoct silly daydreams, sis. This arrangement of ours is temporary. Ellie and I are in agreement on this."

"Would it be so terrible to have someone special in your life again?" she queried earnestly.

That was the wrinkle... Ellie was special. One of a kind. After spending time with her and getting to know her, he was becoming attached. A foolish mistake.

"I had my chance."

"You act as if you don't deserve to be happy again."

"I don't," he scoffed.

"But—"

"Good night, Margaret."

Spinning on his heel, he retreated to his bedroom, not about to argue the matter.

Ellie was thrilled to see Sally the next morning. Flo shared in her happiness. Sally was part of the Plum Café family, and her absence, however brief, had been difficult in many ways. Alexander had informed Ellie that after today, she was to resume her former schedule. Unwilling to mar his good mood, she chose to delay that particular battle.

Margaret didn't make an appearance until midmorning. She descended the stairs in a casual state, her muslin dress cut in simple lines and her sleek raven hair pulled back in a low bun.

"Good morning." Ellie looked up from the pie dough she was rolling out. "You're looking refreshed."

"Can you believe the time? I'm so embarrassed. I promise this isn't typical. I'm no slugabed."

"You deserved to sleep in after your long journey." Dusting the flour from her hands, Ellie retrieved the plate from the warming box and set it on the opposite table. "I promised Alexander I'd see you fed. Do you prefer coffee or tea?"

Joining her at the stoves, Margaret plucked a kettle from the rear. "Tea. And I'll prepare it myself." She cocked her head. "Alex isn't here?"

Ellie gathered the tea tin, sugar and milk. "He left as soon as the morning session was over. Said our stores of meat are getting low, so he went hunting."

"I see."

Margaret had obviously expected to spend time with her brother. Ellie wondered why he'd chosen to leave but hadn't pressed. She'd sensed he needed a hefty dose of solitude.

"Don't worry, he won't be gone the entire day. In the meantime, you could browse the shops." She chose a teacup and saucer painted with lavender sprigs. "There aren't many. However, the ones we do have offer quality merchandise."

Waiting for the water to boil, Margaret crossed her arms and nodded in consideration. "On the way in, we passed a photography studio. I was surprised to see one in a town this size."

"Kate O'Malley operates that. Originally from New York, she's the wife of a local furniture-maker, Josh O'Malley. I haven't personally had any photographs taken, but she has a good reputation."

"Alex looks so different in his business attire. I wonder if he'd agree to have his portrait done so I can show Thomas and the others."

"I don't see why not." Ellie returned to her pie dough and the small mound of pumpkins waiting to be sliced.

"Seeing as he refuses to come home, even for a visit, I suppose a portrait is the next best thing."

"I'm sorry, Margaret. I know how much having him at your wedding means to you."

Margaret carried her teacup across the room, careful not to spill it. Settling in a chair, she ran her fingers over the silverware. "I knew he probably wouldn't agree. Texas holds too many painful memories for him." Clouds passed over her face, and her eyes were haunted by memories, the same memories that tormented Alexander. "A part of me feared coming here and seeing him. He left home a broken man, and his correspondence in the intervening years didn't inspire hope that he'd healed. I'm still a bit dazed by what I've found. He's almost completely restored to the Alex I know and love." She swallowed hard. "I believe I can thank you for that."

Her rolling pin ceased rotating. "Me?"

"I realize I don't know much about you. Nor am I privy to the exact nature of your relationship with my brother. However, I'm deeply grateful."

"Margaret, I can't take the credit. Alexander has had to work through his grief in his own way. I simply happened to be around when he started taking interest in life again."

"I don't believe that," she said gently, "and I don't think you do, either."

Troubled, Ellie left her dough and washed her hands. "I wonder what's been keeping Flo? She went to fetch a couple jars of pickled okra to serve with the noon meal. I'll check on her."

"I'm sorry if I offended you by my plain speaking."

"You didn't." Nodding to her untouched plate, she said, "Enjoy your meal."

Once outside, Ellie tried to push the conversation out of her head. Of course she wasn't responsible for Alexander's renewed interest in his café and the people in his life. The fact that their relationship had undergone changes—from long-suffering boss and pushy employee to friends—at around the same time was a coincidence.

Friends who kissed each other? a pesky voice pressed.

Resolutely not reliving those fleeting, wondrous moments in his arms, Ellie entered the alley between the café and post office, to the side of the building beneath which there was a cellar built into the ground. While the terrain in this area didn't allow for many root cellars, the café's former owner, Mrs. Greene, had insisted upon having one. Fortunately, this end of Main Street was level and

Mrs. Greene got her wish. It was a nice convenience, especially considering there wasn't a stream close enough to support a spring house.

The double slat doors to the cellar were propped open. Ellie peered inside. All she could see were the earth walls and narrow steps descending into darkness.

"Flo? Are you down there?"

Silence greeted her. Strange. Glancing about, she saw no sign of the older woman. On the far end of the alley, pedestrians along the boardwalk were few and far between. She studied the cellar again. What if Flo had swooned? She'd complained of a headache that morning.

Well, there was nothing for it. Ellie held tight to the railing as she awkwardly maneuvered the stairs. A cobweb snagged in her hair, and with a shudder, she batted it away.

"Hope there wasn't a spider connected to that web," she muttered.

She called for Flo again and got no response. At the bottom of the steps, she advanced into the cellar, nose wrinkling at the still, musty air. Crude shelving crowded with jars of preserved fruits and vegetables lined both walls. Ellie wasn't claustrophobic, but that didn't mean she enjoyed dark, tight spaces. Edging deeper into the cellar, she peered around the corner to the wardrobe-sized spot where barrels were stored.

Her fellow employee wasn't down here. She must've gotten hailed by a friend and sidetracked from her task.

Ellie was turning around when the cellar doors slapped closed and the slide of the latch scratched over wood.

Chapter Nineteen

She froze. Complete and utter darkness entombed her.

Seconds passed as her mind tried to sort what had just happened. A rustling in the corner spurred her forward. Arms stretched straight in front of her, she shuffled in the direction of the stairs. Not being able to see *anything* was unnerving. Ellie refused to dwell on the many creepy critters who called this hole in the ground home.

"Hello?" she shouted. "Is anyone out there?"

By the time she located the stairs, her heart was pounding, her neck was damp with sweat and her stomach muscles were stretched tight. The baby flipped and kicked. A response to her heightened emotions, perhaps?

She wanted to dash up to the opening but didn't dare. Being trapped alone was one thing, being injured with no one the wiser was quite another. Forcing herself to go slow, she encountered multiple rough places on the railing and would likely have splinters to show for her misadventure.

Had Flo returned and, thinking the cellar empty, closed the doors? Where then were the okra jars? Ellie didn't recall seeing any on the ground outside, and it didn't make sense that she'd carry an armful to visit with a friend.

Reaching the top at last, she pounded on the sturdy wood with one fist while steadying herself with the other. No amount of pounding or hollering yielded results. The longer she stood there, the harder it was to remain calm. The thought that this had been a purposeful act nagged at her. But who would do such a thing? A group of kids out for a laugh? Or one of Nolan's family members?

She dismissed Ralph immediately. He was sympathetic to her plight. Howard wasn't a likely culprit, either, which left Gladys and Nadine. Those two wouldn't think twice about pulling a prank such as this.

The rustling in the corner sounded again. Closer this time. Images of rats the size of her boot bombarded her. Her scalp prickled. Ellie brushed her hand over her neck, certain she'd encounter an insect.

Her legs were growing tired trying to balance on the thin step. Her stomach felt hard and heavy.

She started beating at the doors, taking turns with her fists as they were growing sore.

Margaret would come looking for her, right? How long would she linger over her breakfast? Maybe she'd sit there and drink the entire kettle's worth of tea. Maybe Sally had come in the kitchen and engaged her in a lengthy conversation about Texas and her upcoming wedding.

They could talk for hours.

"Can anyone hear me?" she yelled again, her throat scratchy. "Why can't you hear me?" A sob snatched her voice away.

Her knees threatened to give out. Carefully, slowly, she returned to the base, sank onto the bottom step and blanked her mind to the possibility of snakes in addition to every other creature she'd imagined. She concentrated on good things, like the huskiness of Alexander's laugh and the endless blue of his eyes when he'd been about to kiss her.

Ellie wouldn't give in to the fear. If the Jamesons were indeed behind this, she wasn't about to let her enemy succeed in their purpose.

He'd forgotten a key item in his quest for venison—ammunition. Who in their right mind took weapons without ammunition? Heaving a sigh, Alexander opened the door and halted on the threshold. The scene in his kitchen was like something out of a tragic play.

His heart climbed into his throat as he noted the very real fright in his sister's eyes. Sally's complexion matched their new snow-white aprons. Flo's mouth was thinned into a barely-there line. And at the center of the group was the woman who'd dominated his thoughts for weeks.

Seated at the table closest to the stairs, Ellie's hair was in disarray and her eyes huge in her face. Flo was bent over her, using tweezers on her palm. He felt her wince to the tips of his toes.

He closed the door with more force than necessary. "What's happened?"

"Someone played a rotten trick on Ellie," Flo answered, her jaw tight.

Wringing her hands, Margaret met him in the middle of the room. "She was locked in the cellar, Alex."

He could literally feel the anger building inside him like a volcano ready to explode. His gaze locked on Ellie, he gritted, "For how long?"

"About thirty minutes," Margaret said, distraught. "I was eating breakfast and became engrossed in the newspaper. I lost track of time. I should've checked on her when she didn't immediately return."

"It's not your fault, Margaret." Ellie finally spoke up.

His stomach dropped to his toes. Her voice had a husky quality, which meant she'd yelled for quite some time in order to get someone's attention. Bypassing Margaret, he walked over and looked down at her hands. One was still in Flo's grasp, the other curled atop the table. They were bruised in places, pink and swollen in others. A single knuckle was busted.

His blood thundered in his ears.

"Alex."

He was going to ride to that cove and—

"Alex, look at me."

Ellie's soft demand drew his gaze to her face, somber but untouched.

"I'm fine."

"Your hands are a mess." He took in the bottle of salve and gauze and the splinters Flo had already removed. "Are you hurt anywhere else?"

"No. The bruises will fade. I'm rattled more than anything."

Flo scowled. "This was planned, boss, I'm sure of it. I was about to go in the cellar when a pair of boys rushed up, begging for my help in catching their dog. They rolled out this sorry story designed to pull on my heartstrings. We searched up and down Main Street and along the riverbanks. Never did see a dog. When I came back, the cellar was locked up tight."

Margaret touched his sleeve. "Do you think it could be the work of her in-laws?"

Flo pulled the tweezers away and lifted her head, and he could see her trying to work out the puzzle.

Sally's brows crashed together. "Why would they want to hurt Ellie?"

Ellie sighed and briefly explained their strained relations, not making mention of the engagement. "They wouldn't hurt me, but they're not above trying to intimidate me."

"Now that you know," Alexander said, "you can be on the lookout for these people. I don't want them anywhere near Ellie."

Sally's chin jutted. "You can count on us, Mr. Copeland."

"I won't be duped a second time," Flo added.

"Thank you. Now, I'd like a moment alone with Ellie." He held out his hand for the tweezers. "I'll finish up. Sally, make a sign and hang it on the door. We're closing for the rest of the day."

"Yes, sir."

Consternation tugged at Ellie's features as he dragged a chair close to her side. "That's not necessary."

"I don't want you cooking today."

"But I've already started pies. They'll go to waste."

Margaret, who'd lingered nearby while the others disappeared into the dining room, offered her assistance.

Alexander twisted on the seat. "Since when do you know how to bake pies?"

Propping her hands on her hips, she sent him a long-suffering look. "Since I convinced Rosa to teach me. Lowell will expect to eat decent meals."

"Did she teach you how to make *buñuelos*?"

"As a matter of fact, she did. If you're nice to me, I'll make you a batch tomorrow."

"I'm always nice to you, Margaret." He jerked his head toward the stairs. "Now go upstairs and ready a place for Ellie to lie down." At her arched brow, he tacked on, "Please."

Her former anxiety no longer visible, she grinned. "My pleasure."

When she'd gone, he gently took hold of Ellie's ravaged hand.

"I don't recall agreeing to a nap."

He lifted his head to meet her steady gaze. "After your ordeal, resting for a few hours would do you and the baby good."

"I won't be able to sleep."

"Then read a book. I have plenty you can choose from." When she opened her mouth to protest, he said, "Indulge me, please, Ellie. I'm not ready to let you out of my sight."

She closed her mouth and nodded. The urge to hold her seized him. Fighting it, he turned his attention to his task. He worked with care to remove the rest of the splinters and apply salve to her busted knuckle. As he pictured her in that dark, dank hole, scared and alone, his anger burned beneath the surface.

"We have to tell Shane, you know."

"I know."

"I don't want you walking to and from June's unescorted. I'll accompany you."

"I'm sure you wish Ben and the others hadn't been so helpful during your illness. Or that they'd chosen another winner of the town-wide cooking contest."

Alexander finished wrapping her hand in gauze. "Never." One by one, he brought each of her hands to his mouth and brushed gentle kisses there. Tenderness flooded his hollowed-out heart, along with stronger, intense emotions he refused to examine. "My life is better because of you, Ellie."

Looking dazed, she blinked. "I've been nothing but a burden to you."

"You saved my café."

You saved me.

The thought came unbidden. Shying away from the significance of those three words, he pushed to his feet. "Margaret will be finishing up. Let's get you upstairs."

With a lingering look full of questions, Ellie stood. Together, they proceeded to his quarters. She hadn't seen his private rooms before and made no effort to hide her curiosity. The previous owner had taken everything that gave a place personality—family portraits and paintings, figurines and knitted blankets—and left only the furniture and flowered curtains. Alexander caught her eyeing them.

"I know what you're thinking," he said with mock sternness.

"Customers won't be seeing those curtains. If you're happy with them, who am I to suggest you change them?"

Margaret emerged from the second bedroom and beckoned for Ellie. "The bed's made up. I'll be happy to brush your hair, if you'd like."

Ellie touched a hand to her disheveled hair and glanced at him. He smiled and gestured to the kitchen. "I'll fix you something to drink. How does hot cocoa sound?"

She smiled back at him. "I can't remember the last time I had any."

"Then it's settled."

He waited in the living area until they'd retreated into the bedroom. It was strange having Ellie in his home, but nice, too. Something he could definitely get used to.

The remnants of tension slowly ebbed from her body. The long, gentle strokes of the brush through her hair were making her sleepy. Seated before the mirror, she met Margaret's reflected gaze and smiled.

"Here I was thinking I'd never be able to relax. Now I'm afraid I'm going to fall asleep in this chair."

Holding the brush to her middle, Margaret bit her lip. "Ellie, I'm sorry."

Ellie turned on the low stool. "Please don't apologize again. I don't blame you. Nothing about this is your fault."

"But if I hadn't been reading that newspaper, I would've noticed how much time had passed. And you wouldn't have been stuck down there…"

Ellie suppressed a shudder. She may have only been in the cellar thirty minutes, but it had felt like hours as her ears had strained to identify every scratch and scrape on the earth walls and floors.

Alexander spoke from the doorway. "Who's ready for a chocolate treat?"

The caution in his eyes told her he'd overheard and that he was as unsettled about her ordeal as she was. Did he share her unease? Did he, like her, wonder if there'd be another prank?

Laying the brush aside, Margaret folded back the quilt and patted the mattress. Her expression conveyed her eagerness to make Ellie comfortable. She felt a bit awkward settling into a bed in Alexander's quarters, but his sister's presence alleviated any questions of impropriety. He placed the tray on a trunk at the bed's foot and, once she was propped against the pillows, brought her a man-size mug. When he offered one to Margaret, she declined.

"I have to finish those pies, remember?"

Alexander rubbed his hand along his clean-shaven jaw. "I don't think—"

"I'll leave the main door to the stairs open. And once you've enjoyed your chocolate together, you can come down and assist me."

"I'll be down in ten."

After she'd gone, Alexander left the room and returned with a stack of books. He set them on the bed beside her and stood back, sinking his hands deep in his pockets. His darkened gaze kept going to her hair, then to her hands where she cradled the warm mug between them. The memory of his tender ministrations would stay with her a very long time.

"In case you can't sleep," he said, nodding at the books.

"Thank you." Sipping the decadent drink, she said, "You and your sister know how to pamper a person."

His smile didn't quite reach his eyes. "Thanks to Rosa. She coddled us any time we were ill or simply had a bad day. My father scolded her but didn't try to stop her."

"You can cease worrying about me, you know. I'm perfectly well."

"Physically, maybe."

"I admit I may have a few nightmares after this. But the memories will fade."

Pulling his hands from his pockets, he thrust them through his hair and paced to the window. Taking in the sights of Main Street, he said, "They wanted to scare you. Intimidate you. I don't want to think what they'll try next."

"Me either. However, I have to trust that God will protect me."

Her words didn't alleviate his concerns. Quite the opposite. By the look on his face, she knew he was thinking of his wife and child.

"He's in control, Alex. He has a plan for each and every one of our lives. We may not understand or agree with it. Are you familiar with this verse? 'All the days ordained for me were written in your book before one of them came to be.' It's in the book of Psalms, and I find a unique sense of comfort in that."

A muscle in his jaw jerked. Retrieving his mug from the tray, he spared her a quick glance. "I'm going to supervise what's going on downstairs. I'm not sure I trust my sister alone in the kitchen."

He was passing through the doorway when she called after him. "You won't know contentment until you make peace with their deaths, Alex."

He stopped, head bent, knuckles white. "I don't know how. I don't even know if I want to let go."

"You'll know when you're ready." Ellie longed to hold him in her arms and soothe away the pain he clung to so fiercely. "More than anything, I wish my other babies had lived. I wish I was bringing this little one into the world to join her older siblings."

Alexander dragged his tormented gaze to her, his body unnaturally still.

"That wasn't God's plan."

"I appreciate what you're trying to say, Ellie." Lips pressed tightly, he shook his head. "I can't..." His throat working, he moved into the hallway. "Rest for as long as you'd like."

Then he was gone, his footsteps clipped as he left the conversation and her.

Chapter Twenty

Ellie did have a nightmare. Instead of being trapped in the cellar, she was outside a long, low house engulfed in flames, watching it burn and powerless to save Alexander. Her mood bleak, she blinked the sleep from her eyes and scooted to a sitting position. The hushed conversation in the other room reached her, and she recognized Alexander's and Ben's voices.

Hurriedly putting on her boots and remaking the bed, she found them in the living room. Alexander was seated on the sofa, Ben on one of the cushioned chairs. They both stood to their feet, somber gazes scanning her from head to toe.

"How did you sleep?" Alexander's expression was schooled.

Was he upset with her? Had she been too blunt?

"Deeply." She checked the mantel clock and was surprised to see more than two hours had passed. "Hello, Ben. I suppose Alexander related what happened?"

Hat in his hands, the deputy inclined his head. There was no familiar grin. His green eyes communicated the graveness with which he took the situation.

"I'm sorry the sheriff wasn't able to assist you. He's investigating a robbery."

"We know we're in capable hands with you," she said.

Ben MacGregor's reputation was a two-sided coin—he was known as both a consummate flirt and a serious-minded lawman. Those ladies with eligible daughters condemned his commitment to bachelorhood while others said it was typical behavior for a man his age and that he'd settle down eventually. But as far as his profession went, he'd earned respect across the board. He didn't take his responsibilities to the citizens of Gatlinburg lightly.

"Appreciate that, Ellie. I'm sorry, too, that you were the victim of such a spiteful act."

"I didn't think to ask earlier," Alexander said, "but have they ever done anything like this before?"

"You mean while Nolan was still alive? No. He wouldn't have stood for it. We had our problems, but he didn't express his unhappiness in physical ways."

Ben's gaze was assessing. "You believe their recent verbal threats are because you're expecting their grandchild?"

"Yes."

The men exchanged glances. "I'd like to have a word with them," Ben said. "You know them better than anyone. Do you think the law's involvement will hurt or help?"

"I honestly can't say." She shrugged. "In Kentucky, we kept to ourselves. There wasn't a lot of interaction with other people, and never with the local law."

"Before I go out there, I'll ask around and see if we can find a witness. I'm also going to speak with Flo to try to identify the boys."

Ellie looked at Alexander. "Are you going?"

"Yes."

"No."

The men spoke at once. Ben shifted his stance, the pistol on his hip catching the light streaming through the window. "It's not a good idea."

"They need to know I won't tolerate such behavior directed at Ellie."

His vehemence surprised her. A casual onlooker would take him for a real fiancé defending the woman he loved. Did Ben not know that part of the story?

But no, it wasn't an act. He truly cared about her welfare as his employee first, friend second.

"Not this time, Alexander," Ben said. "Can't risk it."

"Why not?" he demanded.

"You're too emotional."

Alexander's eyes went wide. He looked as if he'd been struck dumb. His gaze shot to her, and she could see he was wrestling with some huge truth. Maybe he was chastising himself for ever letting her draw him out of his self-imposed isolation. He hadn't cared for anyone or anything then. He'd been safe, distanced from the people around him and uninvolved in their problems.

He'd denied regretting helping her, but he was too kind, too polite to willingly wound her.

She suddenly craved privacy. Alexander was likely ready to have his own restored, as well.

"Would you mind escorting me home, Ben?"

"Not at all."

Alexander shook off his stupor. "I'll take you."

"I've interrupted enough of your day. Besides, you never did get to go hunting, did you?"

He made a dismissive gesture. "It can wait."

"Then spend time with your sister while you can."

He moved closer to the stairs, intercepting Ellie. "Take care of those hands."

While they were sore, the damage wasn't as bad as it looked. "The bruises will soon heal."

Ben walked up behind them. Remembering their respective roles, Ellie reached up and kissed Alexander's smooth jaw. "See you in the morning, sweetheart."

She glimpsed his surprise as she turned and descended the steps. The kitchen was deserted. With the café closed, Flo and Sally would've gone home. Margaret's whereabouts were a mystery. Perhaps she'd taken Ellie's suggestion and gone exploring.

Out back, Ben unhitched his horse. "Would you like to ride?"

"I'd rather stretch my legs."

He was lost in thought as they left Main Street behind. Leading his horse along the dirt path, he glanced her way, the top portion of his face cast in the shadow of his hat.

"Um, you should know Shane told me about you and Alexander."

She could feel color creeping up her neck. "I see. So that goodbye kiss was for nothing."

He flashed a grin. "I wouldn't say that. Alexander didn't seem to mind."

Ellie pretended to be captivated by the forest stretching out on their left.

"I won't share your secret with anyone."

"I appreciate that."

The crunch of leaves beneath their boots mingled with birds' chirping. "I noticed Sally entering the café this morning," he said casually.

Grateful for the change of topic, she said, "She asked for her job back."

"Glad to hear it. I regret the upset I caused her. She's a sweet girl."

"She's going to be fine, Ben. Girls her age are resilient." She smiled. "In fact, I saw her dancing with a young man last evening who was most attentive."

"Ah." His smile was at odds with his shrewd look. "Did you know I have four younger sisters?"

"No, I didn't." The farmhouse surrounded by fields, the autumn-arrayed mountain rising behind it, came into view.

"I'm familiar with the fickle nature of young women."

She paused in the break of the snake and rail fence. "It would be wise not to mistake the challenges of knowing one's heart with capriciousness. The transition between child and adult is not an easy one."

"Understood, ma'am." His smile perfunctory, he waved toward the house. "Would you like me to escort you to the door?"

"That won't be necessary. Thank you."

He climbed into the saddle and doffed his hat. "Good day."

"Be careful. I can't predict how my in-laws will react, but I doubt it'll be good."

"Don't worry about me. Focus on taking care of yourself and that young 'un."

Ellie wasn't ready to share her ordeal with June. Maybe after a good night's rest and the fresh perspective of a new day. She was in her room preparing for bed when she glimpsed the envelope protruding from her reticule on the dresser. She'd completely forgotten about the letter she'd received bearing a Kentucky address.

Who could possibly be writing to her?

She unsealed the flap and pulled out a single paper with writing on both sides. The faint scent of rose water wafted upward. The signature belonged to Janice Cooper, the reverend's wife. Ellie's confusion deepened. Mrs. Cooper had always been kind. After Ellie's marriage, the other lady had appeared to discern her situation and sympathize with her.

As Ellie read the message, her anxiety returned. She sank onto the bed, limp with shock.

What else did Gladys have in store for her?

"I can't believe I get to attend a wedding while I'm here," Margaret gushed. "I love hearing the vows, watching the bride and groom's expressions."

"They're strangers to you," Alexander pointed out. And not more than acquaintances to him. He was here for Flo's sake, as it was her only niece getting married.

He tugged on his shirt collar, thankful the day was overcast. The afternoon ceremony would be held outside at the family's expansive farm.

"Doesn't matter," she said, shrugging. Looking past him at Ellie, who was on his other side on the path, she said, "What was your wedding like, Ellie?"

Ellie dragged her attention from the chairs and wooden bower adorned with flowers to his meddling sister.

"Very simple. It was just the preacher and his wife, Gladys and Howard, and Ralph and Nadine."

"Did you have a special cake? What did you wear?"

"I wore my best Sunday dress. I would've liked to have worn my grandmother's wedding dress, but there wasn't time to alter it."

From what he'd gleaned about her in-laws, they'd no doubt dismissed Ellie's wishes regarding her special day.

"The reverend's wife baked a cake." Worrying her lower lip, she averted her gaze.

How many of her past memories were pleasant? He'd guess not many. The knowledge made him want to make all her days special. Treat her in the way she deserved... with respect and kindness and—

The air left his lungs, and he almost stumbled. His mind had almost gone to a place he'd vowed never to go again. He hadn't wanted to entwine his life with anyone else's, and yet here he was, playing fiancé to his widowed, pregnant cook. He absolutely was not going to succumb to fanciful notions about love.

Glancing over at Ellie, delicately beautiful in the same dress she'd worn to the harvest dance, he felt sad at the thought of not spending time with her.

Alexander studied the milling guests on the off chance the Jamesons dared to crash the celebration. Of course he wasn't in danger of falling in love with Ellie. He simply wanted her to be safe and free of harassment. His concern had intensified with the cellar incident last week and was clouded by fear.

After Ben's official visit to their isolated cove, he had related his conversation with both couples to Alexander. They'd denied being in town that day, but the deputy had gotten the impression they were being less than forthcoming.

"The next time around," Margaret said as they drew near the gathering, "you should have wedding memories you can treasure and remember with joy."

"I'm not getting married again," Ellie protested.

Margaret's gaze darted to the people closest to them. "That's not what the people of this town think."

Ellie looked at Alexander in a silent bid for help, only he didn't know what exactly she needed from him. Not for the first time these past few days, he wondered if something was bothering her. Something she hadn't shared. The sparkle in her eyes had vanished, her inherent optimism nowhere to be seen.

Gently drawing Ellie's arm through his, he aimed for a bright tone. "Thanks for the reminder, little sis. I'd forgotten my role. Now, my dear, where would you like to sit? The ceremony will begin in less than fifteen minutes."

They found a spot with a decent view of both the musicians and the reverend. He sat between Ellie and his sister. In keeping with their charade, he draped his arm across her chair and leaned close to whisper in her ear.

"What's the matter, Ellie? You've been preoccupied lately."

Staring straight ahead, she said, "That's because I received a troubling letter."

His body tensing, he eased back a fraction. That was not the response he'd anticipated. "From who? The Jamesons?"

Smiling and nodding at a passerby, she murmured, "No, from my former reverend's wife. Apparently Gladys has been writing what few friends she had in Kentucky and telling them she's about to become a grandmother."

"Why does that trouble you?"

Her gaze, turbulent and dark, cut to his. "She's picked out names, Alex. Ruby Lorraine after her mother if it's a girl. Nolan Jr. if it's a boy."

His mind spun. "That's insane."

The music ceased. Ellie turned her attention to the groom, who was now waiting beneath the bower of mums and greenery, his hands locked behind his back. Stragglers rushed to find seats.

"There's more."

"What?"

"She's saying that the baby and I will be making our home with Nadine and Ralph. That we're one big happy family." She splayed her hand across her bulging belly. "Gladys is scripting my life and that of my baby without my consent. Their possible plans for us keep me up at night."

Scrutinizing her profile, Alexander worked to keep his expression pleasant. They were in full view of the crowd. Anyone looking would assume they were sharing sweet nothings typical of an engaged couple.

"Why didn't you tell me sooner?" he scraped out, frustration pounding at his temples. "I could've—"

"Could've what?" Turning her head, her gaze delved into his. "There's nothing you or anyone can do. They're twisted, Alex. No amount of reasoning will fix things." She huffed out a breath that fanned his cheek. "I was wrong to think being engaged to you would ward them off."

The defeat blanketing her floored Alexander. He floundered for a solution, anything to restore her hope.

"Come to Texas with me," he blurted louder than he'd intended.

The woman sitting in front of them turned to stare. Margaret leaned in so their shoulders were touching.

"*What* did you say?"

Lips parting, Ellie's throat worked. "You don't mean that."

"I…" He stalled, as stunned as the women on either side of him.

"The Wilson and Rogers families would like to welcome you to the marriage of their offspring, Tabitha and Jimmy." Reverend Munroe's voice boomed over the crowd, causing a hush to descend.

Alexander couldn't concentrate on the reverend's speech. Texas was the last place he wanted to be, especially with Ellie. But she'd be far from those trying to control her. What was more important? His state of mind or her safety?

Chapter Twenty-One

The ceremony was difficult in many ways. It was poignant and inspirational. Listening to the young couple's story made Ellie's heart ache for what she couldn't have. Seated beside the man she loved, she listened as the reverend introduced the young bride and groom, launching into their personal history before the vows were spoken. Flo's niece, Tabitha, had lost her first husband to illness within the first year of marriage. Their only child, a boy, died three days after birth. At this point, Tabitha assumed the telling, the sheen of tears mingling with a bittersweet smile as she regarded her captive audience.

Beside her, Alexander shifted in his chair. He hadn't dared look at her since blurting out the offer he clearly regretted. She'd witnessed the warring emotions in his intense blue eyes the moment his mind caught up with his mouth. He wasn't going to Texas, and neither was she.

"My heart was broken," Tabitha said. "I resigned myself to a lifetime of loneliness. I lived in a cloud of despair for months, until one day I discovered a lost little girl on my property."

At this point, the bride turned her full attention to

her groom and the three small children holding hands beside him.

"That was me!" The shortest one piped up, earning chuckles from the crowd.

Alexander leaned forward and propped his elbows on his thighs, intent on the story.

The groom, Jimmy, patted his daughter on the head. "If you hadn't gone wandering off, I might not be standing here today."

Angling toward the guests, Jimmy told how he came in from the fields one day to find a note. His wife had abandoned him and their kids. Furious and hurting, he hadn't known what to do. It had taken many nights on his knees in prayer to forgive her. And longer still to resolve the fact she wasn't coming home. Embarrassed by his divorce, he sank into a pit of self-pity.

"Until you met me." Tabitha reached out and took his hand.

"Until I met you."

The love on their shining faces was something to behold.

Reverend Munroe broke the silence. "Anything is possible with God, isn't it, folks? Sometimes in our darkest hours, we can't see how He'll turn tragedy into triumph."

Throughout the reciting of the vows, Alexander remained unmoving. Try as she might, she couldn't discern his thoughts. On his other side, Margaret dashed tears from her cheeks, no doubt dreaming about her own wedding. When the reverend pronounced them husband and wife, Jimmy whooped and twirled Tabitha in a circle. The children ambushed the pair and, amid claps and whistles, the newly-formed family walked up the aisle.

A yearning took root in Ellie's being to have the same ending to her own tragic circumstances. Margaret's talk of a second wedding inspired thoughts of her grand-mother's dress, which was safely stored in her room at June's. She wouldn't have an occasion to wear it. Now that she knew what genuine love was, she couldn't pledge her life to any other man besides Alexander.

The guests started toward the refreshment tables situated beneath the trees. It wasn't five minutes before she and Alexander were approached with some teasing, some not so teasing questions about their own wedding plans.

"When are you two going to tie the knot?" Claude Jenkins, the banker, addressed Alexander. "Your sister's in town. Perfect time."

Claude's wife, Merilee, stared pointedly at Ellie's stomach. "I'd say the sooner, the better."

Alexander's hand came to rest low on her back. "We appreciate your interest, but we haven't yet decided. We'll make an announcement as soon as we do."

They moved off to join the line of well-wishers. Margaret watched them in obvious disapproval. "Well, that was rude."

Ellie shook her head. "They're simply expressing what everyone else in attendance is thinking."

Turning back, Margaret grasped Alexander's arm, her blue gaze searching. "Tell me, brother, were you serious about Texas? Because Thomas misses you. He doesn't express his feelings to me, of course, but I can tell. And Rosa would dearly love to ply you with *empanadas* and *tamales* and see for herself that you're hale and hearty. Then there's the small matter of your only sister's wedding…"

His mouth twisted with regret. "I spoke without thinking. I have the café to run. Perhaps in the future I could make the trip."

"What about Ellie? Seems to me she'd benefit from putting space between her and those horrid people."

"She's in no condition to undergo such a lengthy journey."

"I'm the one who should make that determination," Ellie said. "Be honest, Alexander. The real reason you don't want to go has nothing to do with me or the Plum."

He finally looked at her, his mood inscrutable. A vein ticked at his temple. He was displeased with her for speaking plainly about his circumstances and for keeping mum about her own. Of course her first instinct had been to tell him about the letter, but what good would worrying him further have done?

"I need cake."

Ellie left the siblings, her gait not as graceful or quick as before. At the table laden with Mason jars full of raspberry shrub, Caroline approached her.

Pleasantries dispensed, she got straight to the point. "With Thanksgiving a couple of weeks away, the society is planning our yearly food basket ministry. I was wondering if you'd be interested in helping?"

"I'd love to."

Caroline beamed. "Wonderful. We're having a meeting on Monday afternoon. My house." She named the time.

"That's perfect." Alexander had encouraged her to get involved. He wouldn't mind. "I'll check with Sally to see if she can help Flo prepare the supper meal."

The sophisticated blonde lowered her voice. "How are things with you and Alexander?"

"Fine. Why do you ask?"

Her concern didn't smack of nosiness like the others'. "I can imagine an arrangement like yours might prove difficult in some aspects. Spending an increased amount of time in each other's company. Putting on a show of affection." She sipped her own drink. "Did you know that Duncan and I were forced to marry?"

Ellie's jaw sagged. "I had no idea. You seem perfectly suited." And very much in love.

She smiled. "We didn't know that in the beginning. We're both stubborn, you see."

Intrigued, she said, "I'd love to hear your story."

"I'll be happy to tell it." Caroline's gaze scanned the crowd, and she inclined her head to indicate Duncan's approach. "Another time."

"Mine and Alexander's situation is far different than yours," she felt compelled to point out. "This is temporary."

At the knowing glint in the other woman's eyes, Ellie shifted uncomfortably. Were her feelings for Alexander obvious?

"There are pitfalls, all the same. The human heart is unpredictable. Just know that if you have need of a friend, I'm here."

Duncan arrived then and, pulling his wife close, planted a quick kiss on her temple. Ellie forced her gaze elsewhere, only to land squarely on her temporary fiancé. He looked uncomfortable and miserable as if he was wishing he could seek refuge in his office.

"Were you ever planning to come and see us?" Margaret demanded quietly. "I don't mean to be insensitive, but it's been three years since we lost Sarah and Levi."

Taking her arm, he led Margaret to the outer edge of the gathering where they wouldn't be overheard. "You're not being insensitive. You're being your usual frank self, and you deserve the same honesty from me. I'm not sure I'll ever set foot in Texas again."

She winced. "But it's your home, Alex. Your heritage. Pa left the ranch to you. Thomas is filling in for you until you return."

Alexander battled mixed emotions. Before the fire, he hadn't questioned his future. It had been mapped out for him since birth. There'd been no question he'd follow in his ancestors' footsteps. In those days, he hadn't given Tennessee a fleeting thought. He certainly hadn't imagined himself living above a café and serving an endless round of meals to hard-to-please customers.

"This is my life now, Margaret. Thomas has to understand that the ranch is his responsibility."

She shook her head in disbelief. "All this time, we thought you were simply grieving and that time and distance would heal your wounds. We've been patient and understanding, despite the fact you basically abandoned us without a goodbye."

"I'm sorry, sis. I truly am. I should've handled the fire and its aftermath differently, but I wasn't thinking clearly. And when I almost killed Cyrus, I knew I had to leave right away, before I did something I couldn't take back."

Her eyes went round. "What are you talking about?"

"Surely you heard." Alexander searched her face. "I knew there'd be talk. Beating a man to within an inch of his life isn't news easily suppressed."

"Alex, I have no inkling of what you speak."

He gazed at the happy guests enjoying the refreshments. Memories crowded in, haunting memories of the night he lost everything—his wife and son, his home, and nearly his freedom.

Crazed with grief and rage, he'd ridden hard and fast to the Pollard spread. He'd hollered for Cyrus to come out and face him. The ranch hands had emerged from the bunk house, unsettled by the sight of a crazed man on the property and prepared to defend their boss. But the arrogant ranch owner hadn't been afraid of a much younger, slighter Alexander.

Cyrus had underestimated his drive for revenge.

"I confronted him," he told Margaret, his voice gruff. "I leaped on him like a savage beast and nearly pummeled him to death."

Her complexion pale, she lifted trembling hands to her mouth. "What stopped you from…?"

"Ending him? I'd like to say I regained my self-control, but it was the ranch hands who put a stop to it. They pulled me off and threatened me with a gunshot to the chest if I didn't skedaddle. At that point, I didn't care whether I lived or died." He hadn't cared for a long time. Until Ellie. Rubbing the spot above his heart, he said, "I just wanted the pain to stop."

His solution had been to flee the only home he'd ever known. Only, it hadn't worked. The pain had traveled with him, hatred and bitterness poisoning his soul.

"Oh, Alex." Margaret hugged him tight. "I wish I'd been able to do something. I've felt so helpless. Truth be told, I still do."

"There's nothing you could've done." He eased away and gazed deeply into her troubled eyes. "I'm glad you came to Gatlinburg. I've missed you. I didn't know how much until I saw you standing in my dining room."

Her smile was tremulous. "I didn't exactly give you a choice. I was afraid if I warned you ahead of time, you'd find an excuse for me not to come."

"My intentions were never to hurt you or Thomas."

"I know." She flicked a leaf from his shoulder. "After you left, weren't you afraid Cyrus would set the law after you?"

"I considered that. Soon after my arrival, I wrote the

sheriff and informed him of my whereabouts. Told him if he decided I deserved jail to come and get me. About two months passed before I received a response. Cyrus hadn't breathed a word to anyone. He certainly didn't bring it to the sheriff's attention."

"He wasn't the kind of man to turn the other cheek."

"No, he wasn't. But he was guilty of murder. Some, if not all, of his employees must've known and that's why they kept quiet."

His gaze drifted to the bride and groom and their small brood, the lot of them radiating happiness. He felt Margaret's fleeting touch.

"You could have that again."

"I don't know."

His attention shifted to the right to where his beautiful, purehearted cook stood conversing with Flo.

"Don't you think it's time to release the burdens you've been carrying around all these years? Forgiving those who wronged you—forgiving yourself—would free you to live again."

"I know what I'm supposed to do," he said. "I'm not sure it's possible, though."

"Remember Ma's favorite verse?"

"How could I not? She hung the stitched sampler beside the door so we'd see it every time we left the house."

"'For with God nothing shall be impossible.'"

"Luke 1:37."

Alexander recognized that holding on to this anger wasn't hurting anyone other than himself. Getting his heart to release it, however, was the problem. To do so would feel like he was failing Sarah and Levi, as if their deaths didn't matter.

I need Your help, God.

The spontaneous prayer felt right. And sort of freeing.

I'm done running from my problems, but I can't work through them alone.

"Do me a favor?"

Margaret's brows collided. "Anything."

"Pray for me."

Her lips curved. "I've been doing that all along."

"And pray for Ellie. Pray her enemies leave her alone to enjoy what's left of her pregnancy. She deserves that."

"I will. Of course I will. But you have to do something for me."

"What?"

"Ask yourself why you agreed to this charade and what exactly Ellie has come to mean to you."

Chapter Twenty-Two

She was getting bigger every day. Ellie tugged on the snug skirt and wrinkled her nose in distaste. "I adjusted this skirt two weeks ago."

"Stop fretting," Margaret admonished good-naturedly. "You're gorgeous."

Together, they climbed the stairs of the stately two-story home belonging to Caroline and Duncan. Slightly nervous about the society meeting, Ellie was grateful for the other woman's company.

"I know Alexander thinks so, too."

Ellie's fingers hovered over the knocker. "Nonsense."

"I know my brother." Margaret tossed her head. "I've seen how his gaze tracks your every move."

"Because I'm too large to miss."

"No, because he's smitten." Her bubbly laughter wrapped around Ellie. "You're perfectly proportioned. Believe me, I've seen some women in your condition blow up like hot air balloons." She inflated her cheeks with air, making Ellie laugh.

The door opened then, and they were greeted by Caroline, who showed them into a spacious dining room done in elegant hues of blue and silver. The long walnut table was littered with baskets, ribbons and mounds of material. Several other women had arrived before them. They welcomed her and Margaret with warm smiles and immediately drew them into the activity.

The group worked for more than an hour, conversation flowing like pan-heated honey as they decorated the baskets that would eventually be filled with preserves, fresh bread and baked goods, canned vegetables, and smoked hams. When Caroline decreed it was time for a break, her cook served a delicious assortment of bite-size cakes and cookies. As Ellie had feared, the focus eventually landed on her wedding plans. The other ladies' interest was to be expected, she reminded herself, and aimed for a pleasant yet concise response.

"Mr. Copeland is dragging his feet, isn't he?" A young mother named Laura studied her with compassion. "Some men are frightened silly by the idea of marriage."

"Or commitment in general," another woman commented. "Our debonair deputy is a prime example."

"But he asked her to marry him," Angela Tate intervened. "That shows he's willing and eager. Are you the one with reservations, Ellie? No one would blame you, seeing as you so recently lost your husband."

Shifting on her cushioned chair, she balanced her small plate on her knees. If she'd been at June's she would've used her tummy as a makeshift shelf.

"Seeing as how Alexander and I have both lost spouses, we've decided to proceed slowly."

"But don't you want to secure your baby's future?" Laura turned to Margaret, who was seated beside her. "You're leaving the day after Thanksgiving, right? You should persuade them to wed while you're here."

"I've tried, but they're both in possession of extremely hard heads," she joked.

An awkward silence descended. Caroline chose that moment to change the subject. Relieved, Ellie excused herself. She carried her dishes to the kitchen and relayed her thanks to the cook. The older woman caught her admiring the side yard with its majestic trees and urged her to explore if she wished.

Ellie exited the house and, bypassing the stables, settled on a stone bench. Margaret found her there a quarter of an hour later.

"I saw you from the window," she said, hands folded at her waist. "I apologize for what I said. I didn't mean to embarrass you."

"You didn't." She shrugged. "An interrogation is the least I deserve for deceiving everyone."

"May I join you?"

Ellie scooted over to make room for her.

She sat and adjusted her skirts. "I wish your engagement was real."

I do, too. "I overheard Alex and you talking that first day. I know how much he loved Sarah."

"Yes, he did. We all loved her. But he's different with you." Angling toward her, Margaret said, "Sarah was sweet-natured but clingy. She lacked confidence and constantly looked to Alex to confirm her worth. I hate to say it, but I believe it would've caused problems later on." She tucked an errant lock behind her ear. "You're not like that. Sure, he's protective of you, but he clearly admires you. You're wise and brave, and I'm convinced you'd be a wonderful wife for my brother."

Her baby kicked and flipped inside her womb. The sensation was strange yet reassuring. Ellie focused on the fact she'd soon have a child to lavish with love who would one day love her in return. Dwelling on what *could be* with Alexander only brought her sorrow.

"Do you love him?" Margaret asked outright.

Ellie's heart skipped a beat. Rising from the bench, she gestured to the house. "We should rejoin the group. They'll be wondering where we disappeared to."

Margaret trailed after her. "You do, don't you?"

Whatever emotions were reflected on her face, they must've told quite a story.

Triumph surged in the other woman's eyes. "You have my word I won't say anything."

Ellie nodded. "I do."

She found herself enveloped in a fierce hug. "I wish I could stay longer. I've relished our time together." Hands on Ellie's shoulders, she straightened. "I wish you could attend my wedding. You'd get to meet Lowell and Thomas. And Rosa would adore you. Most of all, I wish you'd tell Alex how you feel."

"I can't."

"Why not?"

At her crestfallen expression, Ellie said, "You have to understand, Margaret, my marriage was a huge failure. I can't go through that again. I couldn't bear to disappoint Alexander."

Margaret lowered her arms to her sides. "I admit I don't know the details of your marriage. However, I do know that it takes both spouses to make it work. You strike me as someone who's not a quitter. I believe you gave your very best effort."

"I did," she whispered. "And I still failed. That's why I won't tell Alex and neither will you."

Brow furrowing, Margaret started to speak.

"You promised."

"I won't break my promise. But—"

"I'm tired, Margaret. Let's go in for a bit longer and then make our excuses."

"All right."

It was clear she was unhappy. She wasn't the only one.

Ellie hadn't been alone with Alexander for days. Ever since the wedding, he'd kept his distance. He'd been polite and courteous, as always, but the warmth she'd grown accustomed to was missing. She didn't like the return of his guarded nature, but it was for the best.

Anxiously anticipating his and Margaret's arrival— he'd been careful to use his sister as a buffer on their walks to and from the café—she brushed her hair until it shone, arranged it into a twist and tucked a bird-shaped pewter hairpin above her right ear. Settling her gray shawl over her eggplant-hued blouse, she went in search of June. As expected, her spry hostess was at the stove preparing enough bacon and eggs to feed a family of ten.

"Good morning," Ellie greeted. "That smells delicious. Hopefully Snowbell is in an agreeable mood and the milking won't take long."

Lighting a lamp and snatching the pail from the peg, Ellie emerged into the quiet, pre-sunrise darkness. There was a chill in the air that hadn't been present the week before. A shrill bird's cry echoed off the mountainside. She entered the barn and hung the lamp from a protruding nail.

"Snowbell, I'm sorry I'm late—"

Ellie halted, her muscles seizing with apprehension. "What are you doing here?"

Nadine loomed in the middle of the aisle, blocking the entrance to the cow's stall. "I'm not here to argue." She steepled her hands beneath her chin. "I just want to talk to you."

Holding the pail in front of her stomach, Ellie took a

step back. "You could've announced yourself at the house instead of hiding out here."

"You're right." She nodded vigorously, her lank hair slipping forward over her shoulder. "I wasn't sure you'd admit me, so I decided to wait for you."

She narrowed her gaze, trying to project a toughness she didn't feel. "How do you know I'm the one who milks Snowbell? Have you been watching the house? Tracking my actions?"

Nadine didn't answer her question. Instead, she inched closer, her gaze sliding to Ellie's enlarged middle again and again. There was a gleam of something in the depths, something unsettling.

"If you agree to come home, I promise things will be different." Waving her fingers at the animals inhabiting the barn, she said, "You won't have to do any chores. I'll do it all without complaint."

Ellie swallowed a retort. Her former sister-in-law hated to break a sweat.

"I don't think you'd enjoy that for very long. Besides, the cove's no longer my home." *If it ever was.* "My place is here with June." At Nadine's clear confusion, she added, "And ultimately with my fiancé."

Her lips thinned. "You're only marrying him because you don't wanna raise that baby alone. If you'll admit you were wrong to leave us, we'll welcome you with open arms. You'll have four people around day and night to help out with whatever you need."

Ellie suppressed a shudder. The prospect of living with those people again robbed her of breath. The scuff of boots on the straw-covered earth behind her registered. She whirled, half expecting Gladys.

"Alexander."

He advanced into the barn, his gaze—burning with

icy promise—locked on Nadine. Halting beside Ellie, he deliberately shifted his suit jacket to expose the pistol at his hip.

"You were warned to steer clear of Ellie."

Irritation flashed at his intrusion. "I'm not doing anything wrong. I've been congenial, right, Ellie?"

"You should leave," Ellie told her. "You've nothing to gain by coming here again. I will never return to that cove."

"We'll see about that." She strode past them and through the door.

Alexander waited several beats before turning to Ellie, his face taut with anxiety. "I arrived early. June told me you were out here."

"Where's Margaret?"

"She decided our customers deserve a taste of Texas with a bit of Mexican thrown in. She's scurrying around the kitchen, ordering Flo around, who's tolerating such treatment only because of our familial connection."

Moving suddenly, he erased the inches separating them and brought his hands up to frame her face. His roughened palms were gentle and warm against her skin.

"I fear I can't do enough to keep you safe," he murmured.

"We have to accept that my safety is ultimately God's job."

A muscle ticked in his jaw. "That's a hard lesson, one He apparently wants me to learn."

"Concerning me? Or Sarah and Levi?"

Sadness surged. He lowered his hands to his sides. "Concerning my past and present."

Ellie wanted to tug him close again, to give and receive comfort. He'd traveled a hard road. They both had.

"If not for our charade, I wouldn't have stepped foot

inside a church," he said. "I wouldn't have heard God's Word spoken or been reminded of the truths I've learned since childhood—truths I'd lost sight of in the haze of my grief and bitterness. I'm asking Him to help me forgive my enemies and to overcome the guilt I've felt over my role in the whole sorry saga."

"I'm proud of you, Alex."

After this was all over and they returned to their previous ways, her life would never be the same. Her heart would suffer the loss of her one true love. Ellie was comforted to know that something wonderful, something with eternal value, had resulted from their impulsive scheme.

The cow bellowed in her stall, and they both smiled.

"I won't be but a few minutes." Ellie picked up the pail from where she'd let it slip to the ground.

He reached for it. "Let me do it. You've yet to eat breakfast."

"I'll relinquish my task if you agree to eat with us."

"It's a deal."

Ellie returned to the house. In a matter of months, she'd be saying goodbye to this relationship that had enriched her life and given her a glimpse of how it could be between a man and woman who liked and respected one another. All too soon, Alexander's role would end. He'd retreat again, just when she needed him most.

Chapter Twenty-Three

"I can't believe I'm leaving in two days."

Alexander and Ellie exchanged frowns from across the table. No one wanted Margaret to leave, not even Flo, who didn't suffer strangers gladly. It was the day before Thanksgiving, and the café was offering a traditional holiday meal one day early to compensate for tomorrow's closure. The kitchen was bustling with activity. Even Sally had been enlisted to help with the food preparation.

He eyed the clock. Only one hour to go before the supper rush.

Through the windows, he could see dusk encroaching. The late November weather had turned cold this past week, and the stoves provided welcome heat.

"Perhaps you should delay your return. You promised to teach me how to make *empanadas*, remember?" Ellie crimped the crust edges of her pies, always careful to do precise work.

Flo bustled past with a platter of carved turkey. "You're supposed to write down the wedding cookies recipe for me."

Margaret lifted a pot from the stove and poured the mixture of melted butter and spices over a bowl of steamed carrots. Her regret clung to her like fog on an autumn morning.

"There's never enough time to do everything we planned, is there?" She bit down on her lower lip.

Alexander wasn't ready to say goodbye to his only sister. The days had passed too quickly. A longing to see his brother and his former home filled him. At long last, he was finally ready.

"How about I go with you?"

Everyone ceased what they were doing to gape at him.

Hope warred with disbelief in Margaret's gaze. She set the pot on the stove with a clang. "To Texas?"

Flo transferred the platter to an empty space on the other table and jammed a hand on one ample hip. "I thought you were doing good to leave that office. Never thought I'd see you venture past the town border."

"A man can change his mind, can't he?"

"Not according to my pa." Sally snorted. "A man sets his course and sticks to it," she parodied in a low, gruff voice.

Alexander risked a glance at Ellie. Her focus on the pie before her, she'd gone still and silent. He was suddenly seized with conviction. He wanted to make the trip, and he wanted Ellie to go with him.

He set his knife aside and abandoned the oranges he'd been slicing, a special item he'd had Quinn order from Florida. "Sally? Flo? Would you mind checking that the dining room is ready for our supper guests?"

Wiping her hands on her apron, Flo muttered, "All you had to do was say you didn't want us to hear your conversation."

Margaret's mouth quirked. "I'm going to miss that woman."

Alexander circled the table and stopped close to Ellie.

When she looked at him, her brown eyes were darker than usual, her skin pale in contrast.

"I want to go to Texas."

A wrinkle tugged her brows together. "I don't understand. You insisted you had no desire to return. What changed your mind?"

Margaret approached. "I'd like an answer to that, as well."

"If I expect to move forward and embrace the future, whatever it may hold, I first have to deal with my past." He drew in a steadying breath. "I didn't get to see their graves. I need to go to the cemetery and touch the headstones. I need to formally say goodbye."

Margaret slipped her hand around his inner elbow and leaned against him in a silent show of support.

Ellie's eyes glistened with moisture. "I think that's a wise decision. And don't worry, I'll make sure the café's looked after in your absence."

"You misunderstand. I want you to come with me."

"Me?" She pointed her finger inward. "I can't."

"That's a wonderful notion," Margaret cried, straightening. "You'll love the ranch, Ellie. Alexander and I can show you every inch of it."

"We'd have to consult Doc Owens first," he said. "And if he's of the opinion you and the baby would suffer no harm, we'll take the trip in stages. We'll stay in hotels along the way."

"I'm not part of your family," she protested. "I have no reason to go."

"We're friends," Alexander responded, anxious for her to agree. "Besides, Nadine and Gladys can't get to you if you're hundreds of miles away."

Folding her arms over her chest, she said, "What

would we tell your family and friends is the reason for my presence? Would we continue our engagement charade?"

"That won't be necessary." He thought for a moment. "How about we say that our customers enjoyed Margaret's dishes so much that I decided to bring you along to learn more of our cuisine?"

Her gaze skidded away. Was that disappointment on her face?

His sister regarded him with thinly veiled annoyance. Tossing her head, she said, "Well, I for one, want you both at my wedding. You wouldn't even have to buy me a wedding gift."

Ellie carried the unbaked pies to the oven. Alexander hurried over to open the stove door for her. With a murmured thank-you, she returned to her work station and began to wipe the flour from the surface.

He looked to Margaret, who simply shrugged.

"Ellie?"

"Yes?"

"Aren't you going to give me an answer?"

Margaret's brows rose in unspoken reproof. He winced. Perhaps he had sounded like an impatient adolescent. But he could picture Ellie on the train beside him, smiling in wonder as he pointed out the passing scenery. He could see her on the hill overlooking the acres upon acres of Copeland property. He knew, deep inside, that he could face his past if he had Ellie by his side.

She reached to clean the far side of the table, her stomach bumping against the edge. The memory of their one kiss came roaring back and, if not for his sister standing there, he'd wrap Ellie in his arms. The sudden need to taste her rosebud lips again was a tangible thing. He yearned to twine his fingers in her silken hair, press his hand to her belly and be reminded of the life growing inside her.

"My answer is no."

The finality of her words snapped him out of his daydream. He opened his mouth to speak and took a step forward, but Margaret gave a firm shake of her head.

She touched Ellie's shoulder. "Will you at least promise you'll think about it?"

The damp rag in her hand stilled. "Margaret, I—"

"Please. For me."

She sighed. "All right."

Margaret gave her a quick hug and shot him a significant look, one that warned him to drop the subject lest he push Ellie too far.

Later that evening, after the café had cleared out and Margaret had gone to bed, Alexander paced aimlessly through his quarters. He couldn't stop thinking about Texas and Ellie. He hadn't dreamed of going himself, much less with her. The prospect became increasingly appealing the more he pondered it.

What if she said yes? What if they had a satisfying trip? What would happen once they returned? He wasn't convinced he'd be content to resume their present circumstances, Ellie living in a rented bedroom when he had all this space.

Alexander halted on the living room threshold, imagining her in the cushioned chair closest to the fireplace, her hair spilling over her shoulder as she cradled an infant to her chest. Longing for something more than what he'd had these last few years clutched his chest in a vise. He was tired of being alone. Marrying his pretend fiancée would aid them both. He'd gain companionship and a second chance at fatherhood, and Ellie and her baby would have a home of their own.

So much about his life had changed in recent weeks—for the better—and it was all thanks to Ellie. All he had to do was convince her to agree to a marriage of practicality.

This Thanksgiving, Ellie had a lot to be thankful for... new friends, a satisfying job and a safe place to stay. She was determined to focus on God's blessings. She refused to dwell on Alexander's decision to visit Texas and her ridiculous fear he might not come back. Living in the same town once their charade was over wasn't going to be easy, but never seeing him again? That was the stuff of nightmares.

"You're awfully quiet this morning."

Breathing in the crisp air, she switched the basket handle to her other hand and studied the passing scenery. She and June were on their way to the Plum, where they would spend the day with Alexander and Margaret, Ben MacGregor, and a few of June's friends who didn't have family nearby. Alexander had insisted he'd prepare the turkey but that Ellie and June were welcome to bring vegetables and fresh rolls. Margaret was taking care of the desserts.

"It's going to be overcast the whole day, isn't it?" Ellie remarked, not eager to talk about Alexander.

June glanced about at the trees arrayed in their fiery glory. "I don't mind days like this. The gray skies make the beautiful colors stand out." She sent Ellie a sideways glance. "Our lives are like that sometimes. In the midst of the gloomy days, we can more clearly count our blessings."

"You're a wise lady, June Trentham."

"I've lived a long time." She winked. "I would hope I've learned a thing or two."

Passing by the church, they neared Main Street, empty

save for a stray dog trotting along the boardwalk. The shops were closed in honor of the holiday. Ellie vaguely recalled sitting around the Thanksgiving table with her parents and various aunts and uncles. Her mother and father had enjoyed an easy, loving relationship, at least that's what her grandmother had often told her after their deaths. What Ellie remembered most was the way her father had made her mother laugh, teasing her with a certain twinkle in his eye.

Holidays with her grandparents had been different. Because they lived in a different state far from other family members, it had been just the three of them. Ellie hadn't ever been able to shake the sense of loneliness. She'd craved the big celebrations she'd enjoyed in her parents' home. For that reason, she was looking forward to today's meal in spite of how she'd left things with Alexander.

She touched June's elbow. "Thank you, June."

Her brows hitched. "For what?"

"For giving me a home."

"Oh, my dear girl, you've given me far more than I have you." Her eyes shone with affection. "I've loved having you around. It's nice to have someone to share meals with and keep me company in the evenings."

Ellie returned her smile, glad she hadn't been a burden to the other woman. "Seems we've helped each other, then."

They came alongside the café windows. Twin fires in the fireplaces flanking the room beckoned them inside, where the tables had been pushed together in the middle and set with pretty china plates Ellie had seen on the lower storeroom shelves. Glasses sparkled, silverware gleamed and tall candles flickered in silver holders. Pinecones and gourds added texture and color to the tableau. It was welcoming and beautiful.

The door was unlocked, so they entered, calling out their arrival as they discarded shawls, gloves and hats onto one of the unused tables in the corner.

Alexander was the first to greet them. He looked the model genteel businessman in his fitted black frock coat over a tan vest and chestnut trousers with thin blue stripes. A tie pin sparkled in the folds of his silk puff tie. He must've shaved minutes ago, because the woodsy scent of his shaving soap lingered about his person. Brushed off his forehead, his rich raven locks gleamed.

Ellie hung back as he hurried to assist June with her shawl. Over June's shoulder, Alexander's brilliant blue gaze found Ellie's. Instead of the pressing urgency she'd expected—and dreaded—there was soft admiration that put her instantly at ease. That he'd asked her to accompany him on his trip both stunned and pleased her, but she couldn't agree. And ruining this special day with an argument was untenable.

"Welcome, ladies. The food is ready save for one of Margaret's desserts." He tipped his head toward the hallway and took both of their baskets in hand. "It's laid out in the kitchen. We thought we'd go through and fill our plates and enjoy the meal out here."

"It's a lovely scene." June smiled, pleased. "You outdid yourself."

"That was my sister's idea." His gaze encompassing the room, he smiled. "I'm glad I heeded her advice. Lends it a more homelike feel."

His features were relaxed. Contentment radiated from him. How much he'd changed, Ellie marveled, since those early days. Instead of dodging the company of others, he embraced it. Alexander was no longer the untouchable café owner. He had a place in his community. Friends. Acquaintances. Loyal customers.

But was it enough to hold him here now that he was ready to be free of his past?

Setting such thoughts aside, she followed him into the bright kitchen, tantalizing aromas of rosemary-rubbed meat; carrots glazed with cinnamon and butter; and buttery, yeasty bread making her stomach growl. The lavish spread before her was enough for a week's worth of meals, it seemed, and that was before her and June's dishes were added.

"I thought you were only doing the meat," she said to Alexander.

He brought his face close, their shoulders brushing. "My sister never does anything in small measures."

She tried not to stare at his wonderfully dear face. "I guess not."

"Happy Thanksgiving, Ellie!" Margaret, striking in a jewel-green dress, waved from the far stove. "You too, Miss June. I'll be finished in five minutes."

"Good to hear, because I'm about to snag one of these rolls." His customary grin in place, Ben came over and hugged them each in turn. "How are you faring, Ellie?" he said once June and Alexander became involved in a conversation. "You haven't had any more visitors out at the Trentham place?"

"None that were unwelcome. Thanks for paying them another visit. I think perhaps they've decided to leave me be."

She hadn't received any more letters from Kentucky and no more frights in the barn.

"Good." His expression turning serious, he said, "I didn't mince words with them. I laid out exactly what would happen if they continued their shenanigans."

"Ralph hasn't ever been a problem, maybe because he married into the family like I did. Howard is obviously loyal to his wife. He takes her side on matters but doesn't instigate things."

"It's the women who've given you the most trouble."

"Yes."

"I don't foresee any more problems. That being said, continue as you've been doing. Pays to be cautious."

"Of course."

June's friends arrived in a cloud of heady perfume and lilting conversation. Margaret finished her preparations and, removing her apron, called on Alexander to say grace. It was the first time Ellie had heard him pray, and the act moved her to tears. Surreptitiously wiping them away before he'd concluded, she offered her own silent prayer of gratitude. God had taken a closed-off, hurting heart and healed it, as was His specialty.

Conversation bounced off the walls as they retrieved their china dishes from the dining room and returned to fill them with mouthwatering fare. Ellie was maneuvered—by Margaret, of course—to a seat across from her and beside Alexander. Ben found a place amid June and her friends, and he kept them entertained for the duration of the entire meal. The deputy projected a lighthearted demeanor, but at odd times Ellie thought she caught hints of sadness beneath the facade. What Ben might have to be sad about was a mystery. Indeed, she acknowledged she knew very little about his past. Her ruminations were diverted when, while in the kitchen observing the many sweet options, Alexander asked to speak to her alone.

"It must be important if it can't wait until after dessert," she quipped, her heart fluttering with anxiety.

Was he going to tell her goodbye forever? Had he already decided to remain in his home state, surrounded by family and old friends?

"It is."

His voice was huskier than usual, his easygoing manner replaced with an apprehension that was troubling.

"Let's talk in my office."

Once inside, he closed the door and took up position behind his desk.

Nervousness assailing her, Ellie wandered over to the windows. "I haven't spent much time in here lately."

"You'll notice the open curtains."

"That post office wall is a much better view than printed fabric," she tried to tease. She turned to face him. "Admit it, you resented my intrusion into your prized privacy."

He winced. "I used to be a very foolish man."

"You were never that," she defended. "Perhaps it's better to say you were guarded."

His mouth curved into a half smile. "You're a generous woman, Ellie Jameson."

"Enough of the banter." She advanced into the middle of the room, arms hanging at her sides. "What do you need to tell me, Alex?"

His chest expanded with a deep breath. Opening the topmost drawer, he removed a tiny object and placed it on the desk.

"Your wedding band."

"Yes." He plunged his hands in his pants pockets, only to pull them out again. "I'm ready to wear one of these again."

Ellie's heartbeat roaring in her ears, she reached for the cushioned chair nearest her. "What are you trying to say? I—I thought you were going to talk about your trip."

More solemn than she'd ever seen him, Alexander

rounded the desk and joined her, taking her hands in his. He swallowed hard.

"Ellie, I'd like for this engagement to be real. I want to be your husband and your baby's father. What do you say?"

Chapter Twenty-Four

He was fairly sure she was going to swoon.

"Here, why don't you have a seat," he said in a rush, guiding her onto the chair and kneeling before her. "I've surprised you, I know—"

"Surprised?" Gazing down at him with wide eyes, she shook her head. "Alexander, you've yanked the rug out from beneath me. A marriage proposal was the last thing I expected to hear."

Her candor untangled some of the tension he'd been carrying around since last night.

"Why, Alex?" A vulnerable light entered her eyes. "I don't understand."

Needing to steady them both, he once again took hold of her hands. "Getting married makes sense. Everyone already expects a wedding. Why not give them one? You need a husband. I'm ready to have a family again. It's a practical answer to both our problems."

Her throat working, Ellie stared at him with something akin to horror.

"Practical." She said the word with distaste. "I had that the first time around. I will not repeat my mistakes."

Pulling free, she brushed him aside and rose calmly

to her feet. Alexander pushed upright, dismayed by her outright refusal to even consider his offer. This wasn't the reaction he'd hoped for.

"Not all practical marriages turn out like yours. I've personally known couples who've made successful matches based on mutual respect and commitment." He studied her profile but was unable to gauge the effect of his words. "You've become a dear friend, Ellie. I believe we can have a good life together."

Angling her face away, she swiped at her cheek before turning back. Her pretty doe eyes communicated grief that shook him. Why would his proposal sadden her?

"You were blessed to marry a woman you loved and who loved you in return. When—*if*—I enter into that sacred institution again, my husband and I will adore each other. I will accept nothing less."

Alexander didn't try to prevent her from leaving. He stared at the spot where she'd been, one truth eating at him. Ellie wanted someone she could adore, and that someone wasn't him.

Long minutes later, Margaret came looking for him. "Alex, what are you doing in here by yourself? Did you do something to upset Ellie?"

His chest tight with emotion he didn't recognize, he turned toward the door. "As a matter of fact, I did."

Her brow furrowed. "What happened?"

"I proposed."

Margaret's hold on the door frame slipped, and she advanced into the room. Her blue gaze was intense. "You asked her to marry you for real?"

"She was not thrilled with my idea."

"I'd say not. She left without tasting a single dessert."

"She actually went home?" Guilt seized him. "But the day isn't even half over. She shouldn't be alone on

Thanksgiving." He started for the door. His sister blocked his way. "Move, Margaret. I have to catch up to her. At least see her safely to June's." He was hoping to convince her to return.

The Jamesons may have promised Ben they'd leave Ellie alone, but he had his doubts.

"Ben went with her."

"I see." Kneading his stiff neck muscles, he stalked the perimeter of the room. "I can't comprehend why she's upset. I thought my offer would make her happy. I'd take care of her, you know. I'd raise her child as if it was my own."

He couldn't have entertained such a notion even a few short weeks ago. His precious son would always own a piece of his heart, the memories of Levi a gift he'd carry with him the rest of his days. God was slowly healing the holes inside, knitting them with forgiveness and hope. He wanted to be a father again. Truth be told, he already felt protective toward Ellie's child. That she'd rejected him as a husband hurt. That she didn't see him as good enough to help raise her son or daughter wounded him.

"Why don't you tell me exactly what you said?"

He complied. Margaret wasn't impressed. "That's terribly unromantic, Alex."

"Our relationship isn't based on romance." Ignoring the memories of their kiss springing to mind, he said inanely, "I'm her boss."

"Who's been parading as her fiancé," Margaret pointed out. "And acting very protective of her."

"That's no act," he snapped. "Ellie's well-being, and that of her baby, is my utmost priority."

A stirring at the door had them both turning around. June stood in the hallway, obviously worried. "I'm sorry to interrupt. I thought you might know what's bothering Ellie."

His sister spoke first. "Why don't I go and talk to her? I'm confident I can convince her to return. Not many people can resist my pumpkin *empanadas*."

June agreed to Margaret's suggestion, mainly because she had friends in attendance and didn't want to abandon them. Alexander recalled his role as host and, though difficult, managed to engage in a discussion of that year's planned Christmas festivities. But his mind was with Ellie.

I didn't intend to cause her grief, Lord. I ruined her first happy holiday in years. Please let Margaret get through to her. Let the day be salvaged.

And what of their friendship? Could it be saved?

Why was friendship with Ellie suddenly not enough?

"You sure you'll be all right?" June hesitated on the threshold the next morning, wrapped in her thick wool shawl and her basket of sewing supplies tucked under her arm. "I can make my excuses."

"You can't miss the meeting. Christmas will be here before we know it, and the children who'll receive the baskets are counting on those blankets."

June's frown deepened.

"I'm fine," Ellie tried to reassure her. She wasn't fine, of course, but she intended to wallow in her misery without a witness.

"Are you going to say goodbye to Margaret this afternoon?"

"We said our goodbyes yesterday."

Margaret had arrived shortly after Ben's departure. Their conversation had been brief and unproductive. The other woman had expressed her dismay over the whole situation and was convinced her brother cared more for Ellie than he was willing to admit—even to himself. Ellie disagreed. After reminding Margaret of her promise to keep Ellie's feelings a secret, she'd bid her a tearful farewell, aware that she'd likely never see her friend again.

What had started out as a day with such promise had turned into a lonely stretch of time.

June's gaze lit on the coffee table. "Oh, I forgot to tell you. There was a letter addressed to you left on the front porch two nights ago."

Ellie examined the writing. "It's from Kentucky."

"I hope it's not more upsetting news."

June knew about the lies the Jamesons were spreading in their former town. Ripping open the letter, she skimmed the contents.

"It's another letter from my reverend's wife there. Janice received my last reply explaining what's been going on. She's offering me a place to stay free of charge for the first six months."

"What will you do?"

"I don't know."

Kentucky held a mixture of happy memories overshadowed by unhappy ones. The mere thought of leaving Gatlinburg, of leaving Alexander, caused her heart to spasm with pain and denial.

Carefully refolding it, she mulled over the offer.

"You won't do anything rash, will you?" June said.

"I need to think."

"You need to pray."

Once June had gone, Ellie dressed and arranged her hair, glad she wasn't required to put in an appearance at the Plum. Alexander had decided to close for the second day in a row in order to send his sister off in proper fashion. She wondered if he wished he'd bought a ticket for himself. Perhaps he had. Perhaps he'd leave this weekend or early next week. He might not inform her of his plans directly. Ellie had bolted from his office, too crushed by disappointment to gauge his reaction.

I wouldn't blame him for being angry.

Another thought occurred to her, and she put the brush down on the dresser with a clang. What might he construe from her abrupt departure? She hadn't behaved like a mere friend. Someone with platonic feelings would've been flattered by his practical proposal.

Burying her head in her hands, she groaned aloud. A rap on the main door startled her.

"I'm not ready to see him, Lord," she murmured, her pulse leaping as she walked through the house.

But who else could it be? Maybe Margaret hadn't been able to resist one more hug. Half hoping it was the brother-sister duo, Ellie opened the door and immediately wished she hadn't.

"You've made a wasted trip," she sighed. "Go home, Nadine."

Ellie started to close the door, but Nadine blocked it with her body. "Oh, I will. And you're coming with me."

Shoved out of the way, Ellie stumbled and caught herself on the couch arm. Alarm winged through her as Nadine produced a pistol and waved it above her.

"Nolan used to complain about how stubborn you were," she said coldly. "You've tried my patience for the last time."

It was a struggle to stand up and also put distance between them. The blood rushed from her head. Lightheadedness swamped her.

"What are you doing with a gun?" Ellie knew the woman was comfortable with weapons. She'd hunted alongside Ralph, Nolan and Howard. What she didn't know was whether or not Nadine would actually use it on her. "We were family, sisters-in-law, for four years."

"A fact you've conveniently forgotten." She motioned toward the bedrooms. "Time to pack your bags."

"What do you mean to do? Keep me prisoner?"

"You'll soon figure out you're better off with us." She lifted a shoulder. "Once the baby's born, you're free to go, however."

Disbelief rattled her. Nadine's meaning was clear. She, Ellie, would be free to leave. Not the baby. This was the act of an insane person, far beyond anything Ellie could've imagined her former sister-in-law would do.

"You can't hide me for long." Ellie inched farther away, putting the square side table and kerosene lamp between them. Pleading with God to help her remain calm and clearheaded, she attempted to reason with Nadine. "Do your parents know? Ralph wouldn't condone this, of that I'm sure."

"Not yet, but they'll agree this is the best way. You weren't fit to be my brother's wife, and you aren't fit to raise his child." Her blue eyes glinted with disdain. "Ralph always had a soft spot for you. Don't worry, he'll come around. He's wanted a baby for as long as I have."

"This baby belongs to me!" Her voice was high and strained. Panic threatened.

"No more arguing." She leveled the gun at Ellie. "Now, you will pack your bags. Take everything. We're going to make this look like you've decided to take the dear old Reverend Cooper's offer."

"How did you know about that?"

Nadine began to quote, word for word, the contents of the letter.

"You wrote that?"

Now that she thought about it, the handwriting had

been different. And the scent of rose water accompanying Janice's first missive had been absent. Ellie's gaze bounced over the contents of the room, searching for a way out, a weapon she could use to defend herself. But did she dare attempt it? In her advanced pregnancy state, she wasn't as fast as she could be, and the safety of her child was paramount.

"Sure did. A clever ruse, isn't it?"

"Alexander will never believe I left without discussing it with him. We are engaged."

"He will because you're going to write a convincing note, explaining how you still love my brother and couldn't possibly marry another. You crave the comforts and familiar surroundings of home—Kentucky."

Ellie couldn't allow Nadine to take her to that cove. If she wound up there, she'd likely never leave. Begging God for mercy, she said, "I'm not doing it."

Nadine's twin blond brows shot up. "What?"

"I'm not writing that, and I'm not going home with you." Splaying her hands on her belly, she said, "This is your niece or nephew I'm carrying. You won't hurt me. You don't want to put his or her life at risk."

For an instant, Nadine wavered, her gaze dropping to Ellie's belly. Then an explosion rang out. Glass shattered and pinged to the floor. Ellie screamed.

Smoke curled from the gun barrel. Nadine's face had hardened to a cruel mask. "Now we're going to have to clean that up."

Behind Ellie, green-tinted glass shards littered the floorboards, the remnants of a decorative bowl atop a shelf. A bullet was lodged into an eye-level log.

Ellie's spirits sank, her stomach churning dangerously. There wasn't going to be an escape.

Chapter Twenty-Five

Margaret's hug was cutting off his air supply.

"You've got another hour before your driver arrives," he wheezed.

Her hold loosened, and she pulled away to dab at her cheeks with a lace handkerchief. Her blue eyes were awash in sadness. "If only you and Ellie were traveling with me." Glancing about at the wagons rolling along Main Street, she shook her head. "I'd envisioned a very different holiday and subsequent send-off."

"I'm sorry I ruined Thanksgiving for you," he said with regret.

I had no idea asking Ellie to marry me would explode in my face.

Alexander was still wrestling to make sense of the scene in his office yesterday. He'd battled myriad emotions before hurt settled deep in his chest and refused to budge. That, coupled with a feeling of great loss, had left him cranky and absentminded. June and her friends had managed to sustain an atmosphere of celebration, engaging in all sorts of games from chess to charades. If they'd noticed his deflated demeanor, they hadn't commented on it.

"You didn't ruin anything, Alex. I simply want you and Ellie to be happy."

"Well, we're not." He had no idea how to fix this.

"This isn't the place, but it is the time." Taking his hand, she led him to the bench a few steps to their right, located in front of the café windows. Her trunks had been piled beside it. Once seated, she angled toward him. "Why did you ask Ellie to marry you?"

"I told you—"

She held up her hand. "I know the reasons you gave her. Alex, Sarah's and Levi's deaths ripped your life apart. The fact that you're willing to marry again tells me there's more to this than a desire to protect her. I don't accept that friendship is enough to spur a decision like this, not for you."

Alexander sagged against the bench. People hurried about their business, their breaths fogging in the cold air. A stray cat paused for bits of jerky from the elderly men who stationed themselves outside the mercantile each day. A pair of young boys chased each other into the alley beside the livery.

He couldn't focus on their faces because Ellie's dominated his thoughts. Memories of their time together bombarded him.

"I loved Sarah," he uttered, his voice gravelly. "How I feel about Ellie is different."

"Different how?"

Propping his elbows on his knees, he thrust his fingers through his hair. Frustration gripped him. "I don't know how to explain it." Springing to his feet, he paced to the nearest awning post.

His sister followed him. "If you're feeling guilty, please stop. Sarah would want you to be happy."

Margaret was right. His late wife wouldn't have begrudged him a second chance at happiness.

"I didn't realize I was until you said something." He fisted his hands. "Sarah died too young. Her life was snuffed out by an evil man. I tried to save her...but God has the ultimate authority. I can't go on blaming myself any longer. Ellie helped me see that."

She'd helped him see a lot of things.

"I didn't like her at first," he admitted.

Her eyes got huge. "How can anyone *not* like Ellie?"

"I wasn't thrilled about her being hired without my input, first of all. I considered firing her on principle, but her cooking was above standard and had an immediate effect on business. Suddenly, my dining room wasn't big enough to hold everyone. That didn't keep me from complaining about her unrelenting attempts to involve me in every little decision." Smiling wryly, he recalled all those mornings when she'd burst into his office to review the menu. "After the fire, I decided to stop engaging in life. I'd pretty much accomplished that, too. Ellie refused to leave me be. She made me care about the Plum, about Flo, Sally and the customers, and about her."

Margaret smiled. "She's a special lady."

"I admire her more than I can express. I'm happy when I'm with her. I miss her when I'm not."

"Can you imagine your life without her?"

"Absolutely not. No."

"Then what are you waiting for? You have to propose again, but this time tell her everything you just told me."

He ran his hand over his face, inwardly cringing at how he'd botched things with her. "I'm not convinced she'll give me a different answer."

She gripped his upper arms. "I am."

The knowing glint in her eyes gave him pause. "How can you be certain?"

"I gave my word I wouldn't say anything."

"Ellie talked to you about us?"

With an exasperated huff, she linked her arm through his and tugged. "Let's go pay her a visit."

He jerked a thumb toward her trunks. "You'll miss your ride."

"So I'll leave tomorrow."

After locating a young lad willing to watch Margaret's belongings for a small fee, they walked to the Trentham spread. Alexander's nerves jangled with each step. He hadn't allowed himself to imagine loving again. This love for Ellie—intense, wondrous and deep-rooted—had been building inside him, like one brick upon another, each layer going unnoticed until wholly complete. Only when he'd risked making their engagement real and been spurned had he recognized how deeply connected he was to her.

He wanted no other woman by his side. Only Ellie would do.

Question was, would she have him?

She wasn't supposed to be here.

Nadine guided the team onto the cove's winding lane, those same overgrown branches catching on her hair that had almost knocked Alexander's hat from his head. Fear left a coppery taste in her mouth.

Would she see him again?

Would she ever leave this cove alive?

The wagon bumped over the ruts, jostling her, increasing the chances she'd lose her breakfast the moment the wheels stopped turning. Nadine hadn't spoken a word since they left June's. She was coldly silent and determined to carry out her selfish, insane plan. Ellie prayed without ceasing, holding on to hope that Ralph would react as any normal person would and negotiate her release.

The twin cabins came into view, and a tangible blanket of depression wrapped tightly about her. She hadn't ever wanted to return. Now she was back…as a prisoner.

When the wagon lurched to a stop, Nadine leaped to the ground and hollered for her family. Howard was the first to emerge. His scraggly brows lifting slightly, he called for his wife. Gladys joined him, a half-peeled potato in one hand and paring knife in the other. Her gaze narrowing, she descended the steps.

"This the surprise you were talking about?" Gladys looked from her daughter to Ellie.

Nadine's gaze pierced Ellie, stark warning written there. "She's here to stay, Mama."

Ellie remained on the high seat, feeling like a prized steer at auction beneath three appraising stares. Desperate, she appealed to Howard.

"I want to go home," she announced. "Nadine forced me to accompany her at gunpoint."

Scraping his cracked, stained hand over his jaw, he said finally, "She didn't hurt you, though, did she?"

Her head reared back. Why was she not surprised by his apathy? He'd remained a passive bystander since the day she wed his only son.

"That's not the point. I—"

"Cease your bellyaching," Gladys snapped, motioning for her to get down. "Seeing as how you love to cook," she sneered, "you can help me with the noon meal."

Ellie thought about refusing. For a split second, she considered grabbing the reins. But turning the team around would take concentration, skill and time—time enough for Nadine to discharge her weapon. And she had no doubt she'd wound her, not seriously but enough to thwart her escape. A nick on her shoulder or arm, perhaps. She couldn't risk it.

So she climbed down. The moment her boots touched the soil, her future went dark, her hope all but extinguished.

With a gun pointed at her, Ellie had penned two convincing letters, one for June and one for Alexander. Nadine had hovered over her, making it impossible to try to insert clues. The only sign that anything was wrong was her messy handwriting. Try as she might, she hadn't been able to still the shaking of her hands.

"First, we're going to get her settled," Nadine pronounced, going to the rear and taking one of the crates in her arms.

Ellie trudged after her, feeling like a twenty-pound sack of flour sat on her chest. Taking one of the other crates, she went into the cabin she'd moved into after Nolan's death.

"Welcome home."

"This was never my home," she said quietly. "You did nothing to make me feel welcome. In fact, you treated me like an interloper who provided free labor."

Nadine dropped the crate to the floor with a crash. Rounding on her, she thrust her finger in Ellie's face. "You speak to me like that again, you'll regret it."

Ellie forced herself to meet her gaze. She wasn't going to be cowed before her. "Nolan and I had our problems, but he never would've allowed such treatment."

Nadine lifted her hand and would've struck Ellie if Ralph hadn't entered then.

"Nadine!" He advanced into the room, his shirt sweat-streaked and boots caked with dirt. His expression reflected his utter confusion. "What's the meaning of this?"

Quickly lowering her hand, she attempted to pacify him. "Ralph, you and I discussed how Ellie would be better off with us."

"On her own terms," he responded, staring at his wife as if he'd never met her. "Doesn't look like she's here of her own free will." He pointed to the gun belt around her waist. "You took my gun without my permission. What did you do? Threaten her life?"

Ellie kept silent as Nadine walked over and placed her hands on Ralph's chest.

"Sweetheart, you know this is where Ellie needs to be. If she remains in town, we'll be cut off from our kin. That baby is a Jameson, our last and only link to my brother."

A little of the hardness left his face. "You've longed for a baby. I have, too. But this isn't the way to fulfill our dream. You have to let her go."

Pushing him away, Nadine spat, "You've never wanted one as much as I have. You're obviously not willing to do hard things. I am." She flung her arm toward Ellie. "She stays until the baby comes. Then she's free to leave."

He lifted his hands in a placating gesture. "Nadine, this is madness—"

"You're free to leave, too. Nolan would expect me to watch over his child."

Ralph looked ravaged, as if he'd lost his wife and wasn't sure he'd recover her.

"Maybe you're right."

"About?"

"I've longed for a baby. All these years, the disappointments, the ups and downs, waiting and hoping… I had accepted that we probably weren't going to be parents." Ignoring her sharp inhale, he continued, "But maybe this is our chance. Ellie's baby can live here in our home with all three of us."

Ellie's knees gave out, and she sagged onto the bed. *Please let this be a ruse*, she prayed. Because if it wasn't, her only hope of escape had just gone up in smoke.

Chapter Twenty-Six

"This doesn't make any sense." Alexander paced the length of the café's kitchen. "She wouldn't leave without saying goodbye to us."

He stopped to review the letter's contents again, the headache that had been brewing all afternoon hammering at his skull. The others in the room with him remained silent, as confused as he was about her swift and stealthy flight to Kentucky.

"I agree." Margaret peered over his shoulder. "Ellie's not the type to make rash decisions. At the very least, she would've told June of her plans."

Stationed at one of the windows, the older woman turned at the mention of her name. Worry was stamped on her face. "She was completely calm and clearheaded when I left this morning. She said she'd think and pray."

The past two days had been rife with intense emotions. First, he'd ruined Thanksgiving with his botched proposal. He'd feared their friendship was at risk and possibly even their professional relationship. That morning, he'd finally examined his heart. His love for Ellie had filled him with hope for the future.

He and Margaret had been disappointed to find the

Trentham home empty. Disappointed, but not deterred.
They'd assumed the women were tending errands together. A pass through Main Street's shops and businesses had been unsuccessful, so they'd returned to the
Plum to wait. A couple of hours later, June had come to
them with a pair of letters...one for June and one for Alexander...both frustratingly brief.

Gatlinburg's sheriff and deputy were seated at the
table near the stairs, nursing mugs of strong coffee and
wearing matching inscrutable expressions.

"What are you two thinking?" Alexander wanted answers. No, he wanted Ellie here. Safe and happy.

Ben fiddled with his Stetson where it rested on the ta-
bletop. Beside him, Shane sipped his drink and sighed.
"I'm afraid you won't like what I have to say. From what
you've told me, Ellie was very upset. So much so that
she left the holiday celebration early and didn't return."

"You're saying I drove her to make a rash decision."

He held up a hand. "I'm saying that someone in her
position might look at an invitation like the one she received as a tempting solution. An escape, you might say."

Alexander groaned and passed a weary hand over his
face. The thought of Ellie traveling all that distance alone,
and in her condition, made him crazy. He couldn't accept
he'd never see her again.

"Fine. I'm going after her." He had one foot on the
bottom tread when Ben spoke up.

"Wait." Scraping his chair back, he pushed to his feet.
"Before you pack your bags, there's one more thing we
should do."

Shane arched a single brow. "What's on your mind?"

"She would've had to hire a driver in a hurry. Let's
pay Mr. Warring over at the livery a visit."

"Can't hurt." The sheriff grabbed his hat and stood.

Thanking Margaret for the coffee, he strode for the exit. Ben followed suit.

"I'm going with you," Alexander said in a voice that brooked no argument.

"Me, too," Margaret piped up.

He paused on the threshold. "I need you to stay here, sis. In case she shows up."

June came alongside and put her arm around her. "Why don't we whip up a batch of cookies? It'll give us something to occupy our hands while we wait. And I'm sure the men won't complain."

Nibbling her lower lip, Margaret nodded. Alexander reached over and gave her a quick hug. "I'm sorry your trip was delayed, but I'm glad you're here."

"I would've worried myself silly if I'd left."

He pulled away. "You sent the telegram?"

"Thomas and Lowell know I'll be arriving later than expected."

"Good."

Hurrying out the door and into the sunshine, he caught up to the lawmen halfway down the alley. Impatience rode him. Where was Ellie now? Was she okay? The need to hold her, to profess his feelings, had become a desperate ache.

At the livery, Mr. Warring greeted their group with wariness. He listened to Shane's explanation of the information they sought and denied any knowledge of a sudden departure involving a pregnant woman.

"What about your employees?" Shane said. "Mind if we talk to them?"

"Durwood's the only one working today." He jerked a thumb toward the rear entrance. "He's out back unloading grain sacks."

Murmuring his thanks, Shane led the way through

the stable and to the rear alleyway behind this side of Main Street's businesses. The Little Pigeon River flowed between steep banks, with the mountainside rising up sharply behind it.

"Afternoon, Durwood," Shane greeted, going over to relieve the young man of his burden. The hefty sack hit the pile with the others.

"Sheriff. Deputy." His wide gaze bounced between the three of them. Propping his gloved hands on his waist, he said, "Something the matter?"

"I'd like to ask you a question or two. That's all."

Losing some of his apprehension, he wiped the sweat from his brow with a hanky. "Sure."

He gave a description of Ellie. "Did you happen to see her around anytime today?"

His attention shifted to Alexander for the slightest second before snapping back to Shane. "Couldn't miss a lady like that. She came in around ten o'clock asking if I knew of a driver for hire."

Denial rose within him. He took a step forward. "What did you tell her?"

Durwood spat a stream of tobacco in the dirt. "I didn't know of anyone, but the mercantile's regular delivery man from Sevierville was fixing to leave. I told her to ask him for a ride."

"Where was Mr. Warring?" Ben said.

"With a customer."

Shane nodded in the direction of the mercantile's exit stairs, which were visible from their vantage point. "Did you see her leave?"

"I didn't see her ride out of town, if that's what you're asking." He indicated the sacks. "Mr. Warring keeps me busy every minute. Last thing I know, she was walking toward the delivery wagon."

Shane thanked him for his cooperation. Alexander was tempted to linger in this last spot where Ellie had been, to pepper the worker with more questions, but Ben clapped him on the back and urged him onward. They stood in the shade of the livery roof.

"I'm sorry, Alexander." Shane wore a frown. "I know this isn't the news you wanted to hear."

"She hasn't been gone long," Ben pointed out. "Still time to go after her."

Alexander stared at the mountains framed by pale blue skies and grappled to accept she'd actually left without saying goodbye. "Maybe it's best if I don't. She clearly wants distance between us."

"There's a chance she'll get to Sevierville and have a change of heart," Shane offered.

"Yeah. Maybe."

There was no hiding the despondency in his voice. It bled through, permeating his entire being. Ellie was gone. His second chance at love, of having a home and family, was slipping through his fingers, and he didn't know what to do about it.

Ellie stared at the rafters overhead and prayed for sleep to claim her. Three nights she'd been in her old bed, and not once had she slept for more than an hour stretch at a time. Her lack of rest, combined with her constant state of anxiety, couldn't be good for the baby. She lightly rubbed her stomach, comforted by the periodic kicks and pokes her little one doled out.

Shifting onto her side, she squinted to make out the gold numbers on the silver clock face. A deep sigh escaped. Four o'clock. Another hour to go before Ralph would rise to get a head start on the day. Nadine's promises had seemingly been forgotten. While she rose far earlier than in the past, she expected Ellie to fall into their previous routine. Ellie was used to doing chores, but her fragile emotional state made even the simplest of tasks seem insurmountable.

A single tear slid onto the pillow.

"Oh, Alexander," she whispered, her heart aching to see him.

He dominated her thoughts. It hurt to think what he must be feeling. She kept reliving their last moments together and imagining a different outcome. Perhaps she wouldn't be trapped in this living horror story if she had set aside her pride and told him how she truly felt.

A floorboard creaked, followed by a shuffling sound.

Ellie's heart thudded heavily. Pushing the covers aside, she sat up and placed her stocking feet on the ratty rug by the bed. Her fingers dug into the ticking, the dry straw crunching inside.

Muted footsteps drew nearer and halted. Inch by inch, the privacy curtain was slid to the side. The bearded face peering at her registered in the darkness.

"Ralph," she gulped. "What are you doing?"

Edging close, he put his finger to his lips and glanced back over his shoulder. "Shh. Nadine's a light sleeper."

He sank onto the end of the bed, and Ellie popped up, moving until her heels hit the wall. Her brother-in-law used to be on her side—not overtly, but quietly, behind the scenes. That had changed since her return. He fed into his wife's deranged desire for a child, discussing plans in front of Ellie, emphasizing her complete lack of power.

"I didn't mean to frighten you."

She crossed her arms, chilled physically and mentally. "What do you want?"

"To reassure you." Pinching his nose between his

fingers, he said, "I'm going to get you help as soon as I'm able."

Cold air crept up her nightgown. Goose bumps riddled her skin. "You'll understand why I don't believe you," she accused in a high whisper.

"My wife is ill." His shoulders slumped. His voice carried the weight of grief and disillusion. "I've been aware of her deep need for a baby. I just never thought she'd go to this extreme. I won't allow her to keep you here against your will, but I have to be careful. She's in a fragile state, Ellie. I'm not sure what would happen if she found out I was helping you."

A match flared in the living room. Ellie cringed.

Ralph leaped to his feet. "Nadine!"

The flickering flame cast the blonde's face in a disturbing light. Her eyes looked wild.

"You've been *pretending* all this time?" she accused, devastation wracking her. "My own husband lying to my face? Coddling me like an errant child?"

Ellie's knees threatened to give out.

Ralph slowly approached. "Listen to me, sweetheart."

"Don't call me that," she spat. Digging in her pocket, she retrieved a knife and flicked the blade out. Her hand shook. "Don't come near me."

He kept the sofa between them. "I may not agree with what you're doing, but husbands and wives have arguments sometimes. Doesn't mean I don't love you, Nadine." Gesturing behind him, he said, "This isn't right. We can't hold Ellie here like a criminal."

"You don't understand." She shook her head. "You never have."

"Let her go. We'll figure this out together."

Nadine's gaze landed on Ellie, who remained still and

passive. *Please Lord, convict her heart and mind of the injustice of her actions. Protect me and my baby.*

Nadine jutted her chin. "Leave this house, Ralph."

"What?"

"You heard me. I don't want to see you right now."

"You're being rash. Let's have breakfast and a cup of coffee, then we can sort through this."

"First I'm ill. Now I'm rash?" Teeth bared, she advanced with the knife out, moving in Ellie's direction. "If you don't leave my sight, *right this minute*, I'll have my pa run you out of town with nothing but the clothes on your back. Our marriage will be finished for good."

He rounded the sofa toward the door. "Promise me you won't hurt Ellie."

By this time, she'd reached Ellie's makeshift bedroom. "Leave!" Her scream rent the air.

Ellie jumped. With one lingering glance, Ralph hurried out the door, abandoning her to his wife's whims.

Chapter Twenty-Seven

"Alexander." June wiped her hands on her apron and motioned him in. "Have you heard from Ellie?"

His heart heavy, he held his hat in his hands and entered the living room. Being here was more difficult than he'd thought. "I don't have news. I—I'm not certain why I came."

"You wanted to feel close to her," she surmised. "I understand because I miss her, too."

He nodded and glanced around, looking for what, he couldn't say.

"Can I get you tea? Coffee? Or milk?"

"No, thank you." Surprisingly, his ulcer hadn't flared up. "I'm not thirsty."

She situated herself on the rocker by the fire. "Your sister get home okay?"

He remained standing, restlessness eating at him. "I assume so. She's supposed to send me a telegram. I expect to hear tomorrow, or Tuesday by the latest."

"Will you be following her out there soon?"

"I'm considering it."

He was reluctant to leave Gatlinburg. Something inside nagged at him. He was being foolish, of course.

She'd been seeking a way out of town and had obviously found it.

Silence descended. June set the chair to rocking and stared out the window.

"I have a strange request," he blurted.

She turned her wise eyes on him. "Shoot."

"If you don't mind, I'd like to look through her room. I understand it's already been looked at, but I…"

"You'd like to be sure we didn't miss anything." Levering herself upward, she motioned for him to precede her. "I don't mind at all. Look to your heart's content."

"Thank you, June."

"No need to thank me."

She remained in the doorway while he scanned the dresser's surface and inspected the drawers. There was nothing beneath the bed, no clues in the cedar chest. After fifteen minutes of searching, he acknowledged it was a fruitless search.

"There's obviously nothing to find," he said at last.

"Give it time. I believe she'll get to her destination and realize she has unfinished business here. She cares about you, Alexander."

"Kind of hard to believe right now."

They reentered the living room. Alexander's downcast gaze caught a glint of colored glass. He bent to pick it up.

"Break something recently?"

Twisting on his haunches, he held it out for June to inspect.

Brows drawn together, she scrutinized the green-hued shard before turning her attention to the cabinet against the wall. "I can't believe I didn't notice it before." She touched an empty spot. "I had a decorative bowl sitting right here. It's gone."

"Apparently someone tried to hide the fact it got broken."

"We both know Ellie wouldn't have done such a thing."

Alexander stood to his feet and as he did so, noticed a groove carved into one of the wall logs. He passed his fingers over it. "What happened here?"

"I've no idea." By now, June's expression was as grave as his likely was.

"Something gouged the wood. A knife or sharp object." Examining it further, he discovered the damage was deeper than he'd thought. "June, I think a bullet was discharged in here and lodged in the wall."

Worry darkened her eyes. "If that's so, Ellie didn't leave on her own."

Fury momentarily blinded him. Smashing his hat on his head, he strode for the door. "I'm an idiot for not going out to that cove to check for myself!"

"But what about that livery man? His account backs up what Ellie wrote."

"Some people will do anything for the right price."

Slamming out onto the porch, he freed his horse and mounted up.

"Be careful," she called after him. "And bring Ellie home safe!"

"I intend to."

He couldn't cope with any other outcome. Alexander rode hard and fast into town, sliding from the saddle in front of the livery and hollering for Durwood. Warring and the handful of men inside stared in wary surprise.

"What can I help you with?" The livery owner separated from the group.

"Durwood," he snapped, slapping his hat against his thigh. "Where is he?"

Movement out of the corner of his eye distracted him. The young man must've heard the commotion.

"You there!"

Durwood bolted toward the service lane alongside the river. Alexander pushed through the knot of men and raced after him. They'd reached the mercantile when he caught a fistful of his shirt material, jerked him backward and shoved him against the wall.

"You didn't speak to Ellie, did you? You've probably never even met her. Who paid you to lie?"

Panting, he jutted his chin. "I don't know what you're talking about."

There was a telltale glint of unease in Durwood's eyes that contradicted his claim.

Anger collided with fear. He shoved his face close.

"She's pregnant and alone and in grave danger. If something happens to her, you'll swing from a tree."

Beads of sweat popped out on Durwood's forehead. His gaze swung to the men who'd followed them.

"What have you done, Durwood?" His boss, Warring, addressed him.

He paled. "I didn't know she was expecting. I—I thought it was harmless."

"Who was it?" Alexander fought the urge to take his frustration out on the younger man.

"Some blonde woman. Tall. Blue eyes. Kind of rough-looking." He grimaced. "She came to me and offered coin if I'd tell you a story."

Alexander released him.

Nadine. He should've known. Should've at least gone to the cove to rule it out.

God please, I can't lose Ellie. I'd never recover.

He jogged to the café to retrieve his pistol and rifle.

Please give me a second chance to tell her how much I love her.

Back at the livery, he strapped his rifle to the saddle and mounted his horse.

There's nothing I'd rather do than be Ellie's husband, Lord, and be the best father possible to that baby.

"Copeland!"

Alexander blinked the moisture from his eyes and, twisting in the saddle, spotted Ben riding his direction.

"I don't have time to socialize, Ben."

"I heard about Ellie." Beneath his hat brim, his expression was stark. "I'm going with you. Shane will catch up."

Grateful for the assistance, he thanked him.

Ben reached over and gripped his arm. "We're going to bring her home. That's a promise."

Alexander couldn't speak for the emotion clogging his throat, so he settled for a nod. They both knew there were no guarantees she was safe. They were clinging to faith, hoping and praying God had His hand of protection on her and her baby.

Dusk was settling in, another day in captivity drawing to a close. Tonight would mark her fourth night in this cabin, only Ralph wouldn't be around to temper his wife's madness.

The hours since he'd fled had been tense and uneventful. Gladys and Howard had come over midmorning to see why the cows hadn't been milked. When Nadine had explained the scene leading up to Ralph's absence, Ellie had glimpsed the first stirrings of unease in the older couple. Their confusion plain, they'd regarded their daughter with thinly-veiled consternation.

It fueled Ellie's hope. Maybe, just maybe, they'd put a stop to her actions.

The crackle of the fire punctuated the silence between her and Nadine as they sat at the table, both pushing the meat and potatoes around their plates. Seemed Ralph's absence had robbed Nadine of her hearty appetite.

"What was that?" The blonde popped up and withdrew the pistol she'd started strapping to her waist. "Did you hear something?"

"No, nothing."

Putting her fork down, Ellie strained to hear anything out of the ordinary. "Maybe Ralph—"

"Hush."

Creeping to the window with a view of the other cabin, she flicked the threadbare curtains aside and squinted into the shadows claiming the forested mountainsides. After a few minutes, she shrugged and replaced her gun in its holster.

Her gaze pinned Ellie. "Probably a critter searchin' for food." She resumed her seat and dug into her meal with gusto. "Don't know why I thought otherwise. Your beau won't be coming 'round. I made sure of that."

Ellie sipped her milk and focused on keeping her emotions hidden. It wasn't easy. The longer she remained here, away from Alexander and everyone else she held dear, the dimmer her chances of returning to them became. They wouldn't come looking for her. They'd believe her letters—to Ellie's chagrin, Nadine had decided to forego the part about Ellie still being in love with Nolan. If she'd been able to include that, Alexander would've known immediately that something wasn't right.

Tears threatened. She was going to be trapped here, forced to give birth in this prison. After that, she wasn't assured of her safety. Nadine might decide she'd be better off without Ellie around. The mere thought of her baby being raised by these lunatics made her feel dead inside.

An explosion on the far side of the room sent them both scrambling for cover. Ellie huddled beneath the table. Nadine crouched behind her chair, automatically reaching for her weapon. Cold air blasted in through the open window. Remnants of glass clinked to the floor.

Neither spoke for what felt like hours. Ellie prayed feverishly. Could it be that someone figured out her whereabouts?

Going on all fours, Nadine crept to the corner of the couch and peered around the side. "A rock. Someone threw a rock into the window."

Just then, another crash reverberated in the bedroom. Nadine jumped to her feet and would've lunged for Ellie had the door not been kicked open and two men, weapons drawn, poured inside. A third one entered from the bedroom. He barked an order at the others, his voice identifying him as the sheriff. In a blink of an eye, Nadine was face-first on the floor, pinned by a furious-looking deputy. Ben's blazing gaze met Ellie's. He jerked his free hand toward her.

"Alexander."

Familiar black shoes hurried toward her hiding spot. And then Alexander crouched on the opposite side, shoving chairs out of the way to get to her. His beautiful face was drawn and lined with worry, his blue gaze burning with righteous resolve.

Ellie's cry was one of disbelief and joy. When his strong arms closed around her and drew her into his chest, she clung to him and sobbed. He buried his face in the crook of her neck. A shudder wracked him.

"You're okay," he breathed. "You *are* okay, right? Ben

did a bit of surveillance through the window and assured me that rock wouldn't get close to you."

Overcome with relief, she nodded and sniffled. "I'm perfect now that you're here."

He shifted and produced a handkerchief from his pocket.

Nadine let loose a host of threats as Ben hauled her upright and propelled her outside. Shane followed them outside into the dark night and began talking to Howard and Gladys.

Alexander's stubble-heavy features hardened. "I'm just sorry it took me so long."

He helped her to her feet. When he made to step back, she framed his face between her hands. "You're here now. That's the only thing that matters." Her heart fair to bursting, she stared up at him, making no attempt to hide her feelings. The time for secrecy was over. "I wasn't sure I'd ever see you again."

Alexander's hungry gaze roamed her face, and his hands found their way to either side of her waist. "I didn't think you wanted to."

"You believed the letters," she said with regret. "I thought you might, especially after what happened on Thanksgiving."

"It wasn't just the letters. One of the livery workers claimed you'd left town on a delivery wagon. I couldn't shake the nagging feeling something was off. I couldn't believe you'd leave without saying goodbye. I wish I'd discovered the broken glass and bullet hole sooner. If I had, I would've questioned Durwood a lot sooner. Turns out Nadine paid him to lie." A muscle ticked in his jaw. "Did she hurt you?"

"No."

He rested his forehead against hers and sighed. "Thank the Lord, He kept you safe."

Yes, precious Lord, thank You for bringing me through this trial.

"Oh, Alex, I'm tired of pretending."

He lifted his head, his brow furrowing. "There's no longer any need to pretend we're engaged—"

"No, you misunderstand. I'm tired of pretending I don't love you." His eyes went wide as she slid her arms around his neck and, leaning into him, brought her mouth up to his. She poured all the passion and love, tenderness and adoration she felt for him into that kiss. Alexander kissed her back, his ardor matching hers.

Her heart soared. This wasn't the response of a man who wanted a convenient marriage. Surely he cared for her as more than an employee-turned-friend-turned-fake-fiancée.

A throat cleared nearby. Alexander groaned in good-natured frustration. Keeping his arms firmly around her, he lifted his head to glare at Shane. "We're busy, Sheriff."

"I can see that." His smile was half cocky, half sheepish. "Thought you might like to know we're escorting the family to my office for further interrogation."

Alexander returned his gaze to Ellie. "We're not quite finished here."

Neither paid much attention as the sheriff pulled the door closed and, moments later, the horses left the yard.

"This isn't the setting I'd envisioned, but I can't wait a second longer." Taking her hand, he went down on one knee. The tender, affectionate smile he bestowed on her flooded her with joy. "Ellie, please marry me. Be my true bride in every sense of the word. Let me love you and this baby for the rest of my days."

"Yes, Alex. That's all I want."

His eyes suspiciously bright, he hugged her around the middle, then dropped a kiss on her stomach where her baby lay nestled. When he regained his feet, he caressed her cheek. "I love you, Ellie. I don't want to spend another day apart from you."

"Easily remedied," she said, giddy with happiness. "I happen to know where the preacher lives."

"I thought you'd like a formal ceremony."

"Nolan and I had a simple wedding and, for a while, I lamented the lack of decoration and tradition. I know now that what was truly missing was love...deeply-rooted, selfless love marked with passion, commitment and respect." Tenderly smoothing a lock of his hair off his forehead, she smiled. "I have that with you, Alex. All I need is you." She tilted her head to one side and winked. "And it'd be nice if our dearest friends were in attendance. Flo would have something to say if she wasn't invited. Sally would be crushed..."

"I believe I can arrange for them to be in attendance." Laughing, he hugged her tight. "Every day I have with you will be a reminder of God's grace."

"And second chances."

Epilogue

November 30, 1887

"Aren't you nervous?"

Waiting at the front of the church for his bride to arrive, Alexander smiled and shook his head. "I'm too excited to be nervous. I can't wait to say my vows and make Ellie mine forever."

Ben had agreed to stand up with Alexander despite his issues with the holy institution of marriage. Decked out in his Sunday suit, the deputy looked and acted the part of an anxious groom.

"I'm just glad it's not me," he stated, running his finger along the inside of his collar again. "Don't misunderstand, Ellie's an exceptional woman. I'm sure the two of you will make a fine match."

Alexander kept his gaze on the far doors, impatient to see her. The church had been transformed with a profusion of white candles of every shape and size scattered throughout the room and accented with greenery hinting at the coming Christmas season. Candles in Mason jars lined both sides of the aisle.

"I didn't expect to marry again," he said. "I certainly

didn't dream of finding a love like the one Ellie and I share." Turning toward his friend, he said, "You never know what the future holds, Ben. God specializes in surprises."

He rolled his eyes. "I don't happen to like surprises."

Alexander checked his pocket watch again. What were Thomas and Margaret doing right this minute? He couldn't wait to see them and introduce Ellie to everyone, not as his cook or fake fiancée, but his wife. They were to travel there this coming weekend. He was slightly apprehensive about the trip, but Ellie had agreed to make multiple stops along the way.

They were both anticipating a wedding trip that would diminish the memories of what occurred in the Jamesons' cove. Howard and Gladys had agreed to leave the area in exchange for leniency for their daughter. Nadine would spend the rest of her life behind bars. Ralph remained a free man, solely due to Ellie's influence. He'd apologized for not acting sooner. A broken man, he, too, had chosen to leave the scene of his marriage's breakdown.

By the time Alexander and Ellie returned from Texas, the remnants of her former life would be gone and she'd be free to start fresh with him. He couldn't wait.

Reverend Munroe emerged from his office. "I believe it's time, gentlemen."

The rear doors opened, and Alexander's pulse thrummed as their guests entered and took their seats. Duncan and Caroline; Flo and her husband; and Shane, Allison and their newborn baby boy came in first. Lagging behind, Sally walked proudly with her new beau, William. June, looking misty-eyed, joined the others, handkerchief at the ready. When everyone was seated, the reverend's wife took her place at the piano and started playing. At long last, Ellie entered the church, and Alexander relaxed.

She was more beautiful than he'd ever seen her. Her shining, coffee-hued waves had been restrained on one side with a silver hairclip and allowed to spill over her shoulder. Dangling from her ears were the pearl teardrop-shaped earrings he'd bought her as a wedding gift, along with the matching necklace. She wore her grandmother's sparkling ivory gown, which had been adjusted to fit her new figure. The bodice hugged her curves, the flowy skirts swaying with each step and skimming her ribbon-trimmed ivory shoes.

Her brown eyes shining, she walked toward him with a shy smile. When she stood before him, he enfolded her cold hands in his and gently squeezed. He would've liked to tell her how happy she made him and how gorgeous she was, but the music trailed off and the reverend began the service. Alexander said his vows with confidence, his gaze never once leaving Ellie's. She beamed up at him, her absolute devotion making him feel like the most fortunate man alive.

After the reverend pronounced them man and wife, the well-wishes had been bestowed, and everyone started for the café and the refreshments waiting there, Alexander hung back.

"Hold on a minute, Mrs. Copeland." He brought her hand to his mouth and brushed a kiss on her knuckles. "We can't leave until I've told you how stunning you are."

Twin patches of pink graced her cheeks. Glancing down, she waved a hand over her lush figure. "I don't look like a traditional bride."

"That didn't stop me from quite literally losing my breath when you first walked through that door." His hands on her waist, he urged her closer, smiling when her stomach prevented them from getting as close as he'd like. Lowering his head, he nuzzled her cheek, feeling almost dizzy as the weight of what they'd done sank in. Ellie was his wife, his to cherish, honor and protect.

"I'm a blessed man."

"We all are. You, me and this baby." She slid her hands up his suit lapels and around his neck. With another shy smile, she said, "And any future babies we might have."

Alexander hugged her closer, unable to resist brushing a lingering kiss on her rosebud lips. Levi would always be with him, in his memories and in his heart, but there was ample space for more children.

"I'm envisioning a house full," he teased. "We'll have to build onto the café."

"I like the way you think."

She kissed him, and he forgot where they were for long moments. When she sighed and lifted her head, he left her long enough to retrieve the gift he'd left on the first pew.

"What's this?"

"Something I hope you'll get a lot of use out of."

"You already gave me the pearls." Untying the ribbon, she peeled the fabric away.

"This isn't really for you."

When the pastel, crocheted blanket was revealed, Ellie uttered a cry of delight and clutched it to her chest. "The baby blanket from the harvest festival. When did you get this?"

He smiled, basking in her pleasure. Unlike Ben, Alexander thought surprises had the potential to be good. He was going to relish surprising his beloved every chance he got.

"The day before Thanksgiving. When I'd decided to ask you to marry me for real—the first time—I tracked the lady down and went to her house, hoping and praying she hadn't sold it."

"I love it, Alex. The baby will, too." Caressing his

cheek, Ellie gazed fondly at him. "I can't wait to tell our child how you came to be their father."

Alexander pulled her into his arms, unable to speak for the deep well of gratefulness springing up inside. Their story could've had a different ending. If he'd continued to cling to his bitterness, if he'd refused to release the past, he might've wound up alone and missing out on the greatest blessing imaginable. God—and a certain waif-like cook with an indomitable spirit—had intervened. They'd both been gifted with this new life together, a second chance at love and family neither one would ever take for granted.

* * * * *

Dear Reader,

Thank you for choosing my book! I hope Alexander and Ellie's story was an entertaining one. The Plum Café has been a long-standing feature in my Smoky Mountain Matches series, so it was a treat to write about the employees who spend the majority of their time there. Not much is known about our hero, Alexander, in the previous books. In trying to avoid dealing with his grief and loss, the former Texas rancher has cut himself off from everyone around him. Only a pregnant widow with an indomitable spirit could tempt him to start living again. I came to admire Ellie's faith and optimism. And seeing how Alexander's initial resistance transforms to first friendship and ultimately love was a thrill.

Next up is the final book in this series, one where the debonair deputy Ben MacGregor finally meets his match! For more information about my books, please visit my website, www.karenkirst.com. I'm also on Facebook and Twitter.

Blessings,
Karen Kirst

Get 2 Free Books,
Plus 2 Free Gifts—
just for trying the Reader Service!

Love Inspired HISTORICAL

YES! Please send me 2 FREE Love Inspired® Historical novels and my 2 FREE mystery gifts (gifts are worth about $10 retail). After receiving them, if I don't wish to receive any more books, I can return the shipping statement marked "cancel." If I don't cancel, I will receive 4 brand-new novels every month and be billed just $5.24 per book in the U.S. or $5.74 per book in Canada. That's a savings of at least 13% off the cover price. It's quite a bargain! Shipping and handling is just 50¢ per book in the U.S. and 75¢ per book in Canada.* I understand that accepting the 2 free books and gifts places me under no obligation to buy anything. I can always return a shipment and cancel at any time. The free books and gifts are mine to keep no matter what I decide.

102/302 IDN GLWZ

Name _____ (PLEASE PRINT)

Address _____ Apt. # _____

City _____ State/Prov. _____ Zip/Postal Code _____

Signature (if under 18, a parent or guardian must sign)

Mail to the **Reader Service:**
IN U.S.A.: P.O. Box 1341, Buffalo, NY 14240-8531
IN CANADA: P.O. Box 603, Fort Erie, Ontario L2A 5X3

Want to try two free books from another series?
Call 1-800-873-8635 or visit www.ReaderService.com.

* Terms and prices subject to change without notice. Prices do not include applicable taxes. Sales tax applicable in N.Y. Canadian residents will be charged applicable taxes. Offer not valid in Quebec. This offer is limited to one order per household. Books received may not be as shown. Not valid for current subscribers to Love Inspired Historical books. All orders subject to approval. Credit or debit balances in a customer's account(s) may be offset by any other outstanding balance owed by or to the customer. Please allow 4 to 6 weeks for delivery. Offer available while quantities last.

Your Privacy—The Reader Service is committed to protecting your privacy. Our Privacy Policy is available online at www.ReaderService.com or upon request from the Reader Service.

We make a portion of our mailing list available to reputable third parties that offer products we believe may interest you. If you prefer that we not exchange your name with third parties, or if you wish to clarify or modify your communication preferences, please visit us at www.ReaderService.com/consumerchoice or write to us at Reader Service Preference Service, P.O. Box 9062, Buffalo, NY 14240-9062. Include your complete name and address.

LIH17R2

*When the wrong mail-order bride arrives with another
woman's baby, Trace Warren's marriage of convenience
brings back the memory of the wife and baby he lost.
Can Katherine help him love again?*

*Read on for a sneak preview of
WEDDED FOR THE BABY by Dorothy Clark,
part of her STAND-IN BRIDES miniseries.*

"I'm sorry I've gotten you into this uncomfortable position, Katherine. I never meant for you to be embarrassed
or—"

The baby let out a squall. Katherine rose, then lifted
Howard into her arms. "You owe me no apology, Trace.
I chose to stay to help you keep your home and shop for
Howard's sake. I'm not sorry." She looked over at him
and met his gaze. Tears glistened in her beautiful eyes. "I
may be hurt by my choice, but I'll never be sorry." Her
whisper was fierce. She bent her head and kissed Howard's cheek. The baby nuzzled at her neck, searching for
something to eat. It was the perfect picture of what he had
longed for, prayed for and lost.

His chest tightened; his stomach knotted. He looked
down at his plate, picked up his fork and forced himself
to take a bite of salmon loaf.

"Trace…"

He braced himself and looked up.

"Please hold Howard while I warm his bottle." She handed the baby to him.

He looked at Katherine standing by the stove, holding a towel while she waited for the bottle to warm. Her lips curved in the suggestion of a smile. His heart lurched. She was so beautiful, so kind and softhearted, so brave to take on the care of an infant of a woman she didn't even know. Katherine Fleming was an amazing young woman.

He jerked his gaze away and stared down at his plate. He had to think of an acceptable excuse to leave as soon as the baby's bottle was ready. It was far too dangerous for him to be here alone with Katherine every day.

She set the baby's bottle on the table. "I'm sorry. I just realized I forgot to pour our coffee. I'll get it now. Would you please start feeding Howard before he begins to cry?" Her skirts flared out as she turned back toward the stove.

He swallowed his protest, clenched his jaw and shifted the infant to the crook of his arm. The baby's lips closed on the offered bottle; his tiny fingers brushed his hand and clung, their touch as light as a feather. Pain ripped through him. The pain of a broken heart vibrating to life again. It was his greatest fear coming true.

Don't miss
WEDDED FOR THE BABY by Dorothy Clark,
available August 2017 wherever
Love Inspired® Historical books and ebooks are sold.

www.LoveInspired.com

Reward the book lover in you!

Earn points from all your Harlequin book purchases from wherever you shop.

Turn your points into **FREE BOOKS** of your choice
OR
EXCLUSIVE GIFTS from your favorite authors or series.

Join for FREE today at
www.HarlequinMyRewards.com.

Harlequin My Rewards is a free program (no fees) without any commitments or obligations.

MYR17